THE
AWAKENING
OF
ARTEMIS

Jeff,
Hope you enjoy
this story

John Calia

JOHN CALIA

Contents

Contents

PART 3

CONTENTS

PART 4

Author's Note

THIS BOOK MIGHT CORRECTLY BE CLASSIFIED AS Science Fiction. But I prefer to think of it as Science Future. I have endeavored to project certain trends into a not-too-distant future including the development and widespread use of technology, primarily artificial intelligence and nanotechnology. While some of what you'll read might sound fanciful – and it is – the technology itself is not too far-fetched.

Every new technology I have portrayed in this novel – from smart bullets to the neural mesh to the embedded chips that keep a cabinet secretary functioning at her peak at the age of 97 – exists today in some form, someplace on a spectrum from concept to prototype. It simply hasn't been developed and adopted on a large scale.

Only time will tell if all these developments are embraced by society as have the iPhone and drones since the turn of the century. In the interim, I hope you enjoy my speculation as to how it might affect us.

—JOHN CALIA

For my granddaughter, Emily Grace Martinez-Calia, the first female in my bloodline in 90 years.

JUNE 20, 2049

TONY RUSSO STOOD AT THE TOP OF THE STAIRS, PEER-
ing down a single flight – which would have been as long
as three in any other building. He always got a queasy
feeling in his stomach at this point in the journey. His queasiness
wasn't from a fear of heights but rather from what he would likely
be asked to do.

The house was as dilapidated as any other in the rundown city
of Erie, Pennsylvania. Needing paint and missing some shingles, a
passerby wouldn't give it a second glance were it not for its size and
placement at the top of a hill. A center-entrance colonial of the
type popular in the 20th Century, one could count 10 windows
across the top floor above the double doors of the main entrance.
Its garden had been neglected so long that the only green shrub-
bery were along the east side facing the sun in the morning . The
rest had gone brown so long ago the branches were showing signs
of rot.

Why would the wealthiest man in town live in this hovel? Tony
thought as he made an approach, something he never did unless

summoned. As the police chief in this town, Tony was charged with enforcing the law. But, like many a small town where most of the land and enterprises were owned by one man, the law often became a gray area where the words written on a page meant little. He had been raised to be a stand-up guy, a guy who would do the right thing. Gray areas were not part of his makeup.

"The General wants to see you," Peggy had said that morning as he'd poured himself his first cup of coffee. She delivered the message with all the drama of a vending machine spitting out a candy bar.

"I know the way," he had said to the goon hanging around in the foyer. He headed down the long hallway, past a ballroom that still showed evidence of its former glory to the unmarked doorway at the top of the stairs. His eyes were still adjusting to the light as he stepped off the last step into The General's office. He glanced around to see if he could detect the scanners, cameras and recorders he knew would be there, archiving the conversation about to take place.

"Chief Russo! How are you this fine morning," said The General jovially. Tony could always tell just how awful his request would be by how cheerfully The General greeted him. *This one will be a doozy* he thought, doing his level best to hide his distaste for the man.

Howard the Geek – Tony didn't know his real last name – was scurrying around the racks of computers behind him doing Gods knows what. Noticing Tony's interest, The General explained that Howard was in the midst of an upgrade. *There's enough computing power down here to run the Pentagon* Tony said to himself. *Why does he need an upgrade? And what does he do with all this processing power?*

Tony wasn't sure if Howard ever saw the light of day. He was never more energetic than when he was scurrying around the glass-enclosed computer room like a rat in a maze. The processors were organized in columns and rows of equal length, making a 10 by 10 square. They were suspended above the floor to allow for maximum cooling and interconnected by a red glow. Tony was vaguely aware that the glow represented the transmission of data between them but wasn't sure how they did so since cables and wires were eliminated from the process years ago.

Howard, whose head was shaved in the middle, making his long orange hair on the sides and back, gelled into a disk around his head, look like the rings of Saturn, reminded Tony of videos of Bozo the Clown his Mom had him watch on an ancient iPad when he was a kid. Paying neither Tony nor The General any attention, poked a translucent globe which he held in his hand . Each time he did, a different processor would light up briefly and a look of mild satisfaction would pass across his face as he moved onto the next task.

"Any spike in crime during this last blackout?" asked The General once the pleasantries were out of the way.

Western Pennsylvania had been experiencing periodic blackouts ever since New York City had been permitted to syphon off as much electric power as they wished from the massive power plant at Niagara Falls. An enormous cable had been run down the trough of the old Erie Canal across western New York State, turning south at the Hudson River to supply Wall Street with enough electricity to keep its billionaires busy trading stocks and bonds 24/7.

"A few break-ins and a stolen motorcycle," replied Tony. "No more than usual despite the length of the blackout."

"I'm surprised there's anything left to steal."

"Well, the break-ins were mostly about making mischief. But I'm sure the motorcycle has been broken down and its parts shipped all over the country by now," replied Tony. "But you didn't call me here to discuss the crime report, did you?"

The General chuckled. "That's what I like about you, Chief. You get right to it, don't you?"

The sooner I get out of here, the better, thought Tony. His queasiness had dissolved, replaced by an urge to punch The General in the solar plexus, an urge he knew he wouldn't indulge.

"I am working on a new technology," he continued, "that will ensure continuity of electric power not only for Western Pennsylvania but for the entire country. Once it's implemented, we can compete with the Podosphere on an equal footing."

"What do you need me to do, Alfred?" asked Tony. A dark cloud briefly passed over The General's face. He hated being called by his proper name.

"There will be some unusual activity to the southeast of where we are. I need you to stay on the other side of town. Focus on maintaining order during the Locomotive Festival, glad-hand a few voters, keep them happy and celebrating . . . that sort of thing," he responded.

Tony hated 'glad-handing' – and any kind of supercilious social engagement – almost as much as he hated the Locomotive Festival, a street fair the Mayor had invented to celebrate Erie's glory days when the General Electric Corporation manufactured locomotive engines. Most of the city's population was too young to recall those days, indeed most wouldn't know a locomotive if they were run over by one.

Unusual activity meant that crimes would be committed in the name of the common good, thought Tony. But he knew better than to ask too many questions. The less he knew, the more likely he was to keep his job.

Upon his return to his office, he knew that Peggy's upraised eye-brow was as close as she would come to expressing interest in anything.

"Don't ask!" he said before she could.

She didn't.

PART 1

"There is no living thing that is not afraid when it faces danger.
The true courage is in facing danger when you are afraid, and
that kind of courage you have in plenty."

— THE WONDERFUL WIZARD OF OZ

CHAPTER 1

THE BATTLE

THE MISSILE HIT JUST AS SHE WAS ACTIVATING HER ground control station. A drone pilot, Captain Diana Gutierrez-Adams was about to fly her first combat mission when she was thrown across the room. Dizzy from the blow to her head, she stumbled to her feet. Points of light prickled in her eyes. The pain she should have felt was overcome by the rush of adrenaline. Looking around, she realized the east end of the building had collapsed, destroying several stations and likely killing the drone pilots. She swung around toward Gabrielle's station. Like Diana, she had been thrown to the floor but, unlike Diana, she was unconscious.

"Gabrielle!" she yelled as she took a step toward her friend. Her head spinning, she tripped forward breaking her fall with her elbows. She crawled across the room and knelt down next to her, placing two fingers on Gabrielle's carotid artery. She was alive! Looking up, Diana realized that Gabrielle's screens were still active. She pulled herself up to Gabrielle's seat, and made a quick assessment. It yielded a startling conclusion. The missiles had been their own. Their fire control system must have been hacked.

She lunged toward the emergency button that would switch the program to manual control. The screen showed that she had successfully broken the satellite link, which controlled the missiles. Using the infrared backup and manual control, she was able to dump the active missiles into the Atlantic before their enemy could redirect them.

What now? Were there more to come? She had read the report that Turkey's missile sites had been destroyed on the previous watch. Yet, they had succeeded in hacking the US missile control system. So, she couldn't be sure their hack hadn't taken control of another round of missiles.

A fire had started at the far end of the control room and was spreading in her direction. Smoke filled her nostrils and stung her eyes. The urge to flee was overwhelming. She was sure she could escape with Gabrielle in a fireman's carry. But would there be another round of missiles? She couldn't know.

There was only one option.

She stumbled toward the flames, her mind fighting both confusion and panic. There was one station that had been used to test a new system and only one person on duty who could activate it. When she stumbled over him, she immediately knew he was dead. But his station was still active. She needed his palm print to activate the biometric bypass and get to the new software. So, she dragged him the 12 or so feet to the station, despite the fact he outweighed her by about 40 pounds.

She activated the link to the football sized lasers that had recently been launched into space, forming a mesh network. They were too numerous for an enemy to destroy without risking counterattack. Yet, she knew they had never been activated. Not until now anyway. She had memorized the coordinates of the targets for today's mission – Turkey's electric power stations — and now entered them into this new system. But would it work?

In three clicks she got her answer. Eighty lasers from different orbits locked on to each target. Pulling the trigger, she uttered a millisecond long prayer and watched as the targets flickered and then vanished. Success! The targets were destroyed. With no electricity, they had effectively been bombed into the stone age.

The flames were like tongues, hissing like a snake as though they were trying to strike Diana. When she stood, they denied her oxygen; so, she crawled back to Gabrielle. She may not get out alive, but she wasn't leaving her behind. So, she draped her over her back and on her stomach and elbows slithered toward the door.

Emerging from the control room , she realized how lucky she was to have survived. Engulfed in smoke and still smoldering, the base was barely recognizable. She stood up, now draping Gabrielle over her shoulders, and headed upwind, expecting any survivors to be found there. Once she emerged from the smoke, she was swarmed by medics who relieved her of Gabrielle's weight. She collapsed to the ground, choking and coughing up smoke. Someone grabbed her and put an oxygen mask over her nose and mouth. She inhaled deeply as though she was taking her first breath.

But she didn't have time to stay still. Ripping off the mask, she stumbled toward HQ, the operations center, refusing further treatment. She tripped several times, once over a dead body, another over a disembodied leg. At one point she even fell to the ground which was hot enough to burn her left hand when she broke her fall. Disoriented, weak and in pain, it took a few minutes (though it seemed like hours) to realize that HQ was gone – completely vaporized. In its place were smoldering ashes. No human remains.

Commanding the operations center that directed all the launch stations that day was Base Commanding Officer, Brigadier General Paul Adams – her father.

"NO-O-O-O-O!" she screamed.

CHAPTER 2

THE SECRETARY
OF DEFENSE

TARA LETO HAD NEVER HEARD OF DIANA GUTIERREZ-Adams before the young officer's heroism had become national news. As Secretary of Defense, hers would be the final signature on the citation recommending the Congressional Medal of Honor for the President's approval. She felt a twinge in her artificial hip as she lowered herself into her seat behind her imposing desk. She'd asked to review only red flagged messages, of which Diana's file was number 3 of 7. An intense woman always stressed by the demands of her schedule, she had intended to only peek at them and then move on to the day's appointments. Instead, she spent more than an hour and a half reading about Diana, her military record and her family history. The file included an analysis of Diana's Culture Index evaluating her suitability for several career tracks. *What a remarkable young woman,* she thought. *I shouldn't be surprised.*

She tapped her left wrist and brought her virtual assistant's image to life in front of her desk.

"Yes, ma'am," said the image.

"Ask Colonel Sakura to join me, please."

Evelyn O'Malley-Sakura hated these impromptu meetings with the Secretary. She was an accomplished career Army officer, a West Point graduate who did not suffer the whims of these temporary political appointees gladly. Instead of doing the important strategic work her position at the Pentagon demanded, she would no doubt be treated as a glorified executive assistant – once again.

She knew the Secretary preferred in-person meetings to the augmented reality commonly used among younger staffers and officers. So, she hustled down the hallway, aided by the wide berth given her by nearly everyone who knew of her nasty disposition.

"Yes, ma'am," she said as she walked into Tara's office. The press had fawned over the appointment of the 98-year-old cabinet member. She brought an extraordinary level of energy to the office. But Evelyn was not impressed. She let her gaze scan the woman who stood before her, resuming her practice of trying to identify all the technology that kept Tara active and functioning: an artificial right hip, chips embedded in each limb to improve quickness of response and strength, a daily cocktail of performance enhancing drugs applied through a transdermal patch . . . . She was less a biological marvel than a miracle of modern technology. Chronological age no longer mattered. *I thought we'd be rid of these aging Baby Boomers by now*, she thought. *Society is riddled with centenarians and their 20th Century values.*

"Good morning, Evelyn," The Secretary greeted her. "Have you seen the file on Diana Gutierrez-Adams?"

"I haven't seen the file but I'm certainly aware of who she is."

"I'd like her reassigned to the Pentagon and I'd like you to take her under your wing. She's a high potential individual. With the right mentor, she could be sitting in my chair someday."

Evelyn recognized bullshit when she heard it but chose not to call out her superior. She didn't look forward to babysitting a 30-year-old junior officer. But she thought it might play into her personal agenda. She was always looking for an angle that would ingratiate her to her superiors despite her colleagues' observation that she was a career brownnose. Still, she wondered why the Secretary was so interested in this young woman. It was totally out of character.

Most of the injured from the 'Hack Attack,' as it had been dubbed in the press, had been sent to the U.S. Air Force hospital in Colorado Springs. Diana, Gabrielle and a few others with minor injuries had been sent back to their inoperable base in the Nevada desert. They were itching to move on. Diana wanted new orders – to get back to the action. Her injuries had been minor, and her recovery had been swift.

The Department of Defense had decided to decommission the outpost where they'd been carrying out their drone operations rather than rebuild it. So Diana and the other survivors spent most days poking at checklists on virtual screens, inspecting the tasks that had so far been completed by salvage crews. Evenings were spent with her fellow officers, downing a few beers, complaining about their military masters and wondering where they would be sent next. It was an easy assignment. But Diana hated easy.

Time flowed like cement. Diana wondered if boredom could be fatal.

And, then their orders arrived. About six or seven of them received a simultaneous alert on their wristband. Eddy Pulaski-Martinez was the first to pop open the virtual envelope.

"Oh, shit!" His reaction got everyone's adrenaline pumping. "I've been assigned to the Pentagon," he said, a note of resignation in his voice.

"Me too," added Gabrielle looking toward Diana.

"And me, as well," said Diana. This was not good news. She had heard too many stories of careers destroyed by office politics or from simply having the misfortune of being assigned to a project that was defunded by Congress. And, of course, it might be the only assignment more boring than her current one.

DEPARTMENT OF THE SPACE FORCE
WASHINGTON, D.C. 20301
TO: MAJ. DIANA GUTIERREZ-ADAMS
SUBJ.: ORDERS, MILITARY
DESCRIPTION: Special Orders No. 111, Relief and reassignment

You are hereby relieved of your duties in U.S. Space Force Air Combat Division 1439 pursuant to reassignment. You are to report to the Office of the Deputy Assistant Secretary of Defense for Strategy and Force Development not later than 18 Jan 2049 . . .

Diana didn't bother to read further. Gabrielle, reading over her shoulder, said, "Same here. Well, I guess the good news is we'll be together."

"Yeah," replied Diana. "Misery loves company."

CHAPTER 3

THE
WASHINGTON,
D.C. POD

IANA'S SELF-DRIVING CAR WAS HAVING A NERVOUS breakdown. While the traffic around her moved nose-to-tail like bullets being shoved into a chamber, Diana guided her chariot worm-like through the gaps, accelerating where circumstances allowed. The car's software objected but Diana just hit the override switch on the side of the joystick – repeatedly. In the five months since she had been reassigned, she still chafed at the constant monitoring — facial scanners reading her expression, algorithms that endeavored to meet her unarticulated needs — and vehicles that piloted themselves.

She recalled the horror she felt when the Podosphere was announced as a public works project to pull the nation out of the second Great Depression – GD2, as it was called. Each pod was a self-contained ecosystem walled off like gated communities against the potential intrusion of the small percentage of the population that chose not to join the majority.

"That's not allowed, Diana," whined the automated voice. *I need to choose a better voice option*, she thought. *Perhaps a French accent would be funny instead of annoying.*

"Speed limit exceeded by 12.3 miles per hour," said the voice. *Oh, shut up.* She flipped the bypass switch – the one her boyfriend Jeff had installed — allowing her to jump off the under-highway charging grid.

"Mobile scanners ahead, zero point seven miles."

"At last, some useful information," she uttered under her breath. Slowing to what felt like the pace of a tortoise, she successfully navigated the scanners as she passed through the exit gates from the D.C. pod.

She rushed into her apartment, dying for a shower after her workout, and was confronted by her augmented reality assistant – her ARA, Courtney. "Yikes!" she yelped, taking a half step backwards.

"Pardon me, Diana," said Courtney, the edges around her image glowing.

"You scared the crap out of me!" Diana found herself mentally plotting to kill the avatar – part of the technology package included in her monthly rent.

The facial scanner read her startled expression which prompted Courtney to ask, "would you like me to change the Entry Settings for you?"

"What?" said Diana, her heart still pounding from the rush of adrenaline. "Change them to what?"

"Well, there are three Entry Settings," came the reply. "If you would prefer that I not greet you as you enter, you can have the scanner read your expression and the algorithm will determine how best to meet your needs."

"And the third option?"

"No greeting at all," replied Courtney matter-of-factly. "Only 7.3% of the population choose this option."

Blessed relief. "I'll join the minority. Thanks . . . "

"Very well," said Courtney who disappeared, turning to electronic dust. *Of course, the scanner will still be reading my expression and calculating and recalculating my wants and needs, even if I don't want what the algo says I need.* This new life within the pods promised to be challenging.

After years as a drone pilot living in the desert, she had been plunged into the Podosphere — each of 15 pods a walled city-state which collectively housed more than 80% of the population. It was a world people had opted into. There was a seductive vibe to it. A natural evolution from social media like Facebook and Twitter. People had become accustomed to being fed information and advertising based on their "Likes." Now, they could live in a world where one's "Likes" were determined by artificial intelligence and they would be confronted with a steady stream of opportunities to have their needs satisfied. No clicks involved. The scanners read their expressions. Their embedded chips analyzed the hormonal secretions in their bloodstream. And the AI delivered. It was not a life she would have chosen. But having been reassigned to the Pentagon, she was part of the Podosphere whether she liked it or not.

"You have two new messages," said Courtney's overhead voice. "First message: your Culture Index dropped slightly from last week. You were overheard making a politically incorr . . . "

"NEXT!" yelled Diana, exasperated.

It's incessant! she thought as the next message took the form of an augmented reality image of Jeff, appearing as though a genie had popped out of a lamp. Instinctively, she knew what was coming. They had been together barely two months and Jeff had already started to complain – no, whine – about Diana's dedication to her routine. When she wasn't working or sleeping, she was working out. At least, that was Jeff's assessment.

"Diana, I'm sorry but . . . " Diana shut it down before he could finish. She had heard it before and didn't need to hear it again. Jeff was just the latest. He was too weak to handle a woman like Diana, too needy to be with someone who didn't put his needs above hers. Nevertheless, she felt a lump rising in her throat like a frog was about to emerge from her mouth. She stifled it.

She would not shed a tear – not one – on a man. Not any man and certainly not Jeff.

Diana's commute to the office was interrupted by a protest outside the Capitol building. Inching her way through the crowd, one protester waved a sign in front of her windshield – RAISE THE BASIC INCOME. She made a mental note to take a different route to work.

By the 2030's, jobs lost to artificial intelligence had exceeded 40% of the workforce. First it was long haul truck drivers, journalists and accountants. Then it was low-level engineers, medical assistants and call center operators. The first attempt to implement a Universal Basic Income came in the late 2025. But the opposition to a massive transfer of wealth to the unemployed was too fierce to overcome. By the 2030's, the economic damage was too robust to ignore. Now, in 2049 with nearly 60% of the population depending upon UBI to make ends meet, Oobies, as they were not-so-affectionately called, were marching in the street demanding more.

The unattended Starbucks kiosk in the lobby had received data predicting Diana's arrival time. As she walked past it to the elevators, a robotic arm reached out to hand her a Grande Frappuccino and a scone charging her account as it did so. She grabbed them without losing her stride. In the elevator, two young women were gushing about some shoes.

"I saw the shoes on my social feed and my ARA knew I loved, like over-the-moon loved them. And my car took me straight to the store. They were sitting on the counter in my size when I arrived."

"Yeah," said her friend. "I love the latest update. It makes life so much easier. Last week, it sensed that I needed some comfort food, and had the recipe for meatloaf projected above my kitchen island when I got home. Then it queued up my favorite movie and started it as soon as I walked into my living room after dinner."

Geez, thought Diana. *It's amazing how people are willing to give up their privacy in exchange for a slightly easier life.*

Flustered and a bit late, she arrived at her cubicle and as she sat down was logged in automatically. Her virtual screen materialized from thin air. Before she could take a sip of her coffee, a pop-up disrupted her routine.

"NEW ORDERS"

A hard message to ignore, she thought, and one that would certainly focus her mind on something besides an ex-boyfriend. Yesterday, the president had made an announcement: satellite guidance systems and those football sized lasers that Diana had deployed would now be controlled by an algorithm. This clearly did not bode well for Space Force pilots' careers. Pilots of Unmanned Aerial Vehicles – UAV's — would be replaced by artificial intelligence.

Despite Diana's heroics, the source of the hack that had turned US missiles on their military masters had not been discovered. Last night's news described how the new algorithm would detect intrusions and eliminate the need to have humans manning the stations, the risk that Diana or someone like her might not be around to thwart the next attempt.

Diana wasn't sure what to make of it. When she was assigned to the Pentagon, she thought of it as temporary. It was common for career officers to do a tour in Washington between field assignments. She had always assumed she would be transferred to a combat unit at the end of this tour. Still, she was only a few months into her assignment at the Pentagon. She didn't expect to be reassigned so soon. And, with pilots' careers now in limbo, what could she possibly be reassigned to?

The virtual image of Evelyn's assistant, Margaret, appeared over her workstation, hovering as a floating head. Diana had never met Margaret in person and wasn't even sure if she was a real person or an ARA. But Evelyn was Diana's immediate boss. So, she was used to seeing Margaret – or at least Margaret's head – whenever Evelyn summoned her.

"Colonel Sakura would like to see you, Major," said the head.

"Okay. I'll be there as soon as I read my orders." New orders were the one thing that would stop anyone in his or her tracks. New orders were disruptive. They often meant you could be packing your entire household and moving to another city or another country. The timing was nearly immediate and scant attention was paid to the personal impact – kids switching schools or relationships interrupted. Everyone would drop what they were doing when new orders came in.

"Your orders are why the Colonel wants to see you." The head turned to electronic dust before Diana's eyes and then vanished into thin air. Diana took the hint and headed to Evelyn's office but not before taking a quick glance at the orders. Special Operations was the headline, but the details were omitted. "TOP SECRET" was printed in bold type. The document simply confirmed what Margaret had said: report to Colonel Evelyn O'Malley-Sakura. "I guess I'd better go see Colonel Sakura," she mumbled to herself.

As she navigated the now familiar hallways toward the cavern of Evelyn's inner sanctum, all she could think of were the mistakes, real and imagined, she had made during her brief tenure. She had always been impolitic – a bit too loud at officers only parties, fraternizing with enlisted people or letting her temper get the better of her at the wrong moment.

Being a wiseass was her natural defense mechanism, especially on days like today when she had emotions bubbling inside. In the last twenty-four hours, her career had been sidelined and her boyfriend had broken up with her. On her journey from home to office, she had been confronted by several reminders of why she hated life in the podosphere – cars that drove themselves, Oobies demonstrating in the streets and 'girls' squealing their delight over software that made shoe-shopping frictionless.

As she walked, she exchanged insults with the men that passed by her.

"Hey, Diana. A thought just crossed my mind," Eddy said when he spotted her coming down the hallway.

"Must have been a lonely journey," she interrupted. A few chuckles arose from the adjoining cubicles.

Insults were the only language men understood and Diana spoke it fluently.

"What are you gonna do now that you can't play video games in the desert?" Eddy continued, trying but failing to hide a smirk.

"I think I'm about to find out."

CHAPTER 4

EVELYN
O'MALLEY-
SAKURA

E VELYN STUMBLED OVER SOME CRACKED PAVEMENT AS
she reached the doorway. "Shit," she muttered under her
breath as she groped around the unlit entrance for a door
handle. When she found it, she clicked an RFID fob to unlock it.
Ancient technology, she thought. *Why hasn't it been replaced yet?* It
was as though no one had a clue what lay behind the door. The
entrance on H Street between 15th Street and Vermont Avenue led
to a tunnel that was constructed in 1919 to connect the Internal
Revenue building to the Treasury headquarters across the street,
ostensibly to protect cash carrying employees from armed robbers.

Seeking a safe space for FDR and his family during World War
II, another tunnel had been built to connect the East Wing of the
White House to the Treasury, where a sturdy granite vault had

been carpeted and furnished for the president and his family. Never used and in disrepair, it now served as a way for Evelyn and the new president to meet without fear of discovery by electronic monitoring.

President Kathleen Porter emerged from a White House elevator, wearing workout clothes with her hair pulled back. She had ordered the workout room to be moved from the third floor to the basement so she could expand the music room. Now it served as her secret passageway. She slipped into the tunnel through an undersized doorway behind the stationary bicycles, pushed open the door to the sleeping quarters and waited a few minutes for Evelyn to arrive.

"How did it go?" she asked.

"It went well," whispered Evelyn, and then wondered why she needed to be so quiet.

"She had no questions?" The president sounded surprised. She stifled a sneeze as the mildew of this long-forgotten room invaded her sinuses. Evelyn took a handkerchief from her bag and offered it to the president whose gratitude was expressed as a noisy nose-blowing.

"Well, yes, she had loads of questions. Apparently, Diana didn't even know her grandfather had been cryogenically frozen. She was only six years old when he died. She seemed a little shaken. Her mother died in the accident too."

"Sounds like it might have been a difficult conversation."

"Yes, it took a while to take her through it. She was fighting back tears. Losing your mother at any age is tough. And losing her at that age had a huge impact on her life."

"What about her grandfather?"

"He was living with them when he was killed. So, they were very close," she continued. "I let her vent for about an hour before we got into the details of the mission."

"Was she able to focus on that?" asked the president. "Did she understand why we wanted her to lead this mission – to venture outside the pods?"

"Eventually, yes. But she wondered why we weren't sending a platoon of Marines if we were concerned about a risk of attack."

"How did you handle that?"

"I told her that Marines would be too visible. They'd quickly be discovered by the press who would speculate on their mission and portray the activity as a military action against our own citizens. Better for it to be low key. Anyway, I told her, there's no risk of physical attack. Perhaps some tomato-throwing protestors at worst. No one was going to attack the woman who saved our nation."

"And she bought that?"

"Well, yeah . . . I had to embellish a little bit."

The president raised an eyebrow, telling her to continue.

"It's inevitable the press will find out about this mission," Evelyn replied. "So, I told her the optics of a war hero leading this mission will be a net positive for all concerned."

"That's great!" said the president. "And it has the advantage of being true. Will you be able to pull together a team for her? One that is unlikely to put up a fight when they are attacked?"

"Should be easy," replied Evelyn. "I've been delegated complete control of the mission."

And, what about Tara?"

"I don't think the secretary suspects anything. She still questions why we wouldn't just send a small, secret paramilitary force, which is undoubtedly better qualified to navigate whatever awaits them. But your phone call was critical to her sidelining her objections. Your insistence that it be Diana sealed the deal. I doubt she wants to use any political capital to fight over something as trivial as this."

"So, you're confident?"

"Yes, I'm confident," Evelyn asserted with a bit more emotion in her voice than she intended. The president looked taken aback.

She continued, "We've been surveilling the travel route by satellite for months. There has been no organized militia activity, just a handful of protestors from time to time. Our best course has been to leave them alone. They eventually lose interest and go home."

"Sounds good. What do you see as the risks?"

As Evelyn rolled her thoughts around in her head, a drop of cold water fell from the ceiling into her hair. It served as a necessary diversion that broke the tension.

"Jesus!" she exclaimed.

The president chuckled as Evelyn obsessed for a few seconds. "You're experiencing life in the 20th Century down here," she wisecracked. "It's, shall we say, imperfect."

"More like the 19th," Evelyn replied.

"So . . . risk?" said the president getting the conversation back on track. Suddenly feeling tired, she glanced about for something to lean or sit on that wouldn't leave a telltale smudge on her Lululemons. Seeing nothing, she shifted her weight but remained standing as, of course, did Evelyn.

"There are a few potential leaks. First, there are the teams preparing the Armored Personnel Carrier – the APC – for the mission."

"They can't possibly know."

"Right, they can't. But they might wonder why they were installing a cryogenic capsule in an APC and a small saltwater battery to ensure it has continuous power."

The president scrunched up her face sending a clear signal of her concern – even without the help of a scanner.

"Then, there are the doctors and biologists at the National Institutes of Health who will try to bring this genius mathematician back to life . . . "

"Will they know who it is?" interrupted the president. "Will they know it's Nick Adams, Nobel winning mathematician?"

"Probably not," continued Evelyn. "But you asked about risks. It's possible one of them will recognize him. He was a pretty famous figure in his day."

Evelyn wondered why she was being asked all these questions now. They had been over them many times before. *Even presidents need reassurance,* she guessed.

"Haven't they been cleared for Top Secret?"

"Yes, Madam President, but, again, you asked about risks. I'm just listing them. They are only slight risks. No one has been briefed on the entire scheme. So, there is very little risk that some-one will figure out the big picture and leak it."

"Right. Anyone else?"

"There are the scientists who have partnered with us to create the diversion."

"In Pennsylvania, right?"

"Yes, the national lab in Erie."

"If they need some special attention, I don't want to know about it."

Evelyn understood the president's not too subtle indirect direc-tive. She had already found the perfect man for the job.

CHAPTER 5

GABRIELLE

D IANA WAS ALREADY PULLING ON HER BACKPACK
when Gabrielle pulled into the parking lot of Sky
Meadows State Park. She would have preferred something further away from any hint of traffic noise. But Diana being
Diana always had a reason — a task list to complete or a goal to be
achieved — that precluded them from traveling too far from the D.C.
Pod. She knew her friend was in turmoil. She sensed it, as if some faint
aroma in the air had changed subtly. Her maternal instinct consumed
her. Diana had saved her life and so she took it upon herself to save
Diana's soul. She wouldn't take no for an answer.

"Okay, I'd rather go further away. But we'll hike Sky Meadows
on one condition," she had said. She waited until Diana locked
eyes before outlining her expectations. "We'll engage in a forest
bathing session once we're far enough away from civilization."
Diana had rolled her eyes and smirked as she often did when
Gabrielle tried to drag her into one of her New Age exercises.

They hiked up to the highest point in the park. It was a weekday, and the weather was a bit clammy. They encountered no other

hikers on their walk, and soon, they found themselves surrounded by trees. The quiet penetrated their souls. They had left behind all the electronic distractions of modern life that they could. The chips embedded at the base of their necks, on the other hand, were not so easy to leave behind. They wandered somewhat aimlessly, letting their bodies lead them where they wanted them to go. When they reached the peak, they sat quietly contemplating the beauty around them, feeling the breeze caress their faces, listening to the rustling of leaves and the occasional scurrying of a small animal through the underbrush.

"I wonder what life would be like if we could live someplace like this instead of the Pods," Diana said.

"You mean someplace without the constant intrusion of digital whatever?"

"Yeah," she said. "Someplace where you're not constantly monitored and fed a steady stream of stimuli."

"Let me entertain you . . . constantly!" Gabrielle mocked, wondering how a well-educated populace became convinced they should turn every conscious moment over to their electronic overlords.

It wasn't until they had kicked off their boots and were consuming ketogenic snacks – a combination of turkey, yogurt and berries extruded into multi-colored cubes – that Diana shared her orders with Gabrielle.

"You said yes?" said Gabrielle. It was a rhetorical response, an expression of shock and dismay that her friend had agreed to 'volunteer' for a special ops mission.

"What choice do I have, Gabs," Diana replied. "Everything I've worked for went out the window with the new algo. Drone pilots are out; satellite-based lasers are in. I've got no job, no family . . . " She choked back an aberrant sob . . . "and no – well, you know."

Gabrielle *did* know. Diana had no romantic interest, no prospects of marriage or a family, no reason to stick around. Gabrielle had liked Jeff, a regular guy with looks good enough to be a movie star were it not for his protruding ears and lanky gait. But she had known that Jeff wouldn't last. She had seen Diana burn through too many like him.

"I didn't realize Jeff was so important to you," she said finally.

"It isn't Jeff exactly," said Diana. "It's family. Or, rather, the lack of family."

"I was wondering when we'd get around to that," Gabrielle responded. "It's been nearly a year since you lost your Dad. I don't think you've properly grieved."

Diana was silent. Gabrielle decided to give her some space.

"It's not just that," said Diana. "I mean, I loved my Dad. He was everything to me, especially after Mom died. It's just that I have no one, no blood relatives anymore, no family. I feel so lonely sometimes."

"Lonely?" said Gabrielle, hoping her friend would have more to say.

"Not lonely exactly. More like alone," she said, her voice fading away.

Gabrielle looked at her friend while composing a response. Diana had always been so mission-oriented, so duty-bound that it was hard to penetrate her thick skull with any thoughts that might dissuade her – that might make her consider alternatives. Most who knew her thought her courage was a given. But Gabrielle was wiser. Behind the bravado, she knew Diana to be consumed by fear – fear of letting go of her disciplined existence and of the entropy that would result if she failed to inject energy into it daily. She also knew that Diana's failure to nurture her soul would lead to burnout someday. Hence, the forest bathing exercise.

"Human beings thrive on connection with others. It's part of how we evolved, how we survived as a species," she began, unhappy with herself for not having something more eloquent to say. "What you're feeling is only natural."

"Yes, I know that," Diana replied. "But there are nights when I feel a sense of panic. It's almost like the world has shrunken away and I am surrounded by a cold void."

"You're always on a mission, Dee – always closed off from the world. It's difficult for others to see you the way I do."

"Closed off?"

"Yes, you come across as too busy or self-centered to have time for others. When you show me your heart – allow yourself to be vulnerable, I see the real hero you are," said Gabrielle. "But others don't see it."

Diana looked stunned. She said nothing.

"I know you trust me and I'm grateful for it," Gabrielle added. She paused to let her words have their desired effect. Then she added, "your best hope is to have the courage to show others your true self."

"You're right, Gabs. I know you are. I just don't know how to do it."

"Life happens. Opportunities arise. You have to hope you'll see it when the time is right."

Diana sat silently; her eyes were moist. The greatest thing about their relationship was the emotional warmth they shared. It was the bedrock of who they were together.

"Too bad we're both hetero," Gabrielle joked, breaking the tension of the moment. They both dissolved into uncontrollable laughter, their emotions in sync as always. It was as though they shared the same pilot light. They sat silently, allowing themselves to synchronize with the pulse of the forest – its dampness, its sounds, its smells. They could feel the magic from their toes to their fingertips.

On their hike back down the mountain, Gabrielle got back to the business of the day. "So, tell me about this secret mission," she said. "Why do they want you for this? Why not . . . "

" . . . a platoon of Marines?" Diana finished her question for her. "Yeah. I had the same question. Apparently, the president likes the optics of sending a war hero. They've been scanning the area for militia activity and think there is no risk of armed confrontation. Just some protesters maybe."

"But it's a Top-Secret mission. There shouldn't be any 'optics.'"

"Nothing stays a secret for long."

Gabrielle absorbed all this while avoiding mud puddles and stepping over logs. The mission was Top-Secret, and they couldn't know the real objective. Their orders would be sent to them piecemeal. At the end of each stage, they would receive an encrypted message telling them what to do next. The first stage was to load a specially equipped Armored Personnel Carrier or APC onto the cargo section of a train from D.C. to Philadelphia.

They would receive orders for the next stage when they had offloaded the APC from the train. It seemed reasonable to assume they would be heading out of the podosphere. Why else would they need an APC, monster wheels and all?

No risk of armed confrontation? thought Gabrielle. *Maybe they're just counting on no one wanting to confront a war hero.* But she didn't need a facial scanner to tell her that Diana knew more than she was supposed to say.

"There's more," said Diana.

"More?"

"Yeah, Evelyn asked me who I wanted as second in command."

"And, you said you wanted me, right?" Gabrielle finished Diana's thought for her with a note of resignation. She didn't like the mission, but she would never say no to Diana, and Diana knew it. They had been together since their swearing in at the

Space Force Academy. They had endured the hazing, crammed for exams together; and, marched to graduation side-by-side. They had seen each other at their best and their worst, picked each other up when the other was down; and, forgiven each other their transgressions. There was no way Gabrielle would abandon her friend.

Gabrielle had always been the perfect complement to Diana. She was soft where Diana was hard. She was empathetic where Diana was analytical. She absorbed her surroundings and responded to them emotionally where Diana was focused like a laser beam on her goals and objectives whether they were long-term career goals or simply getting from point A to point B.

It was the Yin and Yang of their personalities that made them seek each other out. Unlike her smart, focused friend, Gabrielle was an adventurer, was wide open to new experiences. She was a lover not a fighter. She openly and willingly shared her heart with others, with no one more so than Diana.

Diana's sheepish grin gave her the answer to her question. The two sat silently for a moment, gazing at the two-lane blacktop that would take them back to the Pod.

"Well, at least we'll be outside the pods for a few days," said Gabrielle finally. "No Culture Index running each transgression, whether of thought, word or action, into an algorithm." *I would be better off on the outside,* she thought. *Being walled off from nature is like prison.*

"You're right. It will be a blessed relief," replied Diana.

"But why me, Dee? I'm not exactly a good fit for this mission," she asked. "You've trained for Special Ops and have achieved Black Belt status in two martial arts disciplines. If there are problems, your training will come in handy. I've spent all my training behind a computer screen analyzing data. I'm not a good match for this mission."

"Because I know I can trust you."

"Then, trust me!" said Gabrielle. "Tell me the rest. I know you're holding back."

Diana hesitated. "It's Top Secret," she said. "I'm not supposed to tell anyone."

"Dee, I know you," said Gabrielle, her tone more demanding now. "I know that the details of the mission are carried in your mind like a vial of volatile liquid. You'll have to tell me eventually. So, you might as well tell me now."

Diana gave in to the inevitable.

"We're retrieving my grandfather," she began.

"Your grandfather?" Gabrielle exclaimed. "I thought he was dead."

"Yes, I thought so too. He died in the car accident with my mother."

"What? Wait a minute . . . "

"Gabs, give me a chance," said Diana. Gabrielle took a deep breath and resolved to hold her questions until Diana had told all.

"He's cryogenically frozen in a vault in Pittsburgh." Gabrielle felt like her eyeballs were about to pop out of her head. "Our mission," Diana continued, "is to retrieve him . . . to bring him back so he can be brought back to life."

"Holy shit!"

"Yeah, I know."

"But why?" asked Gabrielle unable to hold her tongue. "And why now?"

"I don't know," said Diana. "It's classified."

"Didn't he win the Nobel for something?"

"Yeah, but I was too young to really understand it."

"Maybe that has something to do with it," mused Gabrielle.

"Yeah, maybe," said Diana. "But why now and why was he kept in a cryogenic state for twenty-five years?"

"And why was it kept secret?"

CHAPTER 6

THE CRIME

T ONY RUSSO HAD NEVER SEEN A CRIME SCENE LIKE IT.
The entry scans showed only the two scientists had
entered the secure basement laboratory. No one else had
entered and no one had left. And now the FBI forensic team was
telling him that the two blotches of gray goo on the laboratory
floor were human remains. He was incredulous.

I'm trying to believe you, he thought. *But the murders I've seen
before always featured blood and gore.*

He was unaccustomed to the attention of the federal authorities as they rarely dealt with crimes outside the pods. When he
had arrived on the scene, they paid him little notice. The Erie
city budget had long been unable to accommodate such luxuries as police uniforms. So, he dressed in blue jeans and a T-shirt
adorned with a silk-screened police badge long faded by too
many washings. He didn't even have an official police vehicle.
He drove a jacked up early 21st Century Chevy Tahoe Hybrid.
The city reimbursed him for miles when cash flow allowed,
which wasn't often.

Two agents – an older male and a younger female – were standing over the mess or the bodies or whatever they were. The older agent greeted Tony with an expression suggesting someone had dumped a pile of manure on his doorstep.

"Are you burning gasoline in that thing?" He asked, pointing at Tony's suv. "That's been outlawed for years."

Tony felt his jaw tighten. He didn't like the fact that the FBI has arrived on the scene before he learned about the crime. And he didn't like the pedantic tone of the jerk confronting him.

"If you pod dwellers weren't hogging all the electricity, our grid would be reliable enough to keep a fully charged battery," he replied a bit impatiently. *Was this really why the FBI was here?* He thought. *To find violators of the Green Energy Act.* He wasn't planning to make any new friends. So, he didn't press the point, deciding to stick to business. His focus was solving this murder, if that's what this even was.

The federal government had taken over the hospital building, which had been abandoned by the University of Pennsylvania in 2025. It had been repurposed as a national laboratory conducting God-knows-what Top-Secret experiments. Maintaining the building and keeping it clean were among the few jobs available to locals. Tony had always thought some rich guy would buy the site to take advantage of its fabulous view of Lake Erie. But no one was going to bring their bags of money to a down-on-its-luck, rundown city like this – not now and after these murders, maybe not ever.

"Why are you guys here?" Tony asked, not expecting a straight answer.

"It's a national lab under federal jurisdiction," said the elder of the two. "Once we've completed our forensic investigation of these deaths, we'll turn the data over to you so you can find the culprit."

Doublespeak thought Tony.

"So, if it's under federal jurisdiction, why are you expecting me to find them?" asked Tony, trying to imagine how he and his two deputies were expected to solve a crime like this one.

"Those are our orders. We're stretched a bit thin," he replied with no further explanation.

Tony knew he had to suppress his urge to speak his mind and focus on what he could learn from these two agents before they left town with him holding the bag. Still he wondered how it was possible that the government support of the podosphere could extract all the resources from rural communities like this and then whine they were "stretched a bit thin."

"What do you know so far?" he asked.

"It looks like an experiment gone wrong. We think the nanobot technology these guys were working on ran amok."

Tony's head was spinning. He had heard of nanobots but had no idea what they were, much less how they could kill their human masters.

The younger agent noticed his look of consternation. "It's a Top-Secret experiment. We've already told you too much," she said in as condescending a tone as she could muster.

Her partner suggested she move on to the next phase of the investigation: inspecting the electric transformers in the basement. Once she was out of hearing range, he took Tony aside.

"Look! I'm not supposed to tell you this. But these guys were working on a process that would use nanobots to convert coal into diamonds. That's why they located the lab here in Erie. Lots of coal in the ground nearby. My best guess is that they got their wires crossed somehow. The nanobots would have seen them as just another source of carbon and flattened them."

"Wha . . . ? How could . . . ?"

"I don't know. They were only supposed to program the nanobots to learn to reproduce. Transplanting them to a processing plant and feeding them coal was supposed to happen in the next phase of the experiment."

"Whoa . . . wait! You'll have to slow down for me. What are nanobots and what were these guys doing with them?" asked Tony. He wasn't sure if the agent was trying to help him or mislead him. The more he heard, the more he worried about having to solve this crime.

"A nanobot is a self-propelled machine that has artificial intelligence. They are about a billionth of a meter in size, the size of a speck of dust. They are programmed to perform a task by their creators. Then they are on their own to perform the task," he said, simplifying what Tony guessed was a very complex topic.

"Perform the task?" asked Tony, unable to hide his incredulity.

"They actually grow legs and can move through electrical circuits."

Tony's brain was working hard to absorb this information. The task of applying his knowledge to a murder investigation would have to wait till later.

"We may have reached the point of artificial super intelligence where computers can bootstrap themselves past human intelligence," the agent continued. "If that's happened, the computer can create plans and priorities. Nanobots could be used in place of soldiers to carry out orders."

"So, the nanobots could have killed their creators?"

"Not sure. That's why I sent Debbie down to inspect the transformer."

"So, you're thinking they might have jumped from circuits to humans somehow?" If Tony was incredulous, his FBI counterpart was even more so.

"We know they can travel through living organisms. Our biologists have injected nanobots into lab rats successfully, got them to clean out arterial plaque." Then, after a pause, he added, "Crazy, right?"

"Yeah. Crazy," said Tony, wondering what he would do when the FBI report was handed off to him. "If you're right, these geniuses were like little kids playing with a bomb. But why does the federal government need diamonds?"

"Crazy, right?"

Again? Tony thought. *What is this guy still not telling me?*

CHAPTER 7

THE MISSION

T HE MASSIVE STRUCTURE OF UNION STATION STOOD
before them, defiant in its 20th Century glory. The classic façade had been preserved for over a century despite
the transformation of train travel from steam to electric to magnetic levitation. As a girl, Diana would pester her Dad to visit this
glorious building whenever they visited the nation's capital. The
massive columns, so imposing as she approached, gave way to an
atrium that took her breath away, every time she saw it. Walking
through the entrance, she would feel as though her spirit expanded
to fill the space – a space that drew her eyes upward where the
archways and dome made her feel as though she was connected to
the heavens.

Dressed in civilian clothes, Diana instructed each of her team
to use a different entrance at staggered times as their mission
began. She had been instructed to ensure they slipped out of
D.C. with their specially equipped Armored Personnel Carrier
undetected. The APC was located on a loading dock several levels
below the main floor of the station. So, Diana had devised a sort of

cloak-and-dagger approach to assembling the team without being noticed.

Their training had been brief and was not without its challenges. Few people like expending their energies in an effort the goal of which is unknown to them. The military is no exception despite the "Take the Hill!" approach embraced by their commanders. Diana had always taken exception. Her approach was to tell them the goal and why it's important. In this case, of course, the objective could not be known to her small squad because it was classified.

Their efforts were not aided by the skeptical attitude of US Army Sergeant Ian Filian, a career complainer whose incessant bitching eroded the unit's confidence like a fast-moving stream wore down a rock – slowly, steadily and without retreat. Diana was accustomed to dealing with bad eggs but found this Sergeant particularly annoying. Gabrielle had overheard him complaining to his subordinates about the "video-game-playing, so-called pilot" who would lead them into "God knows what shitstorm".

The challenge to her leadership was exacerbated by the addition of a new team member late in the training cycle. Mateen Ibrahimi was an odd choice to join a military adventure. Middle aged, paunchy yet brilliant beyond the comprehension of the dullards whom Diana commanded, he didn't bother to try to fit in other than to introduce himself using his anglicized nickname, Matt.

Matt had grown up in Kabul Afghanistan. By the time he was 18 years old, he could speak 8 languages not counting the dialects of his native country which he could also speak. In the early days of the Internet, he would steal away to the Kabul Library and scour

Wikipedia and other sites to learn what he could of the world outside Afghanistan.

It was during one of those library visits that his home was destroyed while his family were playing a game of Chinaaq. He later recalled running around the neighborhood believing that he had come home to the wrong address. *It was someone else's home,* he thought while still in shock. *It had to be. I can't have lost everyone I love in a millisecond.*

Squatting in front of what used to be the only place he had known, he was empty – alone and feeling nothing – numb and oblivious to the dangers around him. Before he could think, a US soldier grabbed him by the collar and dragged him out of harm's way, the fire fight that continued in his neighborhood. He hadn't wanted anyone to save his life but that's what happened. Within seconds a mortar shell exploded in the spot he had been kneeling.

Homeless and destitute, Matt applied to be an interpreter for the US Army. As the US reduced its military presence, he found himself in danger. He was a target, a traitor who was helping the enemy. A US Army officer – Alfred Braxton Bragg — to whom he was assigned, fought the Army's bureaucracy to make sure Matt got out of the country safely.

In the US, he found serial employment in government agencies that were in dire need of a polyglot: the CIA, NSA, FBI and, finally, the Department of Defense. But Matt was unhappy and didn't enjoy American culture as much as he thought he might. After a dozen years working for bureaucrats and demagogues whose bigotry was barely contained – *"what's the towelhead doing here?"* — he left government service and became a contractor. Whatever his mission of the moment, it was always shrouded in mystery.

Diana's team all arrived at their rendezvous point within a few minutes of each other. Once they were all present, they boarded a freight elevator that would take them to their APC.

The bowels of Union Station were nothing like the glory of its public face. As Diana and her team exited elevator, the smell of urine smacked them in the face. Gabrielle and Matt took an involuntary step back. As their eyes adjusted to the dim lighting of the loading dock, they took in the sights and sounds that complemented the aroma – the area was dominated by rusty steel beams, discarded and broken pallets and a floor so greasy they almost needed to learn to walk anew. At its center was an alloy container so new and clean it could only be their APC.

The place seemed deserted except for a homeless woman asleep in a dark corner. Were it not for her half-asleep mutterings, they might not have noticed her. She was clothed in a pile of rags so saturated with filth and grime that Diana speculated on the odds of it bursting into flames by spontaneous combustion. Hearing them approach, she popped up like a Jack-in-the-Box surprising her uninvited guests with her agility. She scurried about like a trapped rodent trying to gather her items of value – plastic bags filled with empty bottles, a man's ski jacket obviously pilfered, a canvas tote bag containing God-knows-what – continually glancing sideways at them as though assessing an existential threat.

Diana ignored her and turned to Filian. She had tamed the cynical old sergeant by maintaining a coldly efficient approach – abrupt and correct in every detail of the operation. By the time they were in action, his misgivings about her, if not their mission, had been set aside.

"Let's get started," she said.

Sergeant Filian knew what was to happen next and barked a few commands in the direction of his crew. Utilizing the forklifts that were available on the loading dock, they moved the container to the freight elevator. Two of them rode the elevator up to the loading platform — donning yellow vests and hard hats as they did so — and loaded it onto the rearmost car of the train. The team scattered once again, each of them boarding a different car on the train.

The pods were connected by a hyperloop operating in an above ground vacuum tunnel. Trains freed of the friction of contact with rails traveled between pods by magnetic levitation at nearly 760 miles per hour – the speed of sound. Their train arrived at Philadelphia station within a few minutes of strapping themselves in, and then they followed the same protocol in reverse. When they were finished, they found themselves on another freight dock opening the container and preparing the APC for their adventure into unknown territory.

This was the first time they had seen the vehicle that would be both their mode of transportation and their home for the next week as they headed west toward Pittsburgh. They all looked stunned when they saw the cryogenic capsule except for Matt whose technical expertise was critical to its safe operation. Diana briefly considered revealing the true objective of their mission, just to settle their nerves a bit. *Fear of the unknown always leads to problems* she thought. *Maybe I'll tell them once we've cleared the Philadelphia pod.*

Suddenly a light burst forth from a door no one knew was there. Some of Diana's team reached for their sidearms instinctively but were calmed by Gabrielle who recognized the woman who entered.

"At ease," she commanded, and they holstered their weapons.

"Madam Secretary," Diana said when she recognized their boss. She was stunned as were they all. They stood in silence as Tara Leto strode toward them with the confidence and bearing common to military leaders.

"Diana, may I speak with you privately?" she asked.

As though I have the option of saying no, thought Diana.

When they had separated from the others to ensure they wouldn't be overheard, Tara did something rare – for her at least. She spoke to Diana as a mother would to a daughter.

"Diana, I know you haven't been happy working at the Pentagon . . . "

"I prefer to be in action," interrupted Diana. She chided herself silently. She knew better than to interrupt someone as senior to her as Tara. *Keep your mouth shut, Diana,* she thought.

"I know, Diana," said Tara. "It was I who wanted you in Washington. That's why you got those orders. I think you're a very special person."

Diana's head was spinning. *Special person?* She thought. *What kind of way is that for the Secretary of Defense to talk? And why is she here? And why me?* People at the top of the pyramid always spoke in terms of one's potential or the abundant opportunity to work on a particular mission. 'Special person' wasn't part of their vocabulary. *It's as though she feels some emotional bond with me.*

"This is an extremely important mission," Tara continued. "But I want you to know that it's important to me personally as are you," she said as she reached into side-slit pocket above her left breast.

She handed Diana a velvet pouch that was cinched by a drawstring. "Please take this. It was handed down to me by my grandmother, a woman who I loved, a woman I learned from, a woman who was a great influence on me. Keep it close to your heart."

Diana was stunned. She half turned toward Gabrielle who she saw was watching intently from a distance. When she turned back to Tara, she was already walking back to the doorway from which she had entered. Diana watched slack-jawed as the Secretary vanished behind the closing door.

"What is it?" asked Gabrielle, as Diana fished the object out of its pouch.

Diana held a pendant in her hand. At first glance it appeared to be a teardrop. But careful inspection revealed an icon in the shape of a woman. Answering Gabrielle's question was less important to her than understanding why the Secretary of Defense had shown up at this moment – had skipped over the chain of command – to give her something seemingly unimportant to their mission.

Diana held the leather lanyard on which the pendant hung aloft, and Gabrielle cradled the teardrop in her hand. "It's Gaia," Gabrielle said.

"Who's Gaia?" asked Diana.

"She's from Greek mythology. Gaia is the mother of all life on earth."

"An earth mother," scoffed Diana. It was her usual reaction to anything connected to emotions or symbolism. "Well, I'm not wearing it. It'll just get in the way while we're operating equipment."

"No worries," Gabrielle said as she slipped it over her head. "I'll hang on to it for you."

"Suit yourself."

PART 2

SEPTEMBER 2049

"You're capable of more than you know."

—GLINDA, THE GOOD WITCH
FROM OZ THE GREAT AND POWERFUL
BY L. FRANK BAUM

THE PLOT

D ESPITE THE OPPORTUNITY TO WORK ON ANYTHING anywhere any time, Evelyn preferred to stay late in the office. There was something about the half dark bull-pen and hallways that allowed her to concentrate. Here she could shut down all sources of distraction. Her position at the Pentagon afforded her the option of shutting down facial scanners, digital assistants and always-on video. Her staff viewed her as "old school," a description she rather enjoyed. So, on this particular night, no one thought anything of Evelyn being the last to depart.

Evelyn didn't bother to look up when the last member of staff called out to say they were leaving. She just gave a half-hearted "Good night.".

She logged into the KrypComm system, a communication network with a level of encryption that was impenetrable. The system used blockchain and biometric two-factor identification to ensure secure communication. To login, Evelyn submitted to both a retina and handprint scan. She secured her video message with a password that would be transmitted to its intended recipient using a separate photonic channel.

In addition to the KrypComm system, Evelyn had ensured another level of security through a physical device that she had spirited away under the guise of a phony mission. The messenger who had delivered it to The General's emissary months ago didn't have a "need to know" regarding what the mission was or any of its details. Accustomed as he was to such tasks, he never questioned why he was handing off a plain-brown-wrapped package to a teenaged girl who, in turn, handed it off to a courier who delivered it to The General.

The package carried an AI-powered shirt that would detect the DNA of the person wearing it, validating his or her identity. So, The General, whom Evelyn had never met, was the only person who could unlock the password and receive the message.

"Where are they now?" asked The General, his manner brusque. He was accustomed to being the man in charge. Evelyn ignored his tone in the interest of maintaining focus on their mission.

"They've cleared the Philly pod and are heading west on what used to be the Pennsylvania Turnpike," she responded, her image with a bit more pixilation than expected.

"The pavement starts to break apart around what used to be called Harrisburg," he said. "They'll be roughing it from there to Pittsburgh."

"Will you be ready to intercept them as we planned?" she asked. She had the president's concern in the back of her mind and her words came across sounding more worried than they should be.

"I've told you we will," he replied. His annoyance showed in his tone of voice. They had covered the details many times before during their weekly calls.

Undeterred but growing impatient, Evelyn continued to confirm. "Let's make sure they see nothing on the trip out that will raise their suspicions."

"They won't," he replied without hesitation. "Has there been any news coverage of our raid on the armory?"

"Militia raids on armories have become commonplace," replied Evelyn. "The prevailing political wisdom is for the authorities not to react. We'd rather have the militias hiding and waiting to defend themselves from a government attack that would never come."

"Didn't you say there was a secret committee investigating it?" he asked.

"Yes," she replied. "They suspect a militia but haven't been able to find any real evidence to connect you to it. Or anyone else for that matter. The Secretary has pulled some of their investigators and reassigned them to one of her pet projects. So, I would guess she's not under much pressure to find the culprit."

"When will we get the funds for the equipment we need?" he asked.

"The logging crane? I've got a slush fund that I've designated for a classified project. I'll initiate a blockchain transaction by Wednesday. You can use the same decryption technique as you do for this communication channel to get the funds," she replied, trying to hide her annoyance. *We've been over this a hundred times!*

"WEDNESDAY? That's cutting it close, isn't it? If you want to be sure nothing will be noticed, we should have the funds available to transfer by tomorrow."

"I'll see what I can do," she replied.

Frustrated though he was, he held his tongue and signed off.

KrypComm deleted the video record of their conversation as soon as they both logged off, first sending them to a folder labeled "RECEIVED_VIDEO_MESSAGES" then retitling the files with a .NOMEDIA extension. The designation resulted in deletion of the file in a matter of a few seconds.

The pavement on what was once the Pennsylvania Turnpike had been broken and rough throughout their journey. Now, as they arrived at a little village called Adamstown about fifty miles east of the former state capital, the pavement nearly completely disappeared. The village itself reminded Diana of a ghost town as it may have been depicted in an old Western movie. In front of her, the dusty main street lined with falling-down buildings was complemented by a few rusty fuel tanks and a sign on a storefront, hanging by one corner. Adamstown Pharmacy and Bait Shop, it said. It was a dead end. They would have to calculate a different route.

Using satellite imaging as their guide, Gabrielle recommended trying U.S. Route 30 toward York. They would be roughing it from there. No discernable roadways after that point. They skirted York near the old on-ramp to Interstate 83, noticing that despite the city having been abandoned for nearly 10 years, the sign proclaiming it to be the Barbell Capital of the World remained alongside the iconic statue of a weightlifter performing an overhead press.

The Pennsylvania countryside was beautiful, perhaps more so because it had been abandoned by the civilized world during the second Great Depression. The remnants of civilization remained but were in a state of decay. Their journey along the picturesque Susquehanna River, on their right as they had briefly headed northwest, was juxtaposed by rotting rowhouses on their left.

So, it seemed odd to Diana when she noticed a very new-looking, bright green machine at the top of a hill near Foxburg as they neared their destination.

They had been rotating driving duties so they could drive longer days and spend less time by the roadside. Sergeant Filian relieved Diana as the machine came into view. His eyes followed her gaze and instinctively answered the question on her mind without her having to ask.

"It's a logging crane!"

"How do you know that, Sarge?" she replied.

"I grew up in Oregon," he said. "My Dad was a logger."

It was an idle question. Diana was too preoccupied with the oddity of brand-new heavy equipment in the midst of all this decay to care how he knew.

"Why the hell is it here?" she wondered aloud but under her breath, not expecting a reply.

By the time they arrived in Pittsburgh, they were exhausted. Diana's schedule had kept them moving nearly non-stop. She had made a plan to have them arrive a day earlier than expected. She wasn't confident that Evelyn's brush off about the potential of a militia attack reflected the facts on the ground. Even Gabrielle, who would normally find a source of pleasure in camping under the stars, was numbed by the experience.

The sign on the Wharton Street building said, 'The Hormone Center.' Diana crosschecked her GPS position and had Gabrielle confirm this was their destination. "Hormone Center?" she wondered aloud.

"That describes a line of business the company retreated from two decades ago," said Matt who seemed excited for the first time since they started their journey. "In the 2020's, cryogenic therapy was used to treat everything from arthritis to menopause," he continued. "As the technology advanced, the fantasy of freezing one's nearly dead body until a cure for what ails you could be found has become a reality," he added, answering a question no one had asked.

The exterior of the building was as rundown and decaying as those around it. The only sign of modernity was the side door, recently painted and secured with the latest technology. A database had been updated to include the heat signature of each team member. Each of them was allowed to enter the building once their signature had been validated.

Mateen passed through the doorway a half step behind Diana. He placed his palm on a scanner and stood still until a full body scan admitted him to the inner sanctum of this Top-Secret enterprise. Following his example, each of the team did the same. Once scanned, they entered the space that few had ever visited and headed to Cell Number 30609.

Cell Number 30609 was a cryopreservation lab. Its walls were lined nine-foot-tall high-pressure tanks. Each held one frozen human being.

They were all a bit surprised by the lack of human interaction. For all they knew, they were the only people in the building. Undeterred, Mateen focused on the task at hand. He checked all the electrical connections and the flex hoses that extended from massive tanks marked Liquid Nitrogen and Liquid Helium. "All good," he pronounced them. He connected a handheld electronic device to the master control panel and downloaded the data describing the cellular state of their quarry . Other than a handful of power burps, there had been continuous power and supply of the liquids and gases necessary to maintain a cryogenic state. "Remarkable," he said. "Twenty-five years and it – or he – is still in good shape."

Diana's team looked stunned. They hadn't known they were retrieving a frozen body, much less who it was. They only knew they were in an abandoned building in the middle of an abandoned city watching Mateen – who by this point seemed to be a mad scientist – prepare one of its population to make the return trip.

CHAPTER 9

ENERGY FROM
DIAMONDS

THE PRESIDENT'S IMPATIENCE WAS PALPABLE. THE PRE-senter, Priya Siddharth-Carmichael, Director of the Defense Advanced Research Projects Agency, stood at the bottom of the auditorium, her voice echoing in the huge room's hollow shell. She faced not only the president but also a group of aides who were arranged like branches of a tree with the president at its root. *I imagine they naturally arrange themselves according to seniority* she thought.

Like Plato and Pythagoras, Priya had mathematically modelled patterns that recur in nature. *And here they are – government elites unconsciously observing the natural order.*

"So, we've demonstrated that we can capture carbon-14 in diamonds and use them in lieu of batteries," Priya continued. "In fact, Madam President, the drone you flew here to our national lab was powered by one." This information seemed to crack the president's impervious façade.

She had wanted to make sure the president understood that diamond battery power works and she was pretty sure she had made her point.

"What's next, Professor?" said the president as she recomposed herself. She tapped her wrist to get a heads-up display of the time. "I have to be back in Washington in about a half hour."

She's famous for disregarding her appointments. I must be boring her. Best to get to the bottom line.

"Using carbon-14 as an energy source is the best way to offset the downsides of solar and wind. No more interruptions in power flow because of weather. And we wouldn't need vast parcels of land for solar arrays. We could redeploy the land for food production . . ."

"Okay, so we can create renewable nuclear energy from diamonds. I get it," Porter interrupted. "So, what's the problem?"

"Well, technically, we're just using diamonds to hold the energy from the carbon-14. We need to aim a laser beam through the diamond to get the . . ."

The President looked as though her head would explode. "Yes, professor, I understand. So, what's next?"

"Well, Madam President, we're not sure . . ." *Jeez, I've heard about her temper. But her glare could bore holes through the side of a battleship.* "We haven't figured out how to scale it."

"And what do you need from me?"

"There is some classified data . . ."

"Okay, you've got it." She stood and turned to leave, her retinue a half beat behind, turning like geese in a V formation. "Parminder, see that the professor gets what she needs."

"Yes, ma'am," came a voice from the middle of the pack.

Priya never mentioned that the author of classified documents — the genius behind the research – was none other than Diana's Nobel Prize winning grandfather, Nick Adams.

THE LOGGING
CRANE

DIANA CHECKED OUT THE SPOT WHERE THEY HAD seen the bright green logging crane. Noticing its absence as Sergeant Filian ascended from the lower level of the vehicle to take over driving duties, she wasn't sure if she should be worried or not.

"It's gone!" said the sergeant, reading Diana's mind.

"Yeah. What do you think that means?" she asked. The bright green machine was anomalous when they had spotted it on the way out. The fact that it was gone on their return journey meant there was activity of some kind in the area. *But what?*

"Could mean nothin'," Filian replied. "Or it could mean somethin'."

"Thanks for your great wisdom, Sarge," she replied sarcastically. She gazed at the spot where the logging crane had stood as though that might yield an answer.

"Well, it's just that my Dad told me that he's heard some loggers had started cutting trees again," he added. "So, I don't know if we should be surprised to see logging machinery or . . . "

"How long has logging been outlawed?" she interrupted.

"I would guess about 20 years. It was part of the Green Energy Law passed in the 20's."

"So, why are loggers starting up again?"

"It's been long enough for trees to grow back in some places. And there is black-market demand for real wood."

"Black market? It'd be kind of hard to move timber without anyone noticing, wouldn't it?"

"I doubt the lazy bastards living inside their walled cities are going to risk a confrontation just because a few guys are cutting down trees," he said. "Besides, it's only rich guys who are buying real wood. And they can make sure people look the other way."

Makes sense, thought Diana. But she had a queasy feeling in her stomach. It was a feeling she only got when something didn't quite fit. With Filian in the driver's seat, Diana turned her attention to Mateen as he adjusted the settings on the cryogenic capsule. Diana helped with his checklist as he inspected the oxygen and nitrogen lines. There were over a hundred sensors, more than half of which were implanted to ensure the temperature of the internal organs of the capsule's occupant remained constant.

The pile of logs was hard and unforgiving when it dropped, seemingly out of nowhere, on top of their vehicle. As the APC ground to a halt, the last thing Filian saw was a massive 28-inch diameter tree trunk crash through the windshield. When the log pile hit, Diana was thrown to the floor, hitting her head against a stanchion. Her head throbbing, she lifted herself off the deck of the APC, covered by a pile of eastern hemlock. There was a sharp pain in her left side as she inhaled which suggested a broken rib or two. She stumbled to where Filian was sitting in the driver's seat.

Two logs had smashed the windshield crushing his left side. She placed two fingers on his carotid artery. He was dead.

She had no time to react as the overhead hatch was blown open and a well-armed and well-armored warrior dropped down onto the deck and turned his weapon in her direction. Unarmed and a bit woozy, she had no chance to resist. A second soldier dropped through the hatch and turned toward her team, which was now emerging from the darkness below. Some had drawn their sidearms but placed them on the deck when ordered. Although there were only two attackers, their automatic weapons and body armor were too overwhelming to counter. Diana felt herself losing consciousness. She struggled to stay on her feet. Someone was giving commands – commands she couldn't understand much less obey. The world seemed to be spinning around her as she slumped to the floor.

The throbbing in her head was the first sensation to hit Diana as she struggled to regain consciousness. Looking around the sterile room, she couldn't focus her eyes. She was vaguely aware of someone calling out.

"Welcome back," said the someone as two doctors, accompanied by a huge guy – he looked like a burly gym rat – burst into the room. The gym rat looked like he was ready for action until he realized that Diana could barely stand without help. He stood back as the doctors tended to her, shining lights in her eyes, asking questions.

"How many fingers?" one asked.

What happened? Where am I? How did I get here? Her vague memory of a crash provided no answers. She eyed the gym rat wondering why he was here if she was in a hospital.

"Three. Where the hell am I?"

"She's back," said the first doctor.

"Thank God!" said the second as he injected something into her left shoulder.

They stayed with her until she could sit upright. Her head pounding, she tried to get up, but her knees buckled from the effort.

"Is someone going to tell me what's going on?" she said with an effort that threatened to cause her to lose consciousness again.

"We're just the medical team," said the oldest of the three. "Someone else will be in to brief you soon."

"What about Brutus over there," she said pointing at the gym rat. "Is he part of the medical team too?" If the gym rat was unnerved by Diana's attention, he showed no sign of it. Diana knew why he was there. He was expected to ignore the conversation and apply his physical strength when needed.

"No, he's not," said The General as he entered the room. "And, neither am I." His air of authority and the reaction of the medical team suggested to her that he was the man in charge.

"Who are you and why am I being held here? Why did you attack my team? How long have I been out of action? I want you to let me out of . . . "

"All in due time, young lady."

"Don't patronize me, you jackass. I'm on a mission ordered by the president and, if someone isn't on their way to rescue us, they soon will be." She could feel her blood rising. *Young lady!* She took an immediate dislike to this jerk. She had put up with many like him throughout her brief career. She always felt as though she was required to prove herself worthy, unlike men of similar rank and seniority.

The General's raised eyebrow betrayed his surprise at the mention of the president. But he didn't remark on it.

"They won't find you," he said. "You're being held under 600 feet of granite. We'll let you back to the surface once the neural lace has fully leached out of your skull."

"My skull?" said Diana, instinctively reaching for her head. "What the hell is going on? What's neural lace?"

The General sighed the sigh of an elder who understood the impatience of someone much younger. "If you'll take a breath and hear me out, Major," he started. "I'll explain everything."

Angry and still groping at her scalp, Diana backed down, her curiosity now piqued.

"Those troops you imagine the president sending to save you can't find you without a satellite connection to your embedded chip." Diana knew that everyone who lived in the pods as well as anyone officially connected to the government had an embedded chip that enabled monitoring technology to identify where every individual was at any time.

"Nearly everyone in the pods has had a chip embedded since grade school," The General continued. "Yours – like most military officers – was replaced when you were commissioned."

"What about my team?" asked Diana, as her situation began to come into focus. She had been captured and separated from her team. The means by which her commanders might find her had been disabled. She didn't know why she was here or who her captor was. Nor did she know the whereabouts of her grandfather whose possible revival might have been endangered.

"They're fine and will love hearing that you are fine as well." He paused, waiting for Diana to calm down and pausing to choose his words carefully. "The chip you had embedded at the Space Force Academy was different than most. You were part of an experiment." He paused again.

"What?" Still a bit fuzzy, Diana struggled to focus on The General's words. *What's he saying? What's this about chips? Where's my team?*

"My chip?" she said. "What about my chip?"

"It was replaced at the Space Force Academy," repeated The General.

"Yeah, I know that." *Why is he talking about my chip? Who is this guy?*

"Yes. But your chip was different."

Diana let this sink in for a moment. As she opened her mouth to speak, The General continued.

"The Defense Department, or rather its research arm DARPA, began working on neuroprosthetics in the 2010's. Their goal at the time was to help soldiers who had suffered from traumatic brain injuries by implanting chips in their brains enabling functions that had gone dormant. It wasn't much of a stretch to conceive of implants that stimulated the impulse to fight in dangerous situations."

Why am I being treated to a lecture about chips? Focus, Diana. Focus!

"Are you talking about 'fight or flight'?" she asked.

"Yes. The idea was to ensure that soldiers would respond appropriately in battle. The experiment was abandoned in the 20's due to ethical concerns. Anyway, the military was focused on creating hunter-killer robots by then."

"I've read about those. But what has all this to do with me?"

"I'm getting to that," he continued. "The robots had limited usefulness as warfare went to cyberspace and then to outer space. So, DARPA changed its focus. They had always thought the best way to develop artificial intelligence was by mapping the human brain and collecting data from chips in the brains of military personnel."

"And I'm one of their guinea pigs?!!??" *Why is he telling me this? What's different about my chip?* "Did they map my brain?"

"No," he answered. "By the time they implanted a new chip in you, they already had their brain map. But you're one of their guinea pigs in another experiment."

Diana wanted to scream. *I still don't know why we've been captured. I don't know where my team is. Hell, I don't even know where I am. And now I'm being told I'm a specimen in an experiment involving the human brain.* She wanted to find whoever came up with this bright idea and chose her for the experiment. *Once I find the son of a bitch, I'll kill him.*

"Please let me finish, Major," said The General.

Diana swallowed hard. *He's not going to answer my questions until I've let him finish.* "Go on," she said finally.

"We're all enhanced, Diana. And, we have been for centuries. We drink coffee to stay alert, wear glasses and contact lenses to focus our failing eyesight. In the 20th Century, we developed knee replacements and pacemakers. In this century, we've added embedded chips to improve the reflexes of people who want to remain productive in their later years – the Secretary of Defense for example."

"All very interesting. But, again, what has this to do with me?"

"That additional productivity that has enabled society to provide economic support as we expanded healthcare benefits and housing to those on universal basic income," he continued, warming to his subject and ignoring his audience.

"Why are you telling me all this?" she asked. "Is that why I'm here? Are you going to use me in another experiment?"

"No, Diana," he reassured her. "I'm telling you this because you are at the forefront of the next phase of human enhancement. When the military implanted a new chip in the base of your neck, they also injected a thin thread that created a seamless interface between machine and biological circuitry. It's called a 'mesh electronics' and it forms a neural lace over the surface of your brain. It also creates an electronic signature detectable by satellite. So, we can't let you out of here until it leeches out of your brain. It shouldn't be much longer."

Diana sat in stunned silence. She opened her mouth to speak. But nothing emerged. She couldn't even form a sound.

"The experiment is a combination of leading technologies: nanotech, brain mapping and neuroprosthetics," he continued. "You are the first human being to take full advantage of artificial superintelligence. The military has been tracking your progress for the last ten years."

"All without my knowledge? How can anyone have decided to do this to me and not tell me? It's totally unethical! Who did this? You seem to know all about this. Was it you?"

"No, it wasn't me."

"Well, who then?"

"It was very controversial at the time. I objected but my concerns fell on deaf ears," he continued. "I left the military and the podosphere. That's when I decided to take up residence in this far corner of Pennsylvania. I grew up here. My family built this underground compound in the 1950's as a bomb shelter. It seems quaint now. But man's greatest fear then was nuclear annihilation."

"Well, if you didn't do this, who did?"

"It was General Paul Adams," he paused to let this sink in. "Your father."

CHAPTER 11

DECEPTION

"WHAT DO YOU MEAN WE DON'T KNOW WHERE they are?" Tara Leto asked, her face showing signs of anger she was barely able to contain.

"They were attacked, and their electronic signature was neutralized," replied Evelyn. She was feigning ignorance of their whereabouts while simultaneously demonstrating her expertise, hoping her plot wouldn't be exposed. It was a delicate balance. Tara's fury worked in her favor. Anger typically reduces one's perceptive abilities. "From the perspective of our satellite tracking, it's as though they have vanished."

"Yes, but it's been more than a week," said Tara, the strain showing in her voice. "They should have resurfaced somewhere by now."

Evelyn knew this could be a career killer for people like Tara. Massive failures like this one could haunt a Washington insider forever.

"There are several possible reasons why they haven't been found," Evelyn responded calmly. "Their chips could have been reprogrammed. Or they could have been surgically removed." She paused before stating the most obvious reason. Tara tensed in anticipation of the answer she most dreaded.

"Or, they could have been killed," she said finally.

Tara's face was redder than Evelyn had ever seen it. And, she had been through more than a few of her tirades. She braced herself for the inevitable.

"How could you have let this happen?" She wasn't screaming. But her clenched teeth couldn't contain the spittle that sprayed from her mouth. "You assured me that there was no militia activity in the area. When I suggested we send a platoon of Marines, you talked me out of it. No risk, you said. It would be good to have a war hero leading this mission, you said. What the hell are we going to do now?"

"To be clear," Evelyn said, seeking to stoke the flames rather than calm them. "The President shared my view."

"EXCUSES! I hate excuses. Only results matter and this is a terrible result. As for the President, she's acting like it was my idea, not hers. And, then of course, there's the press."

"They can't have gone far without detection," continued Evelyn, trying to refocus the conversation. "We can . . . "

"That's another thing," Tara interrupted. "Why don't we have satellite photos of the area at the time of the attack?"

"The geo-scans were out of date. Twelve years ago, there were no large trees in the area. Now, there are. And they have obscured what happened when they disappeared. There was a report filed but correcting the error in the geo-scans was a low priority."

Tara was so angry that Evelyn didn't think she cared what her responses were. "And, what about the capsule? How could they have moved the capsule and preserved its inhabitant without the proper equipment?"

"There's no reason why they – whoever they are – wouldn't have the right equipment. Most cryogenic facilities are located in rural towns and stopped operating during the Depression. Anyone with a bit of ingenuity and a lot of ambition, could have absconded with the right equipment."

"How would they have the expertise? They're just a bunch of deplorable, uneducated louts," she said with too much emotion. Her temper was causing her to abandon reason and Evelyn knew it. Tara paused and took a deep breath.

"Well, even if that's true," said Evelyn, "they have Mateen. He could still be managing the capsule."

"You think he's alive?"

"Probably. If they wanted Nick Adams alive, their best course would be to have Mateen alive and well."

"Probably? It was your assessment of probabilities that had got us into this mess in the first place."

Evelyn was silent. *Better to let her make the next move* she thought. *She's starting to calm down. Maybe now I can reason with her.*

"So, what now?" Tara asked after a pause.

This was the moment Evelyn had been waiting for. It was important to get Tara to make the decision she needed. Equally important was for the decision to be Tara's idea – or for her to at least think it was her idea. She started by suggesting a solution she knew Tara would reject.

"Well, we could send that platoon of Marines." Evelyn's voice trailed off as she waited for the response she wanted and received.

"No, that would be worse than if we had sent them out in the first place," Tara replied, now calmer. "We need the equivalent of Fightin' Joe Wheeler."

"Who?"

"He was a Confederate General who volunteered to fight for the US Army in the Spanish-American War. He was in his 60's by then but still in fighting shape. He was put in charge of the cavalry."

"You know him?" Evelyn asked.

"No, I'm not that old!" Tara guffawed in spite of herself. "I'm just a student of history. Fightin' Joe was welcomed by President McKinley at the beginning of the Spanish-American War. He was a former Confederate General."

"So, he could lead blue coated cavalrymen, their horses and artillery through the South without resistance," Evelyn confirmed.

"Right," said Tara. "The Civil War was still a recent memory and the animosity of the losers toward the victors was still palpable."

"So, you're suggesting we find someone who wouldn't raise the hackles of the locals."

"Correct! But, who?" Tara said, her brow furrowed.

Evelyn remained silent for a few minutes so that Tara wouldn't suspect she had a ready answer.

"Alfred Braxton Bragg!" she exclaimed as though the name had just occurred to her.

"Bragg? Yeah, I remember him. He resigned his commission in the 30's over some dust up with the top brass, didn't he?"

"I was too junior to know what happened at the time," said Evelyn. "But he and I were born in the same town – Erie, Pennsylvania. He was famous among the locals."

"Are you in touch with him?"

"Well, I don't know him," Evelyn lied. "But I have an aging Aunt who still lives in Erie. She told me last Christmas that he owns most of the town. So, I would guess we can find him pretty easily."

"I like it!" said Tara. "See if you can track him down. And I want real time updates. Don't wait for the next staff meeting to let me know what's going on."

"Yes, ma'am," replied Evelyn, remaining expressionless despite her glee at having manipulated the situation and been given permission to enlist The General, her partner in crime.

CHAPTER 12

DIANA

IANA WAS A LITTLE WOBBLY AS SHE ASCENDED THE long stairs to the surface. She had been contained in a small, artificially lit space for a bit more than two weeks while she recovered from her concussion.

You can do it! Only thirty more steps, she said to herself as though she was in the gym. When she reached the top, she was winded, a little dizzy but none the worse for wear. Stepping through the door, she gulped fresh air for the first time since she had been knocked unconscious in the attack.

It was Corporal Paul Miller who first reacted to her straightening up at the top of the stairs.

"Major!" he yelped. The rest of the team turned toward her like synchronized swimmers.

Cacophony followed. Whoops and hollering, pushing and hugging. The decorum that was usually required of members of the military was overridden by the joy of the moment, her team thrilled to see that Diana was healthy and able to move about on her own.

Diana noticed Gabrielle was hanging back a bit as though she wanted a clean shot at an enormous hug. When it finally came, the two clung to each other for what seemed like an eternity. The others watched silently.

Once they released each other, Diana looked around, mentally taking a roll call. "Filian?" she asked when she figured who was missing.

"Dead," replied Gabrielle, confirming what Diana was thinking. She took a deep breath and released it slowly to avoid being overcome by lightheadedness. Military commanders were responsible for the safety of those in their charge. But the emotion she felt was more than that. The attack had commenced just a few minutes after Filian had taken the seat she had occupied. Her sense of command responsibility was overtaken by her sense of survivors' guilt. Had Filian been few minutes late, she would have been sitting in the driver's seat when the log came crashing through the windshield.

They were assembled in a huge ballroom, decorated in the fashion of the late 19th Century. Crystal chandeliers and sconces adorned a room that featured woodwork hand carved to a glorious flourish by craftsmen whose skills had long ago been lost in the evolution of manufactured products.

For the first time, Diana took notice of her surroundings. She found herself in awe of the room in which she now stood. *Is that mahogany?* she wondered. It was!

She had almost lost track of how she had arrived in this location – how her mission had been derailed, how she lost one of the men in her charge. *And Matt! Where was he?* She hadn't seen him when she was greeted so warmly at the top of the stairwell.

She was still a bit fuzzy. The concussion had left her unable to process her thoughts clearly. *Or was it the neural lace? Had its removal affected her ability to think clearly?*

"Where's Matt?" she said finally to no one and everyone at the same time.

"We're not sure," said Gabrielle. "He was taken away along with the cylinder."

"So, you haven't seen him since the raid?"

"Oh, we've seen him. But only briefly. We haven't been able to talk with him."

It was all coming into focus again. Her mission, the cryogenic facility, the attack that seemed to come out of nowhere, the conversation with The General.

Why were we taken prisoner? What is there about my frozen grandfather that would cause someone to risk all by attacking a military convoy on home soil? What is Matt up to?

She turned to Gabrielle, wanting to find out what she may know or have figured out during Diana's days underground. But she was interrupted by the stirring of her small contingent, as they all turned toward entrance to the ballroom. A guard – Diana recognized him as the gym rat who had been with her when she awoke – had opened the door. Mateen entered the room, and it soon became clear that he was escorting someone – someone old and fragile.

Her troops parted like the Red Sea and then she saw him. *Grandpa!* She was overwhelmed. He looked not a day older than the last time she had seen him. Of course, he wasn't a day older having been preserved for 25 years. The sight of him reminded her of the last time she had seen her mother, annoyed at having been delegated the task of taking her father-in-law to his doctor on short notice. Her hair pulled back, barely held in place by a pair of barrettes, not having the time to apply her makeup since returning from her morning workout and still wearing her gym clothes, she shot daggers from her eyes toward her husband, too angry to even say "bye-bye" to her six-year-old daughter.

Nick Adams, a bit unsteady on his feet but clearly in possession of his mental faculties, simply looked at her with tenderness in his eyes and said, "Hello, Diana."

CHAPTER 13

THE SITUATION
ROOM

ENERAL MILLER CLARKE HAD NEVER ATTENDED A national security meeting at the White House. He wasn't even sure why he had been invited to this one. Nevertheless, he found himself as part of an entourage headed by the President of the United States, Kathleen Porter. Clarke and the others squeezed into the elevator trying their best not to encroach on the president's personal space. The door opened opposite the entrance to the John F. Kennedy Conference Room – at 5500 square feet, an intelligence management center and conference room – also colloquially referred to as 'The Situation Room.'

"Good morning, Madam President," said Abigail Hayden, the Director of National Intelligence. The chatter in the room died down quickly as the President took her seat at the head of the table. Clarke had met Abigail once or twice at social functions in and around the capital. But this was the first time he was attending a meeting that she chaired. He was forced to recall her meteoric rise to the top of the national security hierarchy.

"Where are we on finding them?" the President started.

"No further than yesterday, I'm afraid," said Abigail.

"Excuse me, Madam President," interrupted Clarke. He was not seated at the massive conference table but rather in a row along the wall. "I'm not clear on why the domestic kidnapping of a small contingent of military personnel, likely by a militia group, has been elevated to a national security matter." The look on the president's face told him he should have kept his mouth shut.

"And you are?" asked the president.

"General Miller Clarke, Ma'am. I lead the Pentagon's Office of Cybersecurity and Surveillance Strategy."

The president opened her mouth to speak but Abigail interrupted her. "I asked the Pentagon to have General Clarke attend today's meeting because of his prior work on both the Hack Attack and the Chinese cyberattack on our power grid."

President Porter paused for a deep breath, as though she was making an effort to control the tone of her response.

"The Hack Attack revealed a critical weakness in our technology infrastructure, a weakness we thought we had overcome, General," added Abigail. "Moving forward quickly to a decentralized grid is an essential step on the critical path. It will ensure we protect the nation from another catastrophic event like the Chinese hack that brought down the grid in the thirties."

"How is that related to this kidnapping?" the general asked. He knew his questions were unwelcome. But he was here for a reason and that reason was his technical expertise. He couldn't make a qualified judgment or give his input if he didn't know what was in the president's head. Something wasn't right here and, like a dog with a bone, he never let go. He wondered if Abigail knew what she was getting when she invited him. He had always been a guy who would do what's right no matter the consequences.

"Does it really matter?" snapped the president, her impatience getting the better of her.

"The team that Major Adams led was a small part of the mission to master a new technology that would enable the deployment of a new grid," added the Secretary of Technology and Artificial Intelligence.

"What new technology?" asked the general, undeterred by the president's temper.

"We believe a new technology that releases the energy from Carbon-14 stored in diamonds can change global energy production overnight," Abby answered, again stepping in. Clarke thought she was trying to thwart a presidential blowup that would derail the meeting.

"And how is Major Adams connected to this development?" he asked.

"She's not. Her grandfather is."

CHAPTER 14

NICK ADAMS

WHAT SHOWED OF THE FLOORS IN THE AREA NOT covered by oriental rugs were hardwood planks about 10 inches wide, cut in saw pits of the type not in use for the last 150 years. The old growth forests in the Eastern United States had disappeared by the late 19th Century. Wide plank floors of the type valued by the wealthy were then commonplace. Logs were cut manually by two men into quarters. They were then cut into "quarter-sawn" planks at a forty-five-degree angle that were stronger, more stable and resistant to cupping.

"How old is this house?" asked Diana rhetorically. She and her grandfather had found a nook in a sitting room on the east side of the big house. They were free to wander without restrictions so long as they didn't attempt to go outside.

"Nearly two hundred years," answered Nick as his eyes scanned the room. "Helluva prison, huh?"

She laughed. "Yeah, helluva prison," she said. Then she added, "reminds me of Newport, Rhode Island."

"I'm surprised you remember that trip," Nick responded. "You were very young."

"After you and Mom were killed in the accident, Dad and I created a scrapbook and a souvenir box to remember you by. I would open that box whenever I was stressed about something. It contained the kind of treasures that have no value except to me. I kept some postcards from that trip."

"What were you stressed about?"

"Oh, you know . . . teenage girl stuff," she recalled chuckling to herself as she dredged up long-buried memories. "What the other girls were wearing, which boys liked us or didn't like us and . . . " Her voice trailed off.

Nick waited a few seconds and asked, "and what?"

"I was an Air Force brat," she said. "Like any child of a military family, we moved every two or three years. I was always leaving friends behind, always having to start over. It was hard me." She swallowed hard, taking a moment to compose herself. "Especially without a Mom," she added, as memories she had long suppressed bubbled to the surface.

Somehow, she felt comfortable with Nick, a grandfather she had never really known. Comfortable enough to allow herself to share her feelings, her life experiences – the history of how she had become who she was. But memories of her mother were buried too deep, and she wasn't sure how she would react if she allowed them to emerge.

"I wouldn't mind going back to Newport," he said as though he sensed he should change the subject. "I always loved it there."

"Too late," she said, happy to move past an emotional moment. His expression told her to go on. "The culture wars of the 20's created a backlash against the wealthy. I was just a kid. But I remember the president declaring the 'The Grand Demolition.'"

"The Grand Demolition?" he was incredulous. "What happened?"

"Artificial intelligence was deployed to rewrite every book, repaint every picture and rename every street and building. The mansions in Newport were demolished."

"A lot has happened in twenty-five years," said Nick, his face betraying a mixture of confusion and concern.

"Yeah," she said. "I wish you had been here to share it with me." And she really did. She wondered how her life would be different – how she would be different – if she had grown up with a mother. Her father loved her and did his best to raise a young girl. But his parental instincts ranged from overindulgence to treating her like a cadet training to be a military officer, which is obviously what she had become.

She wondered what it would have been like having her grandfather around for a few more years too. He was not only intelligent but insightful. And patient. He seemed to know that she wasn't ready to share too much about her mother. And he was willing to wait until she was ready. That's what she thought anyway.

"Me too," he said bringing Diana back to the conversation. "I wish I had been there too."

"Do you remember the accident?" asked Diana.

"I don't have a clear memory of it," Nick Adams replied.

"You don't remember the day of the accident at all?" Diana was incredulous.

"Well, I remember leaving the house. Your Mom and Dad were arguing about something. So, I just headed out to the garage and waited. Your Mom was always very kind to me, but that day she said little. She had a temper that could cause a pride of lions to run and hide. So, we mostly sat in silence in the car. But I don't remember the accident itself or how I ended up enduring twenty-five years of 'Rip Van Winkle'-like sleep."

"Your injuries must have been pretty severe to . . . " started Diana.

"What injuries?" interrupted Nick. "If I had injuries severe enough to warrant cryogenics, how can I be walking around scar-free immediately after being restored from the deep freeze?"

Diana hadn't thought about that. She was so overcome by his return that she hadn't looked at her grandfather critically. If she had, she would have seen a fit, trim, white-haired man in his seventies with a wrinkled face reflecting the wisdom of his years. Someone who had incurred life-threatening trauma would be battered and recovering from broken bones.

"So, what . . . I mean why . . . " Diana was so confounded that she couldn't express a clear thought or question.

"Why was I frozen?" said Nick. "Great question. I've been wondering about that myself. Cryogenics was still in the experimental stage in the 2024."

"Someone wanted you out of action and thought they might need you for something in the future," surmised Diana. "But I don't understand something. If they needed you in the future, why not keep you alive? Why preserve you in the deep freeze?"

"I was dying, Diana. I had – I still have – pancreatic cancer. In the 2020's, that was a death sentence."

Stunned, Diana realized her perspective on both her grandfather's and mother's deaths had been frozen in time. Her six-year-old self remembered being told they had died in a car accident and she had never questioned the facts. *That was why he and Mom were off to a doctor's appointment. Cancer treatment.*

She slumped in her seat, an overstuffed leather easy chair with a high back, faded and a bit cracked from age. She looked around the room, a sitting room of the sort out of fashion for a least 100 years. *None of this makes any sense. Why am I here? Why would anyone have kidnapped my grandfather and frozen him only to retrieve him a quarter century later?*

"And now?" she asked finally. "If you still have cancer, how can you possibly be cured when you're imprisoned in ... Where are we anyway? I still can't figure this whole thing out?"

"I'm being treated with a combination of gene therapy and nanotechnology. The treatment would have been a miracle twenty-five years ago. The General has a team of physicians who ..."

"The General! That's the guy in charge, right?" she cried. "What's he up to? I don't know why I was sent to bring you back. I didn't even know you were cryogenically frozen. I don't know who wants you alive and why."

"I've been wondering that myself. Your guy Matt – is that his name? – has been asking me some pretty tough math questions. It's almost like a test to see what I can recall."

"Math questions?" Diana knew that her grandfather had won the Nobel Prize but had thought it had to do with social justice not math.

"Yes, I created an algorithm that, apparently, is still in use today. It's been embedded in chips and is the basis of much of the artificial intelligence that's prevalent in modern society. At least, that's what Matt has been telling me."

"Matt?" Diana's head was swimming again. *Matt was brought along as an expert in cryogenics. What does he know about math and artificial intelligence?*

"I always thought your Nobel had something to do with justice or society or something," she said.

"Yes, it did. But there was an algorithm at the center of it. When artificial intelligence started to be used in decision making, it analyzed past decisions and applied the learned pattern to future decisions. I found a way to break the pattern."

"I'm confused. What are you talking about?"

"Well, let me give you a couple of examples. Let's say you are in charge of hiring people in a large company. You might have found it attractive to use artificial intelligence to assist in identifying high potential candidates. An algorithm would be created by analyzing data – 'Big Data' it was called at the time – identifying the attributes of the most successful people you had hired in the past."

"Yeah," Diana interjected. "What's wrong with that?"

"Theoretically, nothing. But, in practice, the algo was analyzing data that reflected the bias of human corporate managers over a few decades. So, the algo would come to the conclusion that the most successful candidates were white males. Initially, corporate CEOs blindly followed this advice until they realized that their solution to a problem had made the problem worse. Instead of removing the bias of a few individuals, they had institutionalized that bias."

"And you solved that problem?"

"Yes," he replied unable, despite his best efforts, to suppress a bit of a smile.

"And that's what won you the Nobel?" she asked.

"Well, not exactly. That's what paid for my research. I won the Nobel for applying it in a different setting."

Diana's raised eyebrows told him to continue.

"We – the nation – had a terrible problem. The bias of law enforcement officers and judges had led to disproportionate imprisonment of people with dark skin – African Americans and Latinos. Artificial intelligence made it worse. Before we used AI to make sentencing decisions, a biased judge might negatively affect a few hundred people. Using AI to normalize those decisions affected millions."

"And you fixed that?" His smile gave her the answer. *This is where I come from. This man is a hero – not in the same way people think of me as a hero.* Diana found herself weighing the way society measured her heroism versus the way they might measure Nick Adams' heroism. *Which of us has affected more lives? It's impossible to calculate.*

They sat together quietly for a while, basking in the warmth of the setting sun shining through the tall west-facing windows and the warmth of the rekindled relationship they now enjoyed.

Diana had thought she had lost all of her family. Yet here she was sharing space with someone who had been lost to her when she was a child – someone who knew her family history — someone who cared about her, not because of what she had accomplished but rather only because she had been born. She sat and wondered. *How has all this had come to pass? What does fate have in store for me?*

A whiff of Nick Adams' sweat mixed with Old Spice After Shave triggered a sense memory. She sunk into her chair, relaxing as she had not for longer than she could remember.

CHAPTER 15

THE REPORT

TONY IDLY WONDERED HOW MANY BUCKETS HE WOULD find strewn throughout the dilapidated building that served as Erie's police station. The torrential rain showed no signs of letting up and the leaky roof always brought out the bucket brigade. He had long ago become inured to the soaked carpets and musty smell that always followed a storm. But he didn't look forward to the infestation of ants that would surface when the ground became soaked.

One of the deputies had found a couple of empty paint cans in the dumpster. But they had overflowed. Peggy had become exasperated but not before propping up an umbrella over Tony's ancient computer.

"I'm almost afraid to turn it on," he said. Peggy's expression did not betray her thoughts – it never did – but she backed up a few steps as he pressed the power button. There was only one message awaiting his attention – the FBI report. Tony had never been chipped; so, he selected the option that transferred the data to his handheld device. It was marked for his eyes only, a designation he took seriously in this case. He knew he could trust Peggy to keep her mouth shut. But his deputies had a nasty habit of blabbing to their buddies over a beer after work. He closed his warped office door as best he could and opened the report.

Most of the report provided the details of how the investigators had reached their conclusions: the DNA testing methods, the likely path of the nanobots; and, whether the deaths were the result of a catastrophic accident. Tony skipped to the good stuff – the conclusions. The DNA had confirmed that the gray goo splattered on the lab floor was indeed the remains of the two scientists. Most of the sections describing the programming of the nanobots and the likelihood of foul play had been blacked out and marked classified for national security reasons. It was unclear how the nanobots had made their way from the computers in the lab into the bloodstream of the victims. It was assumed but inconclusive that the tiny perpetrators had human help.

"How long will it take?" Evelyn asked, the tension showing in her voice. It was her first conversation with The General since Diana and her team had been captured. "I'm going to have to show that we've made some progress in our search for Diana or they'll put someone else in charge."

"We can't be precise. But Matt thinks it may take two or three weeks to develop the algorithm. Then we'll have to write the code and lock it away in one of my servers," The General replied.

"Two or three weeks?" Her voice went up an octave, surprising The General who was accustomed to her cool, calculating demeanor.

"Let's go over the timeline again," he suggested.

"We're taking a two-pronged approach," she said. "There's a team at NSA working on reconnecting with an electronic signature. I am not concerned about that for obvious reasons . . . ." *There's no electronic signature to reconnect.* " . . . but I'm under orders to pull together a commando team. We're going 'old school'."

"I'll have to isolate Nick and Matt, so they're not exposed to the possibility of recapture."

"How will you do that?" she asked.

"Easy," he replied. "I'll bring them underground and keep the military squad in the house."

"What about Diana?" Evelyn asked. "You said the two had begun to bond."

"That works in our favor," he replied. "I've convinced him that the work we're doing here is too important to let the government screw it up and that he is critically important to the effort. I'll start working on turning her. If she signs up for our cause, the others will follow."

As concerned as she was, Evelyn signed off.

After disconnecting, The General turned to the dark corner where Mateen sat quietly.

"Have I bought you enough time?" he asked.

"Plenty," he replied. "We should be ready tomorrow."

Finally, thought Tony. It was on page 38, Section III.5.a. The deaths had occurred between the hours of 8 and 11 p.m. on May 18.

Who was in the building then? Should be pretty easy to find it out.

"Peggy!" he bellowed without looking up. As slowly as she moved, he was always astonished at how quickly she showed up at his door when he needed her. She waited, saying nothing.

"Find out who cleans the building."

She raised an eyebrow indicating she needed more information. "The national lab . . . down by the lake."

The answer, when it came back, didn't surprise him. Great Lakes Janitorial Services, Inc. was owned by Alfred Braxton Bragg, a.k.a. The General. He owned most of the small businesses in Erie, having arrived like a vulture following retirement from his military career. In the midst of GD2, many small businesses were failing. Business owners who had borrowed from banks were in danger of losing not only their businesses but their homes. The General was their savior. He used his family fortune to buy companies by paying off their bank debt and providing continued employment to the former owners. Now, some fifteen years later, it was nearly impossible to do business in Erie without dealing with one of his companies.

The rain was letting up as Tony cruised across the desolate city. For blocks and blocks, he was the only beating heart, the only warm-blooded being of flesh and bone. His window open, the only sounds he could hear were those of his tires and a black bird crowing so loudly it was as though it expected its call would bring back people who would leave tasty scraps from their lunch break. Tony couldn't help but remember a time when the falling of the first autumn leaves brought out leaf blowers and the first snow flurry brought out plows. It was a great small city then – a time when people raised their kids, chased their dreams and bought five-dollar coffees from Starbucks.

The drab commercial building that housed the offices of Great Lakes Janitorial was the only one occupied in the row of similarly drab edifices. George Potter, the general manager and former owner, a man whose extravagant obesity left people wondering when he had last seen his penis or how he managed all the things a penis was for, was seated in a chair especially designed to withstand his four-hundred-pound heft. He didn't rise when Tony walked through his front door nor did Tony expect him to.

"Whaddaya want, Chief?" he growled as though visits from law enforcement were a regular occurrence.

Potter was a man whose disposition was so unpleasant he could only have succeeded in a business that required night work and no interaction with everyday citizens. So, Tony responded just as abruptly.

"Names of the crew that cleaned the national lab on May 18."

"You got a warrant?"

Tony waited silently, adopting an expression that told Potter to reconsider his attitude. Cooperate or pay a price down the line, his face said.

Potter's desk was cluttered with the detritus of decades of administrative inefficiency – piles of paper, rubber bands and paper clips and the odd knick-knack. It was a perfect complement to an office furnished with beat up file cabinets, a wooden wardrobe and pictures hung on the wall displaying Potter's prowess as a fisherman in the days before he gained too much weight to board a small boat. At their center was a frayed and yellowed 24" x 36" poster of a scantily clad Victoria's Secret model from an era gone by.

Potter pointed with his left hand and Tony's eyes followed it to a file drawer that was labeled Apr/May/June. Tony pulled a file marked May 18 and handed it to Potter who leafed through it and wordlessly withdrew a timesheet handing it to Tony. Scanning the page, Tony stopped at a red line striking through the name Jeffrey Engels.

"Who's this? Why the red line?" he asked.

"Guy called in sick . . . "

"And?"

"What?" Potter replied like a teenager pretending not to understand.

"I'm not in the mood, George," he replied.

"Okay . . . okay," he said with resignation in his voice. "Guy calls in sick. I say, this is the sixth time this month. I need someone who's gonna show when I need him. He says he's got someone to cover. Says I don't need to worry. They worked it out between them."

"So, you don't know who covered for him?"

"Hey, I don't give a shit. Long as the job gets done."

Tony slowed his suv as he searched for Jeff Engels address. He pulled up in front of a dilapidated trailer bearing the number twelve, it's 2 hanging upside down from one nail. It was late, but a dim light and the flickering of a late-night broadcast told him its occupant was up.

"It's open," yelled Engels when Tony knocked. As Tony's eyes adjusted to the dimness, he spotted Jeff Engels slouching on a brown, plaid couch, its stuffing sprouting from the corners as though a pit bull had been gnawing on it for a decade or so. The room was cramped and cluttered and smelled of stale beer.

"Jeff Engels?" Tony asked as if he already knew the answer.

"Yeah," came the reply. "Who are you?"

"Tony Russo, Chief of Police." If Engels was impressed, he gave no sign of it. "I've got a few questions."

Engels gathered the mess on one of the living room chairs and shifted it to an alarmingly large pile. Tony took the hint and sat down, his weight causing a creaking noise as he settled into the lumpy cushion.

"May eighteenth," Tony began. "You remember where you were?"

"Probably working," answered Engels, with one eye on the day's soccer highlights being replayed on his virtual screen. Tony reached over and yanked the plug from the projector out of the wall. Startled, Engels turned toward him with a deer-in-the-headlights look on his face.

"No, you weren't. Potter says someone worked your shift for you."

"Guy shows up and offers me two hundred bucks to call in sick," said Engels, his voice reflecting more than a bit of fear. "Says he'll work my shift for no pay. I'm gonna say no to that?"

Irrefutable logic thought Tony.

"So, who was it?"

"One of The General's goons," he replied. "Ya know, the one with all the muscles."

"Ronnie Kay?" asked Tony with more alarm in his voice than he intended. He hadn't intended to cross swords with The General. *This is going to get complicated* he thought.

"Yeah, I think that's him."

CHAPTER 16

GENERAL MILLER CLARKE

T HE LOW, SOFT LIGHTING ON THE PATHWAYS TO THE Pentagon entrance steered its visitors to the doorways in the dark. The silhouette of the building itself would not have been discernible were it not for the well-lit American flag draped from the roof, covering the top two floors where, forty-eight years ago this day, a commercial airliner piloted by terrorists had crashed.

It was rare for Tara to take a 6 a.m. meeting. But General Miller Clarke was like a fireman. He only showed up when there was trouble. And she knew him well, having worked closely with him over many years. So, when he demanded the meeting with "extreme urgency," she felt she had no choice. As she rounded the last corner, someone pssted at her from a dark alcove. She jumped sideways involuntarily. *What the ... ?*

"Sorry, Madam Secretary," said the voice in hushed tones. She froze.

"Mill?" she said. She could tell she had said it more loudly than he would have liked. He glanced in both directions and then moved to let some light fall on his face. The anxiety showed in the tension around his mouth and eyes.

"Mill! What the hell are you doing?" she whispered.

"I don't want to be traced to your office."

He's afraid! What could possibly cause such distress in this old Army hand? And then aloud, "I'll shut down the scanners. We can meet in my office. Give me a minute."

When they were settled in her office, somewhat uncomfortably, with the lights off at his request, she asked him why he'd requested this meeting. Clarke could not have looked more uncomfortable if he had a dead skunk hung around his neck. Finally, in hushed tones, he shared his concerns.

"Why are we sending a squad of soldiers to find our missing team when we have technology that can find them within a heartbeat?" he asked. "It's almost as though we don't want to find them."

"Why are you asking *me* this? You should be raising these concerns in the Situation Room."

"I've come across some information that worries me," he replied.

"Okay . . . So, why the secret meeting?"

"It involves the President, and I don't know where it will lead. There's a report, but I can't pull it without being traced. I think you can."

"Wait! Are you telling me that the President of the United States is involved in some plot that has resulted in the kidnapping of a squad of military personnel on our own soil?"

"Well . . . um."

"The better part of valor is discretion, Mill." *He knows that conspiracy theories are easily debunked. If he's developed one, I don't want to know about it unless there is evidence.*

He gulped involuntarily. *He's putting his career on the line,* thought Tara. *Why would he do that?*

"Look, Tara. You and I go way back. I know I can trust you and I know you'll do the right thing."

"What are you asking me to do?" she interrupted again. "I'm not going to start an investigation based on suspicion alone." Her thoughts went to her career. *What if he's wrong and I'm hung out to dry? On the other hand, what if he's right and I've done nothing?*

"Let's leave the investigation for later. I'm suggesting we deploy some new surveillance technology to find out what happened to Adams and her team. Meanwhile, you can pull the report I mentioned. At your level, it can be untraceable."

"If history has taught us anything, it's that nothing is untraceable," she said.

He said nothing.

"Tell me about the surveillance technology," she continued, changing the subject slightly. "I don't want to talk about the report until I've read it."

"As you know, the satellite footage gave us nothing," he said. "We believe someone on the ground has developed technology that blocks our imaging. Under the circumstances, we have three options: satellite, insects or dust. There are pros and cons to each approach."

"So, we could use bugs, right?" she asked. "I know we've used cyborg bees before."

"Drones have been illegal since 2029. And, as tiny as robot insects are, they are detectable. So, if we're found out . . . "

"We'd be breaking two laws: one that prohibits use of drones and another that prohibits domestic spying," she finished his thought for him. "So, tell me about 'dust.' I don't recall it from our last DARPA review."

"The lab rats are calling them 'micro motes,'" he began. "But I like to call it 'smart dust.' Each is a camera about 20 microns in diameter."

"Isn't 20 microns much bigger than a speck of dust?"

"Yes, about 10 times bigger. But still virtually undetectable by humans and easily blown about by ambient breeze."

"In other words, someone would have to be looking for them."

"Yes. And they'd still be incredibly difficult to detect."

"I'm still not sure I would be happy breaking the law on a hunch that something evil lurks in the White House."

"That's the beauty of it. We don't have to."

Tara arched an eyebrow. "The suspense is killing me . . ." *Now we're getting to the good stuff. He's going to tell me what he needs me to do.*

"We have an ongoing test of this technology. It's being deployed from boats on the Great Lakes."

"And, we have them on Lake Erie?" She was intrigued. She had always been fascinated by the military's new technology.

"Yes."

"How is that legal?"

"We're testing the camera and collecting data on its accuracy and effectiveness. We're not saving any data or surveilling anyone."

"Go on." *Sounds like he's found a way around the law.*

"So, we could deploy our smart dust over the City of Erie and see what we can see."

"Well, we'll see a lot, won't we? I mean, there will be tons of data to analyze, won't there?"

"Yes, but the artificial intelligence in our software can respond to commands. We'll tell it to look for activity that resembles military or militia. We'll feed it images of Major Adams and her squad. Then we'll tell it to look for that. So, yes, we'll be collecting tons of data. But we'll ask the AI to look for specific clues. It would take a dozen analysts at least a month to do what the AI can do in minutes."

"But we'd still be violating the law prohibiting domestic spying."

"We'd be walking a fine line."

"A fine line?" Years in Washington had conditioned her not to take risks. And this sounded like a big risk. "If the spin doctors don't see it that way, It'll be like the difference between being thrown off the 18th or 19th floor. Both will kill you."

"Please, just hear me out, Tara," he said. "There is an active test that's been ongoing for months – since well before the kidnapping incident. We've been asking the smart dust to answer these kinds of questions as part of the test."

"What about feeding the facial images into the system?"

"Well, technically, that's not spying."

She knew she had to do what Clarke was asking. But she felt like she had someone else's shadow – uncomfortable despite the knowledge it was the right thing to do.

"Priya's on board?" he blurted out.

"Priya Carmichael?" Some internal alarm system had triggered inside Tara. If Clarke was so afraid of being detected coming to her office, why would he take the risk of sharing all of this with Priya.

"Yes," he replied. "The head of DARPA herself."

"So, you've shared your concerns about the president with her?" she was aghast. If she was to do what Clarke was asking, it had to be in the strictest confidence.

"No! No, I wouldn't do that. Too much risk. I've just asked her some open-ended questions about the technology and showed her the images I'd like to upload."

Tara held her breath involuntarily. *I can't help but do what he's asking of me. But if he's wrong about all this, there's no telling what will happen to both of us. It could be a career-killing scandal or worse. There could be a criminal prosecution.*

"I'm inclined to go forward with your idea," she said. "This one is personal for me," she added, regretting it as soon as she said it.

"Personal?"

She shook her head, ignoring his question.

"Okay, Mill. Let's do it," she said. *What did I just approve?*

CHAPTER 17

THE GREAT
OUTDOORS

GABRIELLE HAD FOUND A WAY TO SPEND TIME OUT-doors – by cozying up to Ronnie Kay, the gym rat who seemed to be in charge of the guards. "Ronnie," she had said to the enormous gym rat. "Put shackles on me. A ball and chain. I don't care. I promise I won't run away. So long as I can be outdoors for an hour or so. Anything to get out of this musty old house."

"Anything?" Ronnie had said as he leered at her, a look she had noticed he always wore when he watched the young women in her crew. She knew the type. *He's a man whose romantic impulses have long been undermined by his inability to articulate his thoughts and feelings.*

"Don't be fresh," she had replied in her most coquettish way, all the while thinking *if I get a chance, I'll stab this asshole in the chest.*

Ronnie had assigned two of his minor goons to keep watch while she was outside, and she emerged from the east side of the house, lifting her head to get the effect of the bright morning sun full in her face. She took a deep breath, enjoying the fall sunshine, the slight chill to the morning air, watching as the first leaves began to turn colors. Her nostrils flared as she took in the day using all her senses: the smell of burning leaves, squirrels scurrying about, the sap rising almost indecently. For the moment, she was conscious only of what her senses could gather.

The sound of crunching dry leaves beneath feet returned her to reality, or rather the reality of her circumstances: a prisoner. Her crime was yet to be declared, her sentence yet to be determined.

The leaf cruncher was Diana. Gabrielle had noticed something different about her since she had emerged from her solitary confinement. Something undefinable, a subtle change in her energy. Her laser beam focus was gone. She stood a few feet from Gabrielle as though she, like her friend, was taking in the sights, sounds and smells of the crisp Fall day.

Gabrielle turned with a glance over her shoulder that told Diana to follow. She stopped near the edge of a ridge and stood admiring the humpback shape of the distant hills. The guards kept their distance, assured that the women would not or could not escape by diving off the cliff.

"Have you figured out how to get out of here?" asked Diana quietly so the guards couldn't hear.

"I guess you figured out my purpose in asking for some time outside," Gabrielle said, smirking a bit.

"I've known you for a long time."

"Well, it won't be easy," said Gabrielle, responding to Diana's initial comment. "I'm not sure how many troops The General has in his little army. But I rarely see the same faces twice. That suggests there's a wider perimeter he's guarding."

"Because they rotate from inner to outer . . . "

"Right! That's my assumption anyway," said Gabrielle.

"What else?"

"Let's assume we can't overpower them . . . "

"Even if we could, we'd take some casualties. I'm not willing to sustain another," Diana replied.

"There's got to be a seam somewhere."

"I was unconscious, but you must have seen how they brought us in from the wilderness."

"Yeah, sort of. We were held at gunpoint down in the hold. It was pitch black. I think we were underground because you could hear the sound of the motor echoing off walls."

"That would make sense," Diana replied. "So, why haven't we been found? Someone was tracking us and should know where we lost contact. It should be easy to find a tunnel."

"Maybe we should use these daily outings to widen our circle, explore what's beyond this narrow perimeter. Our guards would come along to ensure we don't make a run for it. But we'd be able to see what's out there – what we'd be facing."

"I'm not sure we'd be able to see it," said Diana. "It's likely the fencing will be invisible, and we can be traced."

"Traced by what?" asked Gabrielle. "They've removed our chips."

"There's always a way, Gabs. You know that. There must be satellite images."

"And yet the Pentagon with all its resources can't find us."

They wandered wordlessly from the spot they had stood. Gabrielle paused to kick an old decaying log long softened by rot and spotted by moss. They watched as the shadow of a maple tree shifted as the sun rose obliterating the pink of the morning sky. Diana couldn't recall enjoying her natural environment so much.

"I sometimes feel as though I don't know myself since the neural mesh was removed," she said finally. "Have I lost my edge? Who am I?"

Gabrielle pondered that for a moment, rolling it around in her head, mixing it with the varied ingredients of their history – grunting through the obstacle course, sharing wine and laughter, lifting each other up when one was down. She looked at her old friend.

"You're still the same person, Diana."

Diana just stared back in doe-eyed disbelief. "Would I have done all those things in a burning building if I wasn't a human guinea pig? Would I always be so driven, so focused, so closed off from the world around me?"

"You're still the same person, Diana," she repeated. She knew she shouldn't reply to Diana's questions. *No one knows the answers* she thought. They stood in the glorious morning sun, their moods out of sync with the day.

Finally, Diana punctuated their silence with a thought from the recesses of her mind – a thought that might not have emerged if she worked hard to generate it.

"The tunnel!" she exclaimed.

"What?"

"If we came through a tunnel, we can go out the way we came in: through the same tunnel."

"How are we going to do that, Diana?"

"I don't know yet. But it's the only way."

"If we can get to the basement, we might be able to find our way out. But how would we even do that? We might be better off running the gauntlet of detectors from where we stand."

"No, Gramps would never make it. He's too weak after all that time in the deep freeze."

"GRAMPS!! We'll never get out of here if we try to bring Nick with us."

"That's our mission, Gabs. To bring Nick Adams back to the D.C. pod – frozen or not."

Gabrielle looked away, biting her lip, bearing the weight not only of their mission but also to one another. They were like two people who had endured a war while sharing a foxhole. Together they were stronger and more self-assured than each could be on their own. Each lifted the other when they were down. Their time together had been blessed by both laughter and tears. The idea they would split up at a time when they were in such danger was unbearable. But Gabrielle knew the size of the hole in Diana's soul from the loss of her family. She knew, perhaps more than Diana, how badly she wanted to heal that wound. And, now she knew Diana would never leave her grandfather's side.

CHAPTER 18

THE RESCUE
TEAM

WESTERN PENNSYLVANIA WAS ONCE COAL COUNTRY, steel country, a place full of holes. The skeletons of smokestacks still poked up from the underworld. They were a decaying indicator of what once was. Colonel Evelyn O'Malley-Sakura did not care for it. She had never been here before and would be happy to never be here again. Unfortunately, she had no choice but to volunteer to command the unit that would search for Diana and her squad. How else would she ensure that the search remained diverted?

Her unit had been pulled together by Captain Jayden Fischer who, like Evelyn, was a graduate of West Point. But, unlike Evelyn, he was a by-the-book military officer whose naiveté was only reinforced by his baby-face. He had objected to his uniformed troops bearing no insignia indicating their military affiliation. He pondered the legality of their mission out loud.

"Respectfully, Colonel," he had started. "The military may not be used for law enforcement within the United States unless expressly authorized by the Constitution or an Act of Congress."

Is he a man or a robot? wondered Evelyn. *He must have memorized that in a class on Military Law.* She turned toward him; her eyes locked on his. He felt himself leaning backward as she leaned in.

"Our Commander-in-Chief has issued orders," she said with an unwavering conviction, the hair on the back of her neck standing as stiffly as was she. "Our job is not to question them, but to *execute* them."

"But Colonel . . . " His voice trailed off as Evelyn remained silent, like a statue, cold and unmovable. "Yes, ma'am," he said finally.

Evelyn had bigger worries than a tight-ass captain. She hadn't been able to reach The General for three days. So, she didn't know the status of their little scheme to defraud the public much less the status of Diana, her team and Nick Adams. She wondered if something had gone wrong. Worse, she wondered if The General was hiding something from her. *Has he gone rogue? Does he have other plans for the class-leading technology Nick Adams would help him develop?*

The small squad of 10 had spread out, searching for clues and remaining clueless. There was a pile of fallen trees seemingly mortared together by mud. It was as though a giant beaver had built a dam at the bottom of a hundred-foot-high hill. Captain Fischer ordered Privates Diaz and Ramachandran to make their way to the top. They clambered up the side, sticky mud subtracting a half step from each stride. Branches clutched at their clothes and slapped their chests. Their long-standing mano-a-mano competition kept them moving with the energy of a pair of eight-year-olds. When he arrived at the top a pace and a half ahead of his buddy, Diaz stumbled, falling into a ditch that could only have been man-made. Struggling to his feet, he quickly concluded, "Somebody attacked them."

"Of course, somebody attacked them, you idiot. They didn't just vanish into thin air," his buddy replied.

"Who you callin' an idiot?" Diaz said, shoving his much smaller friend just hard enough so as not to knock him head over heels back down the hill.

"Maybe they're under all this rubble . . . "

"Can't be!" said Diaz. "Why would anyone create a landslide and just leave them there?"

"There's no sign of a vehicle moving away from the landslide, is there?" asked Ramachandran rhetorically.

Fischer, who had joined the two soldiers at the top of the hill, could see the pattern. It was obvious there was a landslide from its point of inception. Toppled trees spread from top to bottom like fingers across a piano keyboard, widely separated but attached to the same wrist. What wasn't obvious was what had happened to the APC.

"They were airlifted," said Evelyn when the group had reconvened at the bottom of the hill. She had reviewed the photos taken by Fischer and made her pronouncement without consultation.

"There are other possibilities, Colonel," said Fischer, his brow wrinkled with confusion. "Shouldn't we consider the alternatives before we jump to a conclusion?"

"Nope," she said, hoping to shutdown speculation. She knew Fischer would disagree. So, she adopted an authoritarian manner to ensure there was no further conversation about it. "They were airlifted. They could be anywhere."

A few of the soldiers glanced at each other. It was common knowledge that an aircraft would have left an electronic trail, that they couldn't simply be "anywhere" if they had been airlifted. Modern surveillance systems would tell them exactly where they had gone, and most of all, it was very possible that the group they were searching for were still under that very landslide.

A few hundred yards away, deep beneath the surface, The General sat with Nick and Mateen. The General's IT wizard, Howard the Geek was flitting about in the data center out of earshot, his orange hair flopping back and forth whenever he passed in front of the ventilation system.

"You're telling me that the President is at the top of this pyramid of deceit and corruption?" said Nick, trying but failing to hide his shock and dismay.

"Yes, that's exactly what I am saying," The General replied. Mateen remained silent with his usual stoic posture.

"How can you know that? Just because some mid-level Army officer tells you so?"

"There are certain orders – certain resources – that can only be deployed by the Commander-in-Chief."

"Yeah, but those orders are followed by people down the chain of command who have access to those same resources. It could have been someone else."

"Possibly," he paused for effect. "I knew Porter when she was a mid-level agent at the C.I.A. Her sense of self-interest is monumental. She would do anything to advance her own cause. She lied her way to the top and will stop at nothing to enrich herself."

Nick was a child of a different era. He grew up in the 1950's and 60's when most Americans trusted their government to do what's right, to act in the public interest. At his core, he still embraced the idea of the wisdom of the electorate – that despite the anomalous behavior of bad leaders, from Joe McCarthy to Richard Nixon to Donald Trump, the nation would endure on the basis of its core principles: equal opportunity, the freedoms delineated in the First Amendment and the rule of law. He felt compelled to challenge The General's conclusions about the president.

"Do you have any proof?" he started. "I'm not a big believer in conspiracy theories. Can you draw a direct line from the president's actions to the so-called plot to steal this technology?"

"No one else could have marshalled the resources to have you retrieved from a cryogenic facility in Pittsburg and brought back to life," The General began, avoiding a direct answer to a direct question.

"No one?" challenged Nick. "You seem to have been able to do it without the U.S. Treasury behind you. Surely, the Pentagon has enough money laying around to pay for what you've done."

"It's not just the Pentagon," asserted The General. "Other departments are involved. No one – certainly not a lowly Army colonel – could have coordinated so many government agencies without being detected." Turning to Mateen, he asked, "who hired you, Matt?"

"Generally, I work for the intelligence agencies or the State Department," Mateen answered in his usual reserved manner. Nick wasn't buying it.

"Generally?" Nick challenged. "Who hired you for this project?"

Taking a deep breath and glancing sideways toward The General before answering, he replied, "I was hired through a private shell company. I don't know which agency funded it." His manner told Nick he was lying.

"Look, Nick," said The General before Nick could reply to Matt. "I've known the major players in D.C. for over three decades. I know who we can trust and who we can't. If we're successful, this project will change the world. We simply can't allow it to be stolen. I need you to trust me on this."

Nick didn't trust him. But he recognized the importance of the project. And he knew he could play a critical role in its success.

Besides, what choice did he have? He was still being treated for pancreatic cancer by The General's medical team and there was no telling what might happen should he try to leave.

In the end, The General had to admit that he had no direct evidence that President Kathleen Porter was at the center of a plot to steal the rights to technology that would change the world. He did, however, make a closing argument that Nick found compelling.

"Porter ran her first presidential campaign on small donations from millions of voters. She emerged from a field of a hundred twenty-six candidates as a populist. Four years later, she kicked off her reelection campaign by lending it sixteen million dollars. Where did that money come from? How does a public servant amass a fortune in four years?"

CHAPTER 19

CASING THE JOINT

THERE WAS NO SOUND IN THE HOUSE, NOT EVEN THE sounds that houses make – the furnace, or the stairwell creaking, or the fridge cycling on; nothing but silence. Boots hung round their necks, Diana and Gabrielle tiptoed down the stairs in their stockinged feet, avoiding each of the squeaky spots they had already mind mapped. When they reached the unlit ground floor, Gabrielle stubbed her toe on an overstuffed chair that was one fat guy away from collapse. She bit her tongue to avoid swearing out loud.

Diana wondered if the crystal and brass doorknob was hiding an electronic device; but the solid oak door swung open easily. *Are we walking into a booby trap?* As they crept down the longest flight of stairs they'd ever seen, Gabrielle shut the door behind them carefully to prevent the door from thumping as it closed.

Once at the bottom of the stairwell, the lights turned on automatically. *Are we leaving an electronic fingerprint behind?* As they passed the data center, the entrance to the tunnel was easy to discover. An aluminum gate was unlocked.

They read each other's mind. "Too easy," said Gabrielle. "If there is a secret tunnel for The General's troops to come and go, it shouldn't be so easy to access it."

"Yeah. But maybe the old general has gotten complacent. Who would challenge him on his own turf?"

"Why, then, is the house so well-secured? And all those guards!"

"That's the first level of security," said Diana. "You can't get to this underground lair unless you can get through the front door, right?" She paused for effect. "I would guess no one has gotten this far because no one has ever breeched the exterior of the house."

"Maybe, Diana. But it seems risky to me."

"Yeah, it's risky. But if it's this easy to get this far . . . " She didn't have to finish her thought. She knew it was the only feasible escape plan.

"Okay. Yeah. Maybe."

They stared at the tunnel entrance, its depth unexplored, as though it might yield an answer.

Diana laid out the escape plan for her grandfather over breakfast. Sharing the first meal of the day had become their daily routine. It was a certain way of having confidential discussion with him without raising the suspicions of their captors.

"No, Diana! No way!"

She stared at her grandfather in disbelief. *Huh? . . . We're all prisoners. Why wouldn't he want to escape? Has The General cast a spell on him? What's obligating him to stay?*

"You're not coming?" She had heard him the first time, but the news hit her so hard that she had to ask again.

He sat there eating his toast and drinking from a fresh mug of coffee in silence. *He's still pretty fragile. Maybe he is concerned he won't make it or would slow us down.* She opened her mouth to speak. But he interrupted.

"The work we're doing here is too important."

Diana's temple throbbed. She felt ruffled as though the breeze that rattled the leaves outside the window was shredding the clarity she brought to the conversation. A minute passed, full of nothing but slurps and crunches. Then she asked the obvious question: "What work?"

Nick drummed his fingers on the side of his mug, looking at her across the table. She sat facing him, not eating, but holding her piece of rye toast motionless in midair.

He squirmed under her glare. "I've been sworn to secrecy. I'll have to talk with Alfred before we can share it with you."

She could see her reflection in the bay window; it was drawn and miserable. Her plan may not be perfect. It was fraught with risk. They didn't know where the tunnel might lead nor if their escape might set off an electronic surveillance system. And there was no guarantee they would be safe once they exited the tunnel.

But she had to take her grandfather with her. She was here because of him. He was her only living blood relative. She could not leave him behind.

Unfamiliar doubts and fears fluttered inside her. Long forgotten memories welled up inside. She did not want to remember her pain, her loss or her loneliness. Yet, in this moment, memories came pouring out of the dark recesses of her mind, like buzzing black flies shredding any chance to think clearly.

Death is an elusive concept for a child. When her mother died, she had been told she would never come home. Yet, she awoke each day wishing and hoping for her return.

When is Mommy coming home?

The agony of the unfulfilled expectation, the terror of the knowledge it would never be met, the uncertainty of how to fill the hole left by her absence had all haunted young Diana.

When is Mommy coming home?

She had been euphoric when she'd met her grandfather for the first time as an adult. He had filled that hole without her knowing it. Pain and loneliness had become part of her personal landscape, part of who she was. It resided in her guts like a bolo knot. *Was he feeling what I'm feeling?* Worry lines framed her mouth and tugged at her eyes. Muscles in her jaw bunched. Her mother smiled across the gulf of time.

When is Mommy coming home?

"Dee, we're ready!" Gabrielle looked as though her eyes might pop out of her head. "Whaddaya mean, he's not coming?"

"He says the work he's doing is too important."

Diana knew that Gabrielle was straining to maintain her composure. They used their morning stroll to hatch their plans, pausing at the cliff's edge, speaking into a cavernous valley rather than face each other. To a casual observer, they might have been talking about the leaves turning Fall colors. A raised voice might draw unwanted attention from the brain-dead guards. Diana didn't want to elevate their suspicions any more than they wanted to expend energy beyond the minimum to get by.

"We'll have to go without him," she said looking sideways at Diana.

"I can't leave him behind, Gabs." Tight-chested and trembling, Diana clung to her last link to a blood relative, one she had long thought gone.

"Dee, come on," she said, obviously struggling to keep her voice down. "If we succeed, we'll be rescued and The General and this whole crew will be thrown in jail. Nick will be better off that way, rather than dragging him through a tunnel that leads God knows where. We – all of us – need you to lead us out of here."

Diana felt as though she was being drawn and quartered. Gabrielle's logic was unassailable. Yet, the idea of leaving her grandfather —the double helix of their DNA intertwined — rendered her incapable of motion.

And Gabrielle — their bond unbreakable — had been her only lifeline when she had been drowning in her loneliness. It was Gabrielle that lifted her up when she was down, connected her to her feelings when her brain was on hyper speed, made her laugh when nothing was funny. She had talked Gabrielle into joining this mission, a mission that ended up a fiasco. How could she stay behind? What if something happened to Gabrielle?

Yet, she knew what she had to do. She couldn't leave Nick Adams at the mercy of a nefarious militia leader. Her senses recalled his loss along with her mother. It was too strong a gravitational force.

"You'll have to go without me, Gabs."

CHAPTER 20

THE ARREST

IANA SCANNED THE IMPRESSIVE ROOM AS SHE WAS escorted in. The General's office was much like the rest of his home – reminiscent of the 19th Century. Situated where the sitting room most likely had been in the heyday of such homes – in a front corner of the house near the main entryway – its bay window offered an unspoiled view of the City of Erie over the treetops and beyond to the Great Lakes. The mahogany paneling was well preserved even if it showed signs of wear and the occasional replacement of some panel or another by a modern practitioner of a lost art.

The General – Alfred Braxton Bragg engraved into a brass nameplate facing those who were honored to be his guests – sat behind a massive desk, perhaps of the same vintage as the house. His desk chair, wrapped in burgundy leather that was secured to its wood frame by brass rivets, squeaked a bit when he swiveled, a flaw that could be forgiven as it lent patina to the setting.

What a great home court advantage thought Diana as she sat before him flanked by her grandfather and Mateen. She had been persuaded – no, seduced – into this meeting by The General whose charm had been practiced and perfected over many decades. She was about to learn about the "important work" in which both her grandfather and Mateen had been engaged. A project that was so critical that not only The General but also two of the nation's greatest minds had risked retribution and perhaps prison to accomplish.

The General had barely launched into his preamble when they were interrupted by a fracas in the grand entryway. The shuffling of feet accompanied by the grunts of muscular men gave the impression that the guards were attempting to repel an intruder. All eyes in the office turned toward the door as Diana felt a surge of adrenaline, her conditioned response to the possibility of a fight.

"Where's Kay? Ronnie Kay?" said the muffled voice on the other side of the secure door. The scuffling of boots on the hardwood floors ended when a strong voice ordered his men to back off.

"It's the Chief of Police, you idiots," said someone in charge as the scuffling ceased. "Sorry, Chief . . . "

"Where's Ronnie Kay?" came the reply without acknowledging either the transgression or the apology.

Ronnie Kay – the gym rat Diana had first encountered when she awoke in The General's clinic –emerged from the shadows, surprising her.

Tony Russo barged through the double doors unceremoniously. Everyone jumped out of their seats, uncertain of what might happen next. Diana's eyes opened wide, and she felt herself flush. Tony had the kind of rugged good looks that could stop any woman in her tracks. His bulging muscles and commanding presence got into her bones.

Before anyone could react, Tony declared, "Ronnie Kay, you're under arrest for . . . "

He didn't get to finish his declaration as Ronnie drilled him like a linebacker hitting a quarterback from the blind side, a clean hit driving his shoulder into Tony's ribcage knocking him to the floor and sending his pistol skittering across the floor under the desk.

Diana jumped up out of her seat as The General disappeared through a hidden panel in the bookcase. She had always been quick to engage in battle. Her fight, flight or freeze instinct was preset to fight first and ask questions later. Despite the surge of adrenaline, she found herself strangely frozen on the sidelines. Perhaps it was because she didn't know whose side she should be on or perhaps she had been distracted by the sight of Tony Russo in tight jeans with his muscles rippling through his tee shirt.

A throw rug slipped out from under Ronnie's feet, sending them both reeling to the floor. Tony, unable to catch his breath, nevertheless charged, hoping to subdue Ronnie before he regained his balance. Ronnie, on one knee, threw his forearms up like an offensive lineman blocking a defensive back. Tony sidestepped and came down on Ronnie's arms with one hand while driving his opposite elbow into the side of Ronnie's head, the soft spot high on his temple. With his opponent obviously dazed, he attempted to gain the upper hand by grabbing Ronnie's ponytail. Ignoring the pain, Ronnie rolled Tony across his shoulders and cast him onto the floor like a rag doll. Before Tony could recover, Ronnie was on top of him his hands around Tony's throat. Unable to draw breath, Tony began to see starbursts as his brain and lungs were deprived of oxygen.

Diana – her fighting instincts now aroused – looked around the room for something that would serve as a weapon. She grabbed a bronze urn from a pedestal and swung it with all her might, striking Ronnie along the side of his head.

The "Kabong!" rang through the room resonating like a gong. Ronnie collapsed on top of Tony, barely conscious. As Tony squirmed out from under him, he saw Diana standing over them holding the urn like a baseball bat over her shoulder. He didn't take the time to thank her as the more pressing matter was to immobilize the beast who had nearly taken his life. Gasping for breath, his ribcage shooting pain throughout his torso with each inhalation, he crawled over to Ronnie who was still face down on the floor, blood trickling down the back of his skull from the blow Diana had delivered.

As he cuffed Ronnie, Diana looked around the room, its antique furniture toppled and displaced. Mateen and Nick had taken refuge on the other side of The General's desk and now stood like two pillars of salt aghast at what they had witnessed. The General himself had somehow vanished during the commotion like one of those augmented reality avatars that Diana had hated so much.

Tony twisted Ronnie's arms behind his back, securing them to one another with stainless-steel handcuffs. He took the extra precaution of using a curtain cord as a noose around Ronnie's neck. His head was swimming. He paused to take a deep breath and felt his stomach tighten as he nearly threw up, sending another sharp pain through his ribcage.

He helped the big man to his feet. Despite his physical state, Ronnie attempted to head butt him, but he drove the heel of his palm into the end of Ronnie's nose. A sickeningly loud crack could be heard as he was led stumbling out of the room, rivers of blood running down his chin from both nostrils.

Tony, battered, bruised and struggling to steer Ronnie through the doorway nevertheless glanced over his shoulder at Diana.

"Tha . . . " he uttered, his loss of breath not allowing him to complete a single syllable word.

"Than . . . " he tried again.

Diana, googly-eyed and still holding the urn over her shoulder, said nothing as she gawped at the man whose life she had likely just saved.

CHAPTER 21

ERIE

TARA STOOD NEAR THE DOORWAY OF THE FIFTH-FLOOR kitchenette, her direct line of sight on a bank of virtual screens – each showing a different news channel all running the same story. She tapped her teeth with the wooden stir stick, her mind wandering idly. It was unusual for national news to cover a story outside the pods; but Ronnie Kay's arrest was newsworthy, not because a small-town murder was notable but rather because of the cause of the two scientists' deaths. Talking heads described the remains of the victims as liquid organic matter, carbon puddles or Gray Goo. The description was followed by a brief explanation of ecophagy, the process of molecular nanotechnology consuming the environment. They invariably got the science all wrong as their mission was to scare rather than inform the public.

"And could nanobots consume the entire human race?" asked the talking head on one channel.

"Well, yes, they could," replied the so-called expert, causing Tara to scrunch her face as she doubted the accuracy of that statement.

"They are technically capable as we've just seen. And they are subject to the law of unintended consequences . . . ."

As he babbled on, Tara thought *if they can do that on their own, why is Kay being arrested? Doesn't that imply human intervention?*

Their explanations were less interesting to Tara than the location of the arrest – *Erie, Pennsylvania? Again? Is it just coincidence that Evelyn O'Malley-Sakura's hometown was the site of both the homicides of the two scientists and the kidnapping of Diana and her crew?*

Out of sight but not out of earshot, Tara accidentally eavesdropped on a conversation between two women. Each unleashed a breathy explosion of words — giggling, gasping and gossiping, their manner so foreign to Tara. She had never been 'one of the girls' and had never wanted to be. *Too stuck up for us* one of her contemporaries had said during her Junior High years.

"Erie?" said one, noticing the news broadcast for the first time. "Isn't that where Sakura's mission is?"

"I don't care where she is as long as she's not here," replied the other.

Her reputation as a difficult boss is intact, thought Tara.

"She's not that bad really," said the first. "I ended up on the same flight to Atlanta with her last year around the holidays. We had a nice talk. She's smart and friendly . . . "

"Is that where she's from? Atlanta?"

"Yeah. It turns out we went to the same high school. She graduated about 10 years before me."

Atlanta? She told me Erie was her hometown. She had said she gone there for the holidays. General Bragg was someone known to her family there. Was she lying about that? For the first time, Tara began to wonder if Evelyn might be tangled up in a plot of some sort – of the sort that Clarke had warned her about.

The first of the women leaving the kitchen stopped dead in her tracks when she saw Tara, her eyes seeming to grow to three times their normal size. The two scurried away like little mice, their eyes cast downward as though if they couldn't see anyone, they couldn't be seen. Tara couldn't have cared less.

"The report's available, Madam Secretary," said one of the hundreds of data security pros, whose name Tara couldn't remember.

When she returned to her office, she popped open the report that Miller Clarke had asked her to read on a secure projection. Below the seal and motto of the Federal Bureau of Investigation were the words TOP SECRET. *How would a crime investigated by the FBI become classified with such limited access?*

Turning the page, her heart seemed to stop momentarily. The report was titled ABDUCTION OF NICHOLAS PHILLIP ADAMS, November 22, 2024.

CHAPTER 22

THE TUNNEL

THE STEAK KNIFE WAS THEIR UNDOING.

The plan was to escape by stealth. Carrying weapons was off the table. If they were surrounded, weapons would only lead to a skirmish they would lose. Gabrielle had agreed with Diana's assessment. If they were spotted, they would be overpowered and captured. There was no way they could fight their way out. So, why risk an armed battle when they would undoubtedly be outmatched? It would only lead to more injuries – or worse.

The previous evening, Paul Miller, the young corporal who had first spotted Diana at the top of the stairway that would be their escape route, had grabbed the knife from the kitchen when no one would notice. He reasoned it was an insurance policy, only to be used if their lives were threatened. Now he tucked it into a pocket on the side of his Army fatigues where it would be out of sight but easy to grab.

They arrived at the bottom of the stairs and paused to allow their eyes to adjust to the dim night lights emanating from the data center. Gabrielle led them around the data center to the nearby aluminum gate she and Diana had discovered. They only had two flashlights to light the pitch-dark tunnel, which they were certain would lead them back to where they had been captured. They stumbled and cursed under their breath as they groped their way toward the exit, slipping on wet stones and mud. Miller patted the steak knife hidden in the leg pouch of his fatigues as if to assure himself it was still there.

Diana's only role was to distract the single guard positioned at the end of the third-floor hallway where her squad had been quartered. It was a fairly easy task. Brandishing a key and wearing a juvenile smirk on her face, she suggested to the young impressionable guard they raid The General's liquor cabinet. Although he lacked any appreciation for the quality of the collection of rare, aged scotch whisky, he responded to Diana as she hoped he would.

"Harry, right?" Diana asked the half-asleep guard.

"Uh, yeah," he replied. "Harry Marble."

"Harry, how would you like to help me with a bottle of whiskey?"

"I might get in trouble," he spluttered like a twelve-year-old. But he was already in motion by the time he had finished his faux objection.

"Shh," she giggled flirtatiously and dragged Harry by his sleeve as he stumbled through the door to the temperature-controlled room – a room that held both treasure and the allure of that which was forbidden. By the time Diana cracked the seal on an eighty-one-year-old bottle of Dalmore, her compatriots were down the main stairway to the lower level that housed the data center and led to the tunnel.

Harry kept peeking around the doorway as though he expected his superiors to materialize before his eyes.

"They're asleep," said Diana as she wiped her saliva off the open neck of the bottle with her sleeve. "Don't worry." By the third swig, his inhibitions had vanished

Howard the Geek occasionally slept on a cot at the back of the data center. He had no family and no reason to venture out into the world at large. He was passionate about system architecture, logic gates and hyperthreading. He couldn't care less about things that mattered to most people – family, friends, social gatherings. *No one to talk to. Well, no one who could understand anyway.*

He was also passionate about protecting his creation – a data center with the power to take down Wall Street, the Pentagon and the Bank of China simultaneously. He had no idea what The General planned to do with it and didn't care. He had applied all of his brain power to building it, never stopping to think how it might be used.

The sound of footsteps awakened him. Beyond the orange glow of the processors, he could see silhouettes of — *how many? Six. Eight. Maybe more.* He tripped the silent alarm and hoped for the best: that his masterpiece would be preserved despite whatever might happen next.

The muscles at the back of Diana's neck tightened when she heard the scuffling of boots in the hallway. *What happened?* Harry failed to notice as he glugged the 88-proof brown liquid like it was a glass of water. She left him behind as she moved swiftly on the balls of her feet toward where the troops should be moving in the direction of the rear stairway.

The end of the tunnel was sealed not by concrete but by mud and tree branches. Gabrielle and her squad stood like statues not knowing what to do next. Hopes raised, now dashed. They were crestfallen, not wanting to turn back but not able to move forward.

Their malaise was not long-lasting. The tunnel lit up behind them and their adrenaline surged. They turned to face four silhouettes – average-sized men carrying semi-automatic rifles slung over their shoulders – shining lights into eyes narrowed to slits.

"It's a big house," said the shortest of them, his tone of voice suggesting he was the man in charge. "Easy to get lost."

No one moved.

"Let's go," the short one said as he moved aside to let them pass. Miller pulled the steak knife from his pocket. In a single motion, he lunged toward the biggest shadow and slashed the side of his throat as he lost his balance.

"No," yelled one of the team rushing another guard who had raised his gun. The sound of a gunshot momentarily deafened them as she lurched backward. The bullet had split her sternum, piercing her right ventricle and killing her instantly. Gabrielle swung wildly at the guard nearest her slapping him on the side of his face. It rocked him and she kicked at his groin as he steadied himself. Her boot caught his thigh rather than its intended target and he lunged at her taking advantage of her one-legged stance. The combination of wrestling in the dark as flashlights rolled on the ground and shots were fired left two guards dead, one from friendly fire and the other from Miller's knife attack. Only Gabrielle was left standing among her team. She could see two of them writhing in pain on the ground. She presumed the others were dead.

She felt the steel of a muzzle between her shoulder blades and raised her hands in surrender.

"I'll take her back upstairs," said the one in charge. "You get the doc down here."

"And clear the area of weapons before you leave," he yelled over his shoulder as an afterthought.

They arrived at the top of the stairs as Diana stood slack-jawed, awaiting the worst. Her momentary relief at the sight of Gabrielle, blood running down the side of her face from her left ear — but still in one-piece — was shattered by the realization that none of the others were in tow.

"Sorry, Diana." Gabrielle mouthed the words as Diana hung her head.

Next to her, Harry vomited a mixture of half-digested pizza, bile and the best whiskey on the planet onto the oriental carpet behind her.

CHAPTER 23

AWOL

T HE FIRST-FLOOR MASTER BEDROOM SUITE OF THE
home on Little Haven Road in Virginia Beach was now
permanently subsumed by the Chesapeake Bay estuary.
Long abandoned to the ravages of inevitable sea level rise, its second and third floors now served as HQ for Evelyn's band of mercenaries. She had called upon retired Master Chief Elroy Tecumseh
"Clay" Claymore, a former Navy SEAL with whom she had served
in the Persian gulf early in her military career. The Chief hadn't
hesitated to sign up for Evelyn's cause. Indeed, he didn't really care
what her cause was. He only knew he was promised millions of
dollars to distribute among his troops upon successful completion of their mission.

A war room was constructed on the third floor under the eaves.
Evelyn remained silent sitting in the back of the room as Clay used
a white board and felt-tip markers to lay out the plan of attack.
The old-school technology left no electronic fingerprints or stray
signals that might be detected by satellites or drones. His team,
composed mostly of skilled fighters with whom he had served,

were both intensely intelligent and excessively prone to violence. Rather than lay out a complete plan, he started with an outline of objectives and asked each fighter to propose a contribution they would make. The occasional differences of opinion were easily resolved.

She sat back admiring how Clay and his team debated one another about what role each would play and what weapons they would use in the attack. *These guys have been conquering and killing together for so long they blend their thinking seamlessly,* thought Evelyn.

"The objective is to capture Nick Adams and keep him alive as we extract him, right?" asked Bravo. Each member used a military phonetic letter as a name to ensure their actual names would not be overheard during an operation. "So, we should come in hard and fast with as much force as possible to surprise the enemy," he continued.

"Don't forget the secondary objective is not to kill anyone and keep injuries to a minimum," Clay reminded them.

"So, we'll need to go in at night, neutralize any guards, control the bunkhouse, find Adams and get out as fast as possible," said the one known as Foxtrot, a guy with a wiry build and a deep ragged scar across his left cheek. "Even if we don't want to shoot anyone, we'll need to bring firearms to corral and control them in one room."

"I'm worried we might find ourselves having to take one or more of them out. This is a domestic operation. If we kill someone, it will be first degree murder," another added.

They created a plan to gather all the troops in one location, holding them at gunpoint until they could extract Nick and withdraw using grenades loaded with a mixture of methyl propyl ether and fentanyl to render their enemy unable to respond. Most would merely fall asleep and then suffer from a whopping hangover the next day. The main thing was that they would all survive without injury.

Each of them would carry ceramic knives and sidearms as well as plastic cuffs, gags and gas masks. They would gain entry to the house by first neutralizing the guards. Stealth was essential to success – no gunfire, no yelps or screams, no silent alarms tripped. They would be in and out in a matter of minutes.

Setting out after dark on two purloined stealth boats, they would make their way up the Chesapeake to the Susquehanna River. They would debark near Harrisburg, Pennsylvania and each take a different route to their designated rendezvous in the hills south of Erie. Theft of cars and motorcycles was common outside the pods. So, they assumed they could easily find their own transportation without raising any suspicions of their plot. They would rendezvous the following day at a point that was three hours hike to their target.

The meeting broke up by silent assent. Evelyn was the last to leave the room. She paused at the entrance to the Ready Room noticing traces of black mold invading the wallboard. She expected a musty odor, but the team had the discipline and self-respect to keep themselves and the room clean. The team was already at their individual lockers silently choosing their gear. Delta, the largest of them, strapped a knife to his right leg and secured another in his left armpit above the holster that held his pistol. The man known only as Alpha loaded his rucksack with plastic restraints, which Evelyn had been told were to ensure the prisoners didn't do something stupid and get themselves killed.

There was just one little detail to be taken care of before they executed their plan. Evelyn needed to make sure her activities were untraceable.

"How are you going to neutralize my chip so I can flip it back on when I return to D.C.?" she asked. It was critical that she could construct an alibi without her chip betraying the truth. *I need to return to my desk at the Pentagon with my chip intact. In the meantime, I can't have my movements traced.*

"No problem," said Clay. The two of them peered over the shoulder of the team cyber expert as he programmed nanobots that would perform the task once they were injected into Evelyn's bloodstream.

"Any expected side effects from this?" she asked, wincing from the insertion of the needle.

"Shouldn't be," answered Clay. "We pirated this methodology from a national lab. No amateurs involved its design. The pro's usually get it right."

Usually! thought Evelyn.

CHAPTER 24

THE ESCAPE

THERE WAS A TIME WHEN THE MANSION WAS A CHEER-ful place with bright green shutters on its façade. Towers of shrimp on ice and caviar were spread on a sumptuous buffet while well-dressed waiters served champagne in flutes. The 53-room house with a commanding lake view was the place to be and be seen by politicians and members of high society. It had hosted senators, governors and, on one occasion, the President of the United States. Now, it was occupied by a paramilitary force made up of malcontents, ex-convicts and borderline psychopaths.

Since the attempted escape by Diana's squad, the house had become a fortress. Its ground floor windows had been blackened out and its population of fighters had grown. The squad that had recaptured Gabrielle had been subsumed by a larger force. The two survivors had been wounded severely enough to require surgical intervention, but they were now recovering in private rooms attended by The General's small medical team, each room with a guard at the door.

The Grand Ballroom served as barracks to a group of twenty-three guards who were more disposed to avenging the deaths of their compatriots than ensuring the well-being of their prisoners. Each of the seven entrances was secured 24/7. With Ronnie Kay in the local jail, The General now kept the diminutive leader who had escorted Gabrielle from the tunnel back to the main floor now accompanied The General during every waking hour.

It was either coincidence or kismet that Diana, Gabrielle, Tony and Nick found themselves in the foyer of the house at the same time, as Diana and Gabrielle were being escorted to the office. They all froze when Tony Russo stepped through the front door, as did the guards their last encounter with the Chief of Police fresh in their minds.

"We need to leave NOW!" said Nick. His words failed to rouse any of them. They all looked at each other as though they weren't sure who Nick was addressing. "NOW! I mean it," he repeated as though they all struggled with the English language.

"I'm arresting you on suspicion of conspiracy to commit murder," said Tony. The guards were stunned. Were they being arrested?

Tony grabbed Nick's wrist and clapped handcuffs on him. Nick nodded to the two women, signaling they should go along with his charade. They glanced at one another. Diana just shrugged. Gabrielle smirked in reply.

Tony took his one remaining pair of handcuffs and clasped one half onto Diana's right wrist and the other onto Gabrielle's left. He circled around Diana and Gabrielle holding his arms wide as though he was escorting them to their limousine. They all moved toward the door. The guards stood, jaws agape, staring at them as they walked down the walkway toward Tony's SUV.

They marched with purpose toward the car, restraining the urge to look over their shoulders. Once belted in, adrenaline got the best of Tony, and they lurched toward freedom.

Their circumstances had changed in a heartbeat. Nick from collaborator to independent agent; Diana and Gabrielle from prisoners to free souls; and Tony from law enforcement officer to . . . what? He had no idea.

"Someone wanna tell me what's going on?" Tony asked finally.

"I wouldn't mind knowing the answer to that question," said Diana. Gabrielle nodded her assent. They only knew they were no longer prisoners in the most unlikely of circumstances. There was something else that Gabrielle knew – more a perception than a fact – and that was that her friend became someone else when Tony Russo entered their sphere. Her face flushed. Her manner became more feminine – not quite coquettish but almost.

Nick knew more than any of them. He knew what happened on both sides of the wall that The General had erected between the prisoners and the scientists. He knew about the scheme hatched by the president and Evelyn's involvement. He knew the potential of the algorithm he himself had created. And he had just now initiated their escape after refusing to go along with their first attempt.

He looked at Tony – his eyelids twitching, mouth tightened, swallowing hard – and decided to deliver the bad news as though he was removing a Band-Aid – as quickly as possible. He started with a list of crimes committed by The General and his cohort before getting into the speculation about the president and her plot.

"So, kidnapping, murder, unlawful imprisonment and possibly some other stuff," summarized Tony once he'd heard it. Nick simply nodded his head and said "yes", adopting the manner of an appellate court judge, solemn and dispassionate.

"We can't stay here," Tony said as he turned the car sharply, accelerating to twice the local speed limit. It was as though he had been expecting something like this for quite some time. "The General won't simply abandon his plan. He'll come after us."

They cut through a rundown residential neighborhood. The three passengers, mouths agape, were stunned by the scene that unfolded before their eyes. The despair of life outside the pods was on display – shingles loose and discolored, gardens grown wild with weeds and brambles, the occasional pile of tires on a front lawn. Here lived society's leftovers, presiding over unruly, squabbling children with loud voices. They were the procrastinators, drunks, the stubborn and the poor – those whose idea of leisure was either brawling or gossiping. They all stopped to stare as Tony's black SUV sped by.

Once outside the city, the only sound was tires making sucking noises on the slick roadway. When the pavement ended, they slowed to a crawl as Tony had to pick his way through a slalom of tree stumps, protruding rocks and sagging branches. They pulled up in front of a disheveled cabin. Diana suddenly felt like she had removed a bottom rectangle during a drunken game of Jenga – unsettled and awaiting a disastrous collapse. They all jumped out of the SUV, muddying their boots. Their soles stuck in the muck as they made their way toward the door.

Tony groped around for the master switch. The lights flickered on as they stumbled through the door unsure what to expect. The cabin, which was unoccupied for most of the year, suffered from persistent darkness — sunlight, such as it is along the southern shores of the Great Lakes, blocked by the dense forest, its smallish, dirty windows begrudgingly allowing what light leaked through the trees to filter through the grime. The interior spread out to reveal a single room including what served as living room, kitchen and dining area. The sagging furniture was complemented by various hunting and fishing accessories – a tackle box here, shotgun cartridges there. Two small bedrooms each contained a bunkbed.

"Where's the bathroom?" asked Gabrielle with an obvious sense of urgency.

"Outside," said Tony, waving his arm toward the back door as he fiddled with a junction box, which would connect the cabin to a nearby solar field. The hum of an electric pump pulled water to the kitchen faucet, gasping, choking and coughing.

"What is this place?" asked Diana.

"My hideaway," answered Tony.

CHAPTER 25

FOLLOW THE
MONEY

ARA'S HEADACHE HAD BEEN GRINDING INTO HER
temples ever since she rolled out of bed. The unan-
nounced appearance of her executive assistant as though
she had jumped out of a video game suggested her headache would
not go away any time soon. *She's been programmed to appear only
when summoned unless – well, unless there is something that requires
my immediate attention.*

"The Inspector General has an urgent matter to discuss with
you," she said with a bit more tension in her electronic voice than
Tara was accustomed to. She pulled a bottle of CBD oil out of her
desk drawer before granting permission for him to enter.

Barry Owen was a small man, dressed in the style of a
Twentieth Century accountant — dress shirt buttoned to the top,
a thin necktie in a half Windsor knot pulled up not quite to the
collar so the top button showed a little. His sleeves were partially

rolled up tightly around his forearms so as not to interfere with his operation of various office machines. Although, she was fairly certain he used the most up-to-date tech, she'd always imagined him using a manual calculator, the kind with a hand crank on the side. The tattoo on his neck which occasionally peeked out of his collar suggested there was more to the man than she knew or had the desire to know.

"I found an account with money going in and out without any audit trail," he began. *No social niceties. He's all business this morning.*

He spread out a hand drawn flow chart on the desk in front of Tara. *I can't remember the last time someone used paper in this office* she thought. *And, I don't think anyone has ever given me a report that wasn't produced on a computer.* A cloud passed in front of the morning sun casting a shadow that robbed Tara's office of natural light. She looked up as though the change in lighting was trying to tell her something.

"Why the crayon drawing? Couldn't you produce it on your computer."

"I thought it best not to leave a trace."

Tara thought to ask why but then realized it was better to hold her questions. It was likely the reason would reveal itself in time. "Go ahead," she said finally.

"Money is being siphoned out of each of the accounts in this drawing and it's all going to the one in the middle. The amount of money in each transaction is too small for anyone to notice. But, in the aggregate, it's a substantial amount."

"How much?"

"About a six million New Bucks." New Bucks had been issued in exchange for any cash or dollar denominated assets in 2029 as the second great depression spread its roots throughout the US economy, changing the lives of every human being within its borders. Each was now worth about sixty of the dollars they replaced.

Tara was stunned. She slumped back in her chair, wincing involuntarily when she tweaked her left hip. The expression on Owen's face told her there was more. His mouth was so tense his lips were invisible.

"Don't hold back, Barry. What have you learned?"

"Each of these accounts funds a massive weapons program. As such, there are multiple signatories that have access to the funds. So, it's challenging to trace who is drawing these small amounts of money. There are thousands of transactions every day. Whoever is doing this relied on that to stay below the radar."

"So, how did you figure all this out?"

"I stumbled over it . . ."

He paused. Tara raised an eyebrow to indicate that he should proceed with his case.

"We've had a years-long project to clean up our books."

"Centuries long, more like . . ."

"Yeah," he chuckled. "Anyhow, I found the account in the middle of this chart during a routine review. It wasn't assigned to any particular program. Yet, there's money going in and out all the time."

"You said a six mill went in. How much is left?"

"Nothing . . . It's been emptied."

"Holy shit!" She was stunned at the thought of a parasite within these walls sucking hard cash out of tightly controlled accounts.

"Exactly."

His expression told her there was more to the story. "What else?"

"Well, there were only two signatories in common for each of these accounts. And only one signatory was listed for the account in the middle."

Tara held her breath, waiting for the other shoe to drop.

"One is Colonel Evelyn O'Malley-Sakura. And the other is Samantha Yates."

Tara's shock at the first name was overcome by the need to ask the obvious question.

"Who's Samantha Yates?"

"That's just it. She's a spook, a ghost. As far as I can figure, she doesn't exist"

"So where did the money go?"

"To several hundred accounts, all of them overseas – Switzerland, the Cayman Islands, Singapore and the like. Most of them were in the name of a shell corporation controlled by this mystery person – Samantha Yates."

"And what about Sakura? How did she get to be a signatory on all these weapons programs?"

"She's on the strategic planning board. She has legitimate reason to know how weapons programs are funded. It was probably pretty easy to get low level staff to add her name to the list for each account."

Tara slumped into her chair, casting her eyes aside while she tried to overcome her confusion. She felt a chill in her blood, a coldness that brought the synapses of her brain to a standstill. She looked up at Owen. "What else?" she said, resignation showing in her voice.

"I'm still working on documentation. There's the possibility of criminal activity. But I don't yet have the proof."

"Thanks, Barry," she answered unable to convey any energy through her voice. "Keep at it please. And, it goes without saying, keep it between us."

She turned off the lights after Owen left. Sitting in the dark, she started to pull pieces of the puzzle together in her mind. She had read the FBI report the previous evening and spent a sleepless night contemplating the implications.

Three taps on her wrist brought her assistant to life in front of her desk.

"Please ask Colonel Sakura to join me," she politely commanded.

"She's not in today, Madam Secretary." Tara looked at this electronic version of a human and wished she could take out her frustration on her. She suppressed the urge. Her assistant was emotionless. She wouldn't react. And that would lead to more frustration.

"Where the hell *is* she?"

"We don't know. We've scanned for her chip globally and she isn't showing up anywhere."

"So, you're telling me that a career Army officer assigned to my staff at the Pentagon is AWOL?" Tara simply needed to say it out loud and have it confirmed. She was incredulous.

"Yes, Ma'am."

"One more thing: where is she from?"

"Assuming you mean Colonel Sakura, Ma'am, she's from Marietta, Georgia."

"Has she ever lived in Pennsylvania?"

"No, Ma'am."

"How about Ohio or New York?" she asked, thinking of states that bordered Pennsylvania near Erie.

Her assistant returned the reply in a few milliseconds, after having checked the databases. "No, Ma'am." Tara wasn't surprised at the answer. The pieces of a puzzle were coming together. Evelyn was involved in something nefarious. *It has to be linked to the kidnapping of Diana and her team. But why? What is she up to?*

"Get me General Clarke."

"Which General Clarke, Ma'am? There are seven here at the Pentagon and 103 in the armed forces around the world."

"Never mind," Tara replied as she walked through the electronic image, something she would do when she was frustrated that she wasn't talking to a human being. She didn't get very far before she found who she was seeking. She and General Clarke suffered a minor collision as she passed through the door.

"I've got a 'dust report' for you," he said without bothering to excuse himself for nearly toppling her.

"Dust report?" It took her a moment to figure out he was talking about data acquired by the microdust dispensed over Lake Erie. "You'd better come in."

CHAPTER 26

NANOBOTS

T HE HIDEAWAY WAS A PRISON OF A DIFFERENT SORT. Nick, Diana and Gabrielle had traded confinement in a luxurious mansion for confinement in a dilapidated cabin with no indoor plumbing. It was their introduction to 19th Century living – cooking over flames, hunting rabbits and hauling firewood, lots of firewood.

"Make a pile ten times bigger than you think you'll need," Tony had said. They thought he was crazy until the flame flickered out at 1 a.m. their first night. They'd all scurried out at dawn, their lips blue, their fingers numb, to find fuel for the pot-bellied stove. Once warm and fed, they'd ventured forth again with a clear goal to collect firewood.

Tony had immediately left the three alone in the cabin after getting them settled. He needed to see if his shenanigans had kicked up any dust in the city. His return to the police station hadn't raised any eyebrows.

When he reached the station, the front door hinges emitted their usual squeal, announcing his arrival. Peggy tilted her head to the left about a half inch to see who had entered. Brandon, the more senior of his deputies, brushed by him as he headed for his patrol car to begin his rounds. Amos, the other deputy, who was at that moment absent-mindedly picking his nose while he stared out the window, no doubt waiting for someone to tell him what to do.

"Amos, you got the weekly report done?" he asked. Tony didn't care about the weekly report but rather asked because it pissed him off to see Amos inhaling, exhaling and doing not a goddam thing.

Amos, jolted out of his stupor, said, "Workin' on it, Chief." Tony put it out of his mind, turning to Peggy.

"Anything interesting on the scans?" he asked, trying to sound casual and failing miserably.

"Nope," she replied, squinting and glaring at him.

She knows something's up, thought Tony. *She always knows.*

By day three in the wilderness, they had good reason to admire the results of their hard work on the cabin. A few roof shingles and some tar had eliminated the need for buckets to catch rainwater. Spring cleaning had cured their tendency to sneeze every few minutes. And repairs to the gaping holes along the foundation now prevented the local rodent population from visiting their dining table.

Diana and Nick sat in a pair of Adirondack chairs, which both needed a new coat of paint – a fact they ignored in favor of soaking up the view. The Allegheny Mountains were nearing their peak colors and the evening sky had turned molten brass.

"Dad never talked about my grandmother," said Diana.

She could see him struggling to bring up memories he had long buried, memories he likely preferred not to think about, memories that had been consigned to the deepest, darkest coalmine of his soul. *Is his unwillingness to bring those feelings to the surface overcome by his sense of obligation to his granddaughter?* She had locked herself away in the military just like her father had, in a world where the daily routine was dictated, and feelings were suppressed. A world where those without strong family connections could spend a lifetime ignoring the compelling human need to connect with one another. Now, that need had come to the surface. She felt changed by the rearrangement of her priorities – more confident from the certain knowledge and stability of durable love.

She waited. Patience was not her strong suit. But, on this occasion, she allowed the silence to do the heavy lifting.

We have nothing but time she thought. *I am prepared to wait for my answer.*

"She was consumed by ambition," he started. Then more silence.

"I was this geeky mathematician at M.I.T.," he continued eventually. "I don't know what she saw in me. I was quiet, withdrawn." His voice trailed off. Then he continued, "she was like a force of nature. Men wanted to be with her. Women wanted to *be* her."

Fragments! He's not giving me much to chew on. She felt as though she might explode from the urge to ask a question, ask a million questions.

"I was a thinker. She was a winner," he paused again. "That's what she used to say anyhow."

"Tell me about your lives together," said Diana, unable to contain herself any longer.

"Not much to tell. It didn't last long." He swallowed hard; a vein bulged in the center of his forehead; his throat so tight that he could hardly speak. Nevertheless, he continued.

"She was a powerful lawyer at a Boston law firm by the time your father was born. Being a mother was not in her DNA. She took a year off from work but complained constantly about being 'on the Mommy track.' Eventually, she jumped off."

"Jumped off what?" *He's usually so articulate. Did she jump off a bridge or what?*

"The Mommy track. She just decided she wanted no part of it. She gave me a long lecture about how powerful men, men who earned a lot of money, abandoned their families all the time. And, here she was, a powerful woman who earned a lot of money. So, she hired some vulture of a divorce attorney – Sidney something or other – and paid me off."

"Paid you off?"

"Yeah. They came up with some present-value formula and paid me a lump sum." He stopped, unable to continue for the moment.

His silence was killing her. "Then what happened?"

"She left – disappeared. After that, it was just your father and me. I never saw her or heard from her again. Someone told me she changed her name."

"That's kinda extreme." She could feel the pain – the pain her father must have felt. The pain, no doubt, her grandfather had felt – still felt as was obvious from the difficulty of talking about it after all these years.

"Yeah. I guess it was her way of hiding from me and from your father. He was about four years old when she left." His voice was hollow as though the essence of his humanity had just leached out of him. His pain was palpable. *She could still hurt him long after he thought possible*, she thought.

"I'll show you mine if you show me yours," Tony started.

"Wha . . . ?" replied Nick, startled. The two women looked on wide-eyed and frozen in place, wondering what the heck he was talking about.

"I'll tell you everything I know and then you'll tell me, okay?"

"Well, I don't know . . . " began Nick.

"Look! I've gone out on a limb for you guys. I don't know what the repercussions will be. So, I think I deserve to know what's going on. Capeesh?" He wasn't taking 'no' for an answer.

Nick hesitated. Tony was winning the staring contest. Not moving a muscle, his glare burning holes in Nick's skull while he waited for his answer.

"It's just that . . . " stammered Nick.

"I'll show you mine if you show me yours," Tony repeated.

Nick turned toward the women as though they might relieve him of his burden. "I'd like to know too!" said Gabrielle. Diana nodded her agreement.

Tony started with a brief history lesson.

"The General showed up in the depths of GDII, taking up residence in his family's abandoned mansion and throwing money around like carnival tickets," he said. "I had just got my honorable discharge from the Marine Corps and was looking for work. I met Alfred – he likes to be called The General – while doing gig work for a local security firm. I was guarding the back door when Alfred took a break from his party guests to sneak a smoke." He paused as though he was rearranging thoughts in his head so they would come out in the right sequence.

"I guess The General took a liking to me. Next thing I know he's arranged for me to join the police force."

"How'd you get to be Chief?" asked Diana.

"I'm just getting to that," he answered. "A year and a half later, the local police chief surprised everyone who knew him and retired at the age of 52, leaving town soon thereafter in a brand-new RV." He glanced around to gauge the reaction. All he got was blank stares.

"Before I could blink, the mayor was ringing my doorbell and – poof! – I was the Chief of Police."

"Wow!" was all Diana could manage.

"Sounds like some backroom deals were made," said Gabrielle.

"Yeah," he said. "A brand-new RV for starters. But I was too naïve to figure that out at the time. Since then, Alfred's had me on speed dial as though I'm his personal fixer. So, when he called me in and asked me to turn a blind eye to whatever he was doing on the other side of town, I thought nothing of it. It was routine."

"When was this?" asked Diana.

"Around Labor Day when we have the Locomotive Festival." He noticed the three blank stares. "Locomotives! You know: trains." When he got no reaction, he added, "doesn't matter."

"Labor Day? That's when we were captured," Diana said with a sudden sense of urgency.

"I had no idea he had guests until the day I arrested Ronnie Kay." He nodded toward Diana and said, "thanks for that, by the way". His gaze lingered a bit too long. Diana, whose wardrobe was anything but seductive –an oversized hoodie zipped to the top, her hands stuffed in the pockets – locked eyes with him. Her lips parted involuntarily. *There's something about her* he thought. *Don't stare, Tony!*

"So, you showed up at The General's house and Nick tells you we need to leave right away, said Gabrielle. "What were you thinking?"

"I wasn't thinking," he said. "I just reacted. Something told me it was the right thing to do. Now, I'd like to know what's going on."

All eyes were on Nick.

He began to lay out everything he knew, briefly describing how electricity could be generated from Carbon-14 stored in diamonds.

"Think of the impact of an endless supply of clean energy," he concluded, his eyes wandering off into the distance as though he was creating an image of a clean energy world in his mind.

"Okay," said Diana, snapping him out of his daydream. "So, what's The General up to and why were we kidnapped?"

"He told me he believed that there was a plot among some members of the federal government to steal the technology," he said. "He also thinks the president is involved. And some Army colonel."

"The president?" exclaimed Diana. "How can he know that?" She and Gabrielle exchanged glances.

"Not sure," replied Nick. "And I'm not sure I believe him."

"What about the Army colonel? She have a name?" asked Gabrielle, as though she wanted to connect the dots.

"Evelyn something — compound name — Japanese, I think."

"Evelyn O'Malley-Sakura?" asked Diana and Gabrielle simultaneously, their collective voices up an octave.

"Yeah, that's it."

They sat in stunned silence.

"So, The General is playing a game," continued Nick. "I just haven't figured out what yet."

"Okay," said Tony. "Let's see if we can put the pieces of this puzzle together. We think The General is some kinda double agent, right?"

"I guess you could say that," Nick replied.

"So, he plots with this Army colonel – what's her name again?" Tony asked.

"Evelyn," Diana and Gabriele replied in unison.

"Right. Evelyn. He plots with Evelyn and maybe the President of the United States to steal technology that promises to generate enough green energy to eliminate oil and coal – Finally! – and make the grid less vulnerable to attack in the bargain. Do I have that right?"

"Makes no sense," said Gabrielle breaking a brief silence. "What would they do with it?"

"Well," started Nick. "There are several possibilities. I think it's most likely they would commercialize it through a shell company

– registered overseas – so they can become billionaires overnight." He paused. "That's what I think anyway."

"What a sec, gramps," Diana interjected. "When I first told you about our escape plan, you said the work you were doing was too important. Why, all of a sudden, did you decide we needed to escape?"

"A few bits of information can often lead to a revelation," he said.

"Gramps! Come on," said Diana. "I feel like I'm pulling teeth."

"Sometimes Alfred and I would have coffee together and watch the news. We watched a report on a murder that had taken place right here at the national lab. He got very agitated, and left the room abruptly. Later that day, Tony arrested Ronnie Kay."

"I'm still not seeing it," said Tony, communicating the ignorance that the whole group felt.

"After you left – all of you – I noticed the pictures on The General's credenza. One of them was of a young Alfred Bragg in a combat zone. It was a group shot. One of the men in the group bore a striking resemblance to Mateen."

"So, it's no coincidence that Mateen was assigned to this mission," inserted Gabrielle, confirming what they already knew.

"Or that he flipped so soon after we were captured," added Diana. "So, how do you figure into the plan?"

"The technology to generate electricity from Carbon-14 stored in diamonds has been around for decades," Nick continued. "It was only a matter of time before it could be scaled up cost effectively. They didn't need my algorithm to do that."

"What then?" asked Gabrielle, as they all leaned in, listening intently.

"They needed my algorithm to create an army of nanobots to distribute the technology while protecting their intellectual property rights. In other words, they had no intention of sharing the technology with the world. They wanted to keep it to themselves so they could make a fortune licensing it."

"But they had to know you would figure that out eventually, right?" said Diana. "I don't understand how they would use you to help unless they knew you'd go along with their plot and they were willing to share the spoils with you."

"That's where Mateen comes in," He paused. "Well, you saw what happened to the scientists at the lab." his voice trailed off as he considered his own fate. "They can't figure out how to control the nanobots."

"So, Mateen learns what he needs to know from you and then you are suddenly expendable," said Tony.

"That's my guess," said Nick. "I'm either back in the deep freeze or I'm Gray Goo."

"So, even if we can escape – which is unlikely – they win," said Diana. "They have the tech."

"No," answered Nick. "They don't." He grinned as he said it.

"I'm breathless with anticipation," cracked Tony. *This is the final piece of the puzzle.*

"They don't have the tech. I gave them a bad algo. The real one is stored as data in my DNA." His grin now threatened to break his face.

CHAPTER 27

MOTOWN

THE SUN WAS ALREADY DIPPING BEHIND THE HORIZON when they finished their daily routine of collecting firewood. The ruby-red glow reflected off the bottom of cotton candy clouds. In the few days Diana had spent in the unfamiliar rustic setting of Tony's cabin, she had come to appreciate the nightly ritual of watching the orange sun drop behind the distant hills. She watched the line where heaven touched the earth, and then glanced over her shoulder at where her shadow shrunk toward her feet. Looking back at the horizon, where only a few bright streaks remained, she took in a deep breath.

"Snap out of it, Dee," said Gabrielle.

"Hey, that's my line," she laughed as Gabrielle's smirk dissolved into laughter. It was a moment not unlike many they had shared over the years – moments that had been in short supply over the last few days. They savored the connection, allowing themselves a moment of joy in the midst of a swirling sea of paranoia and cynicism. As the red sky turned sepia, the spell was broken by the sound of Tony's truck approaching.

"Just in time for chow!" exclaimed Gabrielle as Tony jumped out of the front seat.

"Perfect," laughed Tony. "I just came up to help you with the firewood. It's going to turn colder tonight."

"We've got plenty," said Gabrielle. "Been collecting it all day."

"I'll help," said Diana. Gabrielle could only watch, slack jawed as they wandered off into the woods. She had seen them exchange furtive glances. *Was this the next step in their courtship? Would Tony measure up?* she wondered.

"It's almost dark," said Diana. "Not sure how much firewood we're gonna get."

"I love this time of evening," said Tony. *He couldn't care less about firewood*, thought Diana. It was the chance to spend time with her that motivated him to drive up to the cabin. "The cool begins to seep in. You can't help but bundle up. Reminds me of being a kid, growing up here."

"What was it like?" she asked, hoping to get a sense of the man.

"We'd be out on the water all day and light a campfire when we came in. Cook some hotdogs; toast some marshmallows," he said. He took a deep breath as though he was inhaling the memory then added, "You know what I mean, right?"

"Well, no," she replied. "I've lived a very different life. Military brat, traveled the world over."

"Got a glimpse of that when I served," said Tony. "It's not for me. I'm grounded here. Lifelong friends, local rituals. I'm too connected to it."

"I've often wondered what that's like."

"Maybe you should stick around when this is over," he said. "Then you'll know what it's like."

Diana turned to face him, hesitating a moment until his eyes met hers. "I think I might like that," she said finally.

He smiled, slowly. It was like a blossom opening, a smile that came from deep inside. It was calm; it was confident. He didn't flinch or shy away from it. She found such comfort in that moment. A moment that might have been awkward, were it not for each of them allowing themselves to be vulnerable. They both held on to the moment, allowing it to sink in and become part of them.

She wanted this feeling to linger on forever, from now to eternity. Would she have the courage? The courage to overcome the defenses she had built up for so long she no longer noticed them. She didn't know. What she knew was she had never felt such an attraction. She celebrated every mini-second, every beat of her heart. *Can I admit I'm falling for him?*

"We'd better get back," said Tony without breaking his gaze. "It's getting dark."

"Yeah," said Diana, her voice softer than she intended. "Don't want to miss dinner."

They returned to the cabin, settling in for the evening, sharing a meal only Nick could have prepared: chicken cutlets accompanied by boiled red potatoes and green beans. "Nothing too fancy," Nick had said when he revealed he had learned some rudimentary cooking skills from his mother. "She would always say, 'I'm a member of the last generation of women who cook.'"

Their nightly dinner conversation had become a history lesson for Nick as Diana and Gabrielle helped him to fill in the blanks from his 25 years in a catatonic state.

"So, the reaction to the strife caused by social media was an artificially intelligent, real-time fact checker?" he said. "Seems like a sound response to websites like Facebook and Twitter."

"Right," replied Gabrielle. "About 80% of the population wanted something to sort out the bullshit." Diana nodded her agreement.

"Sounds like a good solution. So, how did the government get involved?"

"Well," started Gabrielle. "President Gideon-Mohammed created the FCA – the Federal Certitude Agency – to revise all the history texts."

"Revise the history texts?" he interrupted.

"Well, yeah, the history books left over from the 20th Century had omitted a lot. Textbooks in different parts of the country had different versions of our history. So, the government took over. The FCA was meant to create a consistent version of history."

"A 'Truth Ministry'?" he asked incredulously. "This sounds like 1984!"

Blank stares all around. No one understood the reference.

"Then what?" he asked, feeling his blood rise.

"Well, there were lots of databases containing incorrect information."

"Incorrect according to the revised history published by the government."

"Right!" she continued oblivious to Nick's emotional response. "So, when the fact checking software started digging up old information that was in conflict with the official history, the FCA nationalized it."

"Nationalized what?" he couldn't contain his astonishment. *What's happened to this country? How can anything be nationalized?*

"The software company that published the fact checker."

"They nationalized it. Just took it over so they could control the narrative." It was a statement that sounded like a question. "I can't believe what I'm hearing."

"Right . . . I guess . . . Yeah," said Gabrielle. "I've never thought of it that way."

"If you control the past, you control the future," said Nick in summary. "So, how did the culture index figure into it all?"

"Well, you get points for conforming with behaviors society values."

"And, no doubt, deductions when you misbehave," he said, his stomach growling to match his mood. He was amazed at how 'Likes' on social media had evolved into government control of day-to-day behavior. *We've gone from valuing individual freedom to social media mob rule to government control of individual behavior.*

"Well, yeah," said Gabrielle. "It's kind of a biofeedback loop."

"So, when will they start editing genes to ensure we produce babies who conform?" he asked sarcastically.

"They've started experimenting with that," said Diana.

"I can't listen to this anymore," said Nick, and he pushed away from the table.

Tony's phone buzzed in his pocket, ending the conversation. His sense of alarm when he read the message was contagious. They perked up like a pack of hounds who had gathered the same scent.

"We can't stay here," he said.

"What's happened?" Diana asked looking around as though she was already saying goodbye to her new home.

"Nothing. Not yet anyway. I asked my deputy to message me if he noticed something out of the ordinary," he said. "Seems The General's number two has been sniffing around, trying to figure out what happened to you guys." He began to stare at his phone as though it might tell him what to do next. "Something will happen soon enough. Either The General will reappear with his troops or a unit will be sent from the D.C. pod." He paused for a moment, as if in contemplation. "Or something else we haven't thought of."

"I've been thinking about this," said Diana. "If we can get to either the New York or Philadelphia pod, we can turn ourselves in to the authorities."

The others gave her wide-eyed looks.

"What?" she asked, trying to decipher the reaction. Nick was pretty sure her idea was a bad one but wanted to see if the others agreed. Finally, Gabrielle broke the tension in the room.

"Diana," Gabrielle began. "If we attempt either New York or Philadelphia, we'll run a greater risk that someone will take Nick."

"Well, maybe. But our orders are to bring him back to D.C. So, I . . ."

"I don't care what your orders are," said Tony. "Moving in the direction of D.C. raises the chances we'll be detected. It's a suicide mission." His voice had ratcheted up with a tension Diana hadn't seen from him before.

"So, what are our options?" asked Gabrielle, ignoring the fact that Diana was technically her commander if not the commander of the rest of the group.

"How about Canada?" asked Nick.

"Wait a minute. How does Canada get us to 'Mission Accomplished'?" asked Diana, unwilling to give in just yet.

"Look, Diana," Gabrielle started. "We need to see the mission behind the mission."

Diana rolled her eyes. "Above my paygrade, Gabs."

"Not anymore!" said Nick. "Your mission was to get me back to the D.C. pod so I could be thawed out and put to work on one of society's greatest challenges."

She opened her mouth to reply, but Nick raised his hand to shush her. The gesture was so foreign to Diana that she froze.

"My mission – the mission behind the mission – is to enable a new technology that will address our climate crisis. Your mission – to get me back to D.C. – was deemed an essential first step, but it was only that: a first step. If I'm not working on the problem, the problem doesn't get solved."

Tony and Gabrielle nodded their agreement.

Nick continued, "The General has a different mission: to capture the intellectual property and make a ton of money off it. But he was enabled by a mid-level professional at the Pentagon. The plot may go as high as the president. So, heading in the direction of D.C. is too dangerous. We'll be chased by The General and running into a trap. It's a lose-lose proposition."

He paused to see if Diana would object. She didn't.

"I can do the work from anywhere. Maybe Canada." He turned back to Tony who was staring at Diana to see if she had anything else to say. "What do you think, Tony? You know the region better than any of us."

"I've got a buddy who's a police captain in the Detroit pod," Tony said. "I've got my boat in the water down by the old Sheraton Hotel."

"Can we trust him?" asked Nick.

"Same unit in Afghanistan." He didn't finish the sentence. The fragment spoke for itself. Bonds created in foxholes take precedence over all others. "Anyway, if that doesn't work, we can get you across into Canada."

Nick nodded his assent.

"Isn't the boat ride to the Niagara River a shorter trip?" asked Gabrielle. "We could get into Canada that way."

"I think Canada should be Plan B," said Tony. Buffalo is a ghost town. Our movements there would be easy to detect."

"That's right," added Gabrielle to be sure they knew she was on board with their plan.

"So, Motown it is," said Nick, turning to Diana for a reaction.
"Motown? What's Motown?" asked Diana.

CHAPTER 28

THE ATTACK

C LAY'S TEAM HAD COUNTED ON DARKNESS TO BE
their friend, a darkness that swallowed a person whole.
But the stiff breeze had blown away the cloud cover and
a sliver of moon painted a speckled, shadowy world in grayscale.
Undeterred, they approached The General's hilltop mansion from
all sides.

Each tapped a coded message into their wristband tagged with
their location. They planned to capture one guard each — five in
all –simultaneously to avoid detection. It was three a.m., a perfect
time for a surprise attack.

They hadn't counted on Joe Lopez, a sinewy bundle of nerves and
tight muscles. An insomniac, he had stepped outside to grab a
smoke. A noise coming from the woods perked up his ears. *What
was that? Didn't sound like a deer. Maybe a black bear.* He went

back to his ancient Zippo lighter, thumbing its wheel against the flint repeatedly. He rolled his head back, exasperated by his failure to feed his habit, when motion to his right caught his attention.

"Hey!" he yelled a split second before being tackled from his blind side. He twisted around, losing his footing and crashing elbow first through the ground floor window of the house, taking his assailant with him. Clay's team didn't need any orders to know what to do next. Abandoning stealth, they each jumped through the window, shattering their way into the room where the guards slept, their cots organized in rows. Clay followed his troops with Evelyn close behind.

Most of their intended captives jumped out of bed, motivated by a surge of adrenaline. Those on the perimeter were easily overcome, unarmed and unshod as they were. A few from the center put up a valiant fight. The largest of them charged, reacting before thinking. Moving like a night train, he took out two of Clay's men along with two of his own. Bravo, a man of nearly equal size, thrust his heel into the side of the assailant's knee and grabbed his right wrist as he buckled. He applied his thumb to a pressure point on the back of his hand, twisting it to the left in an upward motion that brought the big man to his knees.

Two smaller men clad in boxer shorts and tee shirts leapt on Bravo's back. On the other side of the room Foxtrot had been knocked to his hands and knees and was scrambling to regain the upper hand. One of The General's soldiers dragged him to his feet. He turned to avoid a kick in the groin and, turning back, banged his opponent's nose with his forehead. He pushed him to create some daylight between them and then tagged him with a right cross which knocked him over the cot.

By the time The General entered the far side of the room, clad in a brocade silk robe with a velvet collar, his troops had been subdued. He turned to Evelyn and said, "Can we call a truce and sit down to discuss what happens next?"

Evelyn, acting on the certain knowledge that she had the upper hand, agreed. Turning to Clay, she said, "Leave Bravo in charge and come with me."

No one could be sure if the truce would be temporary or permanent. The General's men sat on the edge of their cots, under the watchful eye of Clay's team, which stood at their posts along the perimeter of the room. Whatever designs the captives might have had on revenge were tempered by the automatic weapons slung over the shoulders of their captors.

The General huddled with Evelyn in his office, each with their chief henchman hovering behind as though a bell might ring at any moment announcing the next round of combat: Clay, glistening with sweat, his hand on his sidearm; and Peter Kauffman, a dishonorably discharged former Air Force officer, The General's number two, trying to look cool and failing miserably.

"They're gone, Evelyn," began The General.

His words reset everyone's expectations of what might happen next.

"Whaddaya mean they're gone?" said Evelyn, her voice raised. Her heart was pounding, her jaw was slack, and her mind was running in circles trying to imagine how that might have happened.

"Police Chief arrested them." More blank stares. "Not sure what charge. He just waltzed in here and marched them out without ceremony."

Stunned, Evelyn asked, "how could that happen? What can we do?" She was venting her frustration and didn't really expect a straight answer.

"We were in the midst of creating a plan when you invited yourselves to the party," seeming indignant as though she was merely an uninvited guest rather than someone leading an invasion.

"You went dark on me, Alfred. Dropped out of sight, cut off communication. What are you up to? You're not thinking of making off with the grand prize, are you?"

The General was put off by the bluntness of her accusation, but he maintained his composure, unlike Evelyn who was leaning in making it clear that she wanted to reach out and choke him.

"I can understand why you might think that and I'm sorry you feel that way." He paused to let the apology sink in. But Evelyn's posture and expression were frozen. She didn't flinch.

"We can focus on the past and speculate on motives," he continued. "Or we can focus on how to move forward together."

Her left eye twitched.

"I assume they're locked up in the County jail," he continued, doing his best to ignore Evelyn's belligerence. "It's a few miles outside of town and not heavily guarded. The usual residents are lightweight criminals – drunk and disorderly, or the occasional grand theft auto."

"You're suggesting a jailbreak?"

"Let's start with a visit. I'd like to get in without raising any suspicion before we plan anything bigger."

"So, we sign in as visitors and . . . "

"We?" said The General. "Not 'we.' I . . . I will visit them."

Evelyn was determined to reestablish a cooperative relationship, not wanting this adventure to turn into a pitched battle, but she didn't want to be excluded either.

"Look, Evelyn," The General began. "Everyone knows me here. I can gain access to people and information easily. I own half the city."

"And?"

"And, if I show up with you, it will raise suspicions. People will talk. Talk will reach the wrong ears. We want stealth."

"Clay's going with you," Evelyn said. The General looked up at Clay, taking in his appearance, which was more like a professional wrestler than a professional soldier.

"Don't you trust me, Evelyn?"

"Clay's going with you!"

"Are you kidding? Look at him. He's a one-man wrecking crew. You don't think he'll attract notice?"

"Find him some civilian clothes."

The General looked back at Kauffman. Taking the hint, he said, "Well, I can find something. Maybe one of the big guys has something."

Clay looked skeptical. "We can find you something to wear," Kauffman assured him. "You'll look like any other blue-collar guy from town."

CHAPTER 29

SMART DUST

"**O**UR 'SMART DUST' IS SMARTER THAN I THOUGHT." General Miller Clarke's eyes sparkled as he worked to repress a smile.

"What have we found?" asked Tara. She had pulled the door closed and banished her electronic assistant with a password protected cyber lock. *No way I'm risking this conversation ending up in someone's inbox.*

"Lots, as it turns out. There is an array of pictures that I can share with you. They're in a secure file." He tapped his wrist and the images appeared in augmented reality. Each that he highlighted expanded to life size and appeared as though the image was a live person occupying space in the room.

"Where were these captured?" asked Tara.

"There are two arrays I want to show you. The first is from a large house, a 19th Century mansion in the southeastern suburbs of Erie. Most of the houses in the area were abandoned long ago. But this one is not only inhabited but also very active."

Tara's head was spinning. Clarke moved the images so fast – alternately filtering some and enlarging others – that she was unable to focus on any one image, much less figure out what Clarke was hoping to show to her.

"Here's the first shot I want to show you," he said as he froze one image in the center of the array and expanded it. "The soldier lying in bed, obviously wounded, is Corporal Ellen Mahoney. She is part of the squad led by Major Adams." He paused to let that sink in.

Tara peered at the image in stunned silence. *I've expected something like this; so, why am I shocked?*

"Let me show you more from the mansion so you can get a sense of what's going on."

The first few shots looked like a hospital setting, showing at least one doctor and a few other medical professionals caring for Corporal Mahoney and Private Elgin Smalley, another of Diana's team. But it was the activity in the rest of the house that truly had Tara reeling. The ground floor looked like it had been occupied by a conquering foreign Army. Soldiers in various states of dress — some in full uniform others in their underwear and everything in between – relaxing, playing video games or just shooting the breeze. In another room, three men were engaged in a serious discussion while peering at a screen that Tara couldn't see.

"From the body language, it looks like this guy's in charge," said Clarke. He was short and wiry, pointing at a virtual screen while the others looked on, appearing to feign attentiveness.

"I agree. Do we know who he is?"

"First Lieutenant Peter Kaufman — at least he used to be a first lieutenant — US Air Force."

"Tell me about him. Why is an Air Force lieutenant hanging out in a rural mansion, obviously engaged in something illegal?"

"He received a dishonorable discharge in 2046 . . . "

"Unusual for an officer."

"Yes. But not unusual for someone who punches his commanding officer."

"Who was his commanding officer?" she asked stifling a laugh but sputtering like an old water faucet. Her laughter had taken her by surprise. She realized she hadn't laughed since the day of Diana's capture.

"George Pulaski. You know him?"

"Yeah . . . He's a horse's ass but . . . "

"I know," chuckled Clarke, warming to the topic. "But he's dependably a horse's ass."

"I've wanted to punch him out myself a few times," said Tara. They both fought hard, but their cheeks swelled momentarily. It was no use. Their laughter was loud enough to penetrate Tara's door and echo in the hallway. The tension broken, they looked at each other, enjoyed the moment and then jointly resolved to settle down. Tara grabbed a Kleenex from her desk to wipe the tears from the corners of her eyes.

"I needed that," she said finally.

"It's been a rough few days," replied Clarke.

"Weeks! It's been a rough few weeks," she replied, her mood change suddenly splashing cold water on the moment.

"Right. You must be under unbearable pressure," he added.

"It's insane to be laughing," she replied.

"I've been so absorbed in this project that I sometimes lose sight of the larger implications."

"Right," she agreed. "A war hero sent on a 'mission' to Pennsylvania as though it was a foreign land, captured along with six other soldiers, has vanished into thin air. Billions spent on satellite and ground-based electronics designed to track everyone, everywhere and at all times has failed to locate them despite their capture having occurred within a few hundred miles of the nation's capital."

"Yes. I know," he said after allowing her to vent a little bit.

"Before you go on, tell me about the mansion. What do we know about it? Who owns it?" asked Tara.

"Alfred Braxton Bragg."

The name hung in the air like a storm cloud about to throw a bolt of lightning.

"Tara! You okay?" He grabbed her elbow as she started to wobble. She steadied herself as he helped her into a chair.

"Obviously, you know him," he said.

"Yes. And it's much worse."

"Worse? Worse than what?"

"Colonel Sakura is involved in some sort of plot with him." The big picture was starting to come into focus. Evelyn's lies about Erie and Bragg, the money flowing out of government accounts and, of course, the report that Clarke had shared with her. Her heart sunk, her stomach twisted, her head pounded. Her rapid breathing alarmed Clarke and he grabbed both of her arms to steady her.

"She's involved in a 'plot'?" he exclaimed.

"I know they're up to something. But I don't know what." Her anxiety began to ebb. But she was still shaking. "I've been trying to figure it out ever since you shared that Top Secret report with me."

"If the report is relevant, then the president may be involved, right?" he asked.

"I don't know," she said. There were too many gaps in their knowledge of the so-called plot. Perhaps the surge of emotions over the disappearance of Diana – a war hero and her protégée – had affected her ability to be rational. She wondered if she had been so overcome that she was failing to see the bigger picture. It seemed that Evelyn and Bragg were planning something that required Nick Adams participation. *But what?* And the whole enterprise was supported by the president. *Maybe!*

"There's more in the photos," said Clarke. "Maybe it will help."

"More?"

"Yes. I told you I have two arrays to share with you." He poked at the air closing one file and opening another.

Tara eased herself into her chair to prepare for what this array of photos held. The next image was filled with scenery, beautiful scenery. *I have forgotten what raw nature looked like* thought Tara. She briefly yearned to be there. To simply walk away. To retire to some bucolic setting. She chastised herself. *Snap out of it, Tara.*

"Where is this?"

"About 8 miles south by southwest of Erie. It's an uninhabited area popular with hunters and fishermen."

The pictures hung in midair, an array of thousands that Clarke was able to filter through quickly. First, he eliminated those which didn't include motion. That reduced the number to review to a few hundred, some with wild deer on the run, others with badgers, foxes or coyotes. He poked at the air with a sense of purpose to further sort them by geography, finally arriving at the first image he wished to share with a sense of self-satisfaction.

"Our facial recognition software identified Captain Gabrielle Ortiz-Wong. Here's a closeup we cropped from a broader image. And here's the image from which we cropped it. As you can see, she's collecting firewood and walking with an older man. Despite checking multiple databases, we couldn't determine his identity."

"That's Nick Adams," said Tara immediately. She was both elated to see him alive — walking about as though he hadn't been Rip Van Winkle for the last quarter century — and mystified as to what was going on. *What's he doing in the woods eight miles from the people who captured him?*

"THE Nick Adams?" Clarke was incredulous.

"The one and only."

"I thought he was dead," he said.

"Yes, he was. And he will be again if we don't find him."

CHAPTER 30

JAIL BREAK

P EGGY LOOKED UP WHEN THE DOOR SQUEAKED OPEN.
Clay entered first, dressed like a guy he might have punched
out in high school. His expression suggested something
between constipation and diaper rash. The ultra-casual fashion of
the early 21st Century – plaid flannel shirt with the sleeves ripped
off at the shoulder, frayed and baggy cargo pants and a ball cap
turned around – was not a good look for him. Nevertheless, he
accompanied The General to the police station to obtain visitors'
passes for the local jail per the plan they had hatched the night
before.

The locals were accustomed to seeing The General with strang-
ers in tow. Few of them thought much about the small army that
was hiding in his enclave, and those who did weren't quite sure
what to make of it. Peggy was certainly curious, and when The
General and Clay entered the dilapidated building, the vibe in the
air told her that something was amiss.

"Good afternoon, Peg," The General started. He hated having
to deal with the peasant population: store clerks earning minimum

wage, maintenance men shuffling through their day and civil servants who, much like Peggy, clung to the limited power they had – the power to deny those who felt entitled to do whatever they wished, whenever they wished.

Peggy responded with her usual wordless nod. She wished she could unleash the torrent of resentment she felt for this S.O.B. But it was not in her nature. Her hometown had always been divided between the haves and the have-nots. The General had returned at the depth of their misery pretending to be a savior. Now, he was lord of the manor. *Had he not returned . . . well, had he not returned, maybe my father's business would still be in the family, maybe my mother wouldn't have expired from drink.*

She shook it off. Years of resentment had brought her nothing. Any attempt to repair the damage would be too damn little, too damn late.

"We'd like to visit your prisoners."

"What prisoners?" she asked. Two words strung together was all she could normally muster. So, she let the question hang in the air. She could almost hear the wheels turning in The General's head, wondering what she was up to.

"The Chief arrested three guests staying at my home. I would like to visit them." He stood at his most erect as though his body language would elicit a response not otherwise forthcoming.

Peggy stared back, not giving anything away. After a few seconds — which seemed like hours — she said, "none here." The energy drained out of The General's pose, like a slow leak in a tire.

She eyed Clay wondering how someone with his intensity could end up in this hellhole. He took it as an opportunity to interject.

"Diana Gutierrez-Adams, Gabrielle Ortiz-Wong, Nick Adams . . . . Where are they?"

Sticking to her two-word limit, she replied, "Beats me."

The two looked at each other as though they each hoped the other knew what to say next. The silence hung in the air like virga.

"Where is Chief Russo?" asked The General in an attempt to reinflate himself.

"Gone fishing," she said, kicking herself the moment the words slipped through her lips. She had intended it as a wisecrack. But, in this case, she assumed it was true because he had switched off his phone as he always did when he was on his boat. Moreover, in the constant tug of war between not giving a shit about anything and uncultivated loyalty to Tony, she increasingly found loyalty won out. So, dispensing clues should not be part of her repertoire.

"Let's go," said The General. "I know where they are."

As the door slammed shut behind them, Peggy arose with so much urgency that she startled Amos — perhaps the laziest deputy they had ever employed — who had paid scant attention to the goings-on in favor of playing Internet checkers with an anonymous opponent in Oklahoma. She squinted through the dirt-streaked windows until the two visitors had disappeared out of sight.

"Amos, run on down to the docks and tell the Chief that The General is looking for him."

Amos stood assuming his usual slouching posture, his jaw slack, astonished at both Peggy's sense of urgency and her audacity to give him orders. A muscle twitched involuntarily at the corner of his right eye. He tapped his sleeve to bring up his messages – not to read them but rather to act as though he wasn't planning to obey.

Peggy, meanwhile, watched the roadway half expecting The General to double back. Her gaze was unwavering even as her view of the road was interrupted by a phalanx of ants zigzagging its way across the window.

"Be sure you're not followed," she added, turning toward him. When she realized he was just standing there, probably trying to get his feeble mind to come up with a response other than 'yes, ma'am,' she barked, "NOW!"

"We'll need an overpowering presence, so they give up without a fight. I don't want anyone getting hurt," said The General once they were back in his classic Tesla, en route to his mansion.

"Makes sense," Clay replied. "You know where they are?"

"Yeah. Tony – the police chief – has a rundown old cabin in the woods he uses when he wants to go hunting or fishing. That's gotta be where they are."

"How do you know he's not out on that big-ass lake?"

The General wasn't used to being challenged. He tightened at the impertinence of his companion, drawing a quick breath and holding it in long enough to consider what Clay was saying. *I'm surrounded by "yes men." Maybe I should listen to this guy.*

"I can't be certain," he admitted finally, wondering if Tony had access to a boat. "Any ideas?"

"We'll form teams. My team will go with you and your guy, Kauffman, can take your team with Evelyn. That way she has no reason to be suspicious."

"Why would she be suspicious?"

"That you'll make off with the goods." He had the look of a man you wanted next to you when the world is coming apart. He would feel the shockwave and remain on his feet. The General wanted him on his side.

"That's a counterproductive view," he replied, hoping that taking the high road would steer the conversation in a more cooperative direction.

"Counterproductive or not," Clay scoffed. "That's why we're here," he added as The General just grimaced.

CHAPTER 31

GREAT LAKES

T ONY COUNTED ON AMOS' GENERAL CLUELESSNESS AS
the *Bravado* II pulled away from the dock.

He had seen his deputy stumbling toward them, his
arm raised as if to make a declaration, his voice drowned out by
the roar of the motor. *I'm not sure if he's here to warn me or merely
to ask a stupid question. Either way, I'm not slowing down for him.*

It was rare enough to see a small boat on the water this time
of year without the added curiosity of a diverse group of passengers. "Hurry," he yelled above the roar of the engines. "Get into
the cabin. I don't want you to be seen."

The water swirled, making eddies of gray topped by foam. He
squinted as he turned north, unable to tell where the gray skies ended,
and the gray water began. His passengers stumbled down the ladder
into the cabin as Tony gunned the boat away from the dock. Diana
fell forward onto a bench along the starboard side, Gabrielle grabbed
air and fell to one knee; and Nick banged his head on a rafter.

"Careful with that noggin, Nick," cracked Gabrielle. "There's
no backup for what's on the hard drive." Tony steered the boat

to calmer waters. With the cabin closed off from the weather, the gentle rocking was accompanied by the steady thrum of the motor.

Diana had begun to feel a sense of wholeness spending time with Gabrielle, Nick and Tony. She had become accustomed to the satisfaction she felt when talking with Gabrielle. It was more than the words. It was her eyes, her tone and the small gestures – the little shrugs, the knowing smiles – that reflected a deep trust from a lasting friendship. They finished each other's sentences, squabbled over things that didn't matter and defended each other's honor when called upon to do so.

Now, there was Nick too. He was the yin to Gabrielle's yang. He listened as if her words were golden, perhaps some elixir he'd been waiting all his days to hear. She could tell he was thinking so deeply, already with a strategy that was several moves ahead of what she was capable of.

And then there was Tony. *What to do about Tony.*

"This is about the pursuit of justice, Diana," said Gabrielle continuing their conversation about their escape plan while appealing to her friend's sense of what's right and what's wrong.

"Yeah, I get that, Gabs," she responded. "But there are consequences to our actions."

"There always are," Gabrielle interrupted.

"And it could spell catastrophe for us. We are outmanned and outgunned here in the boonies. But back in the pods, we will be overwhelmed by powerful political forces and the media. If we simply follow our orders, we can't be faulted. I think we should return Gramps to D.C. and rely on the system to bring the criminals to justice."

"And, what if Nick is right? What if the conspiracy goes as high as the president? Do you think we'll get justice then?"

Diana always thought of herself as rational and logical. But it was never the logic of Gabrielle's argument that swayed Diana.

It was their connection. They had traveled through life together, pushed on every door. Gabrielle was the only person her instincts could accept – the only person she had learned to trust. *But still.*

"Let's reframe this topic, okay?" asked Nick, looking from Gabrielle's face to Diana's .

"Diana, you've been raised to follow rules," he began. "Rules guide us all to some extent, right?"

"Um . . . yeah," she responded not sure where he was taking the conversation.

"Rules are a reflection of society's standards and provide a safe way forward," he added. "But the world you've described to me has morphed into something else."

"Sorry, Gramps. You've got to break this down for me."

"Rules are now derived from neuroscience. People are embedded with technology that guides them based on cortisol, stress reactions and behavioral responses. There's no more guessing, no more debates about what may be right and what may be wrong."

"Was there ever?" she asked, feeling as though what had always been firm ground was beginning to shift beneath her feet.

"I am sure those who created this paradigm saw it as a way to marry science to an orderly society. I am sure they convinced themselves they were serving humanity."

"You're starting to lose me, Gramps. I want to bring you back to save us from . . . "

"Yes, I understood your argument when you first made it. But there is a larger matter to consider."

"Larger than survival?" she interjected.

"Hear me out, okay?"

The tortured look on her face suggested acquiescence but not openness.

"The world within the pods may seem orderly and it is," he continued. "But the price is freedom or rather the lack of it. The

Culture Index rewards those who obey the rules and makes them afraid to color outside the lines. The freedom we once enjoyed is now restricted because opportunities to earn a living are tied to behaving a certain way."

"Restricted?" she challenged. "How is it restricted?"

"Artificial intelligence identifies dissent and penalizes it. Venture outside the walls to enjoy nature and pay a price."

"Yes. And I don't understand why," she said. He had touched a nerve, something that had bothered Diana since she had moved into the podosphere. *Why are they trying to control our behavior?*

"Someone – 'They' – don't want you to have experiences not on an approved list. Experience leads to creative expression. The rules we are coerced into following are antithetical to a free society. Our government has become a service business."

"A service business?"

"Yes, the product is an orderly society and the government's programs assure it. People always give up some freedom as part of a social contract. But how much freedom do you have to give up in order to live in the luxury of the pods?"

"Wait a minute, Nick," said Gabrielle. "What has any of this to do with our current predicament?"

"We were once governed by principles. We were free to express any idea, to move about the country, to worship something other than a set of guidelines. Now, it's principles be damned. We're governed by a set of rules. And rules change based upon the whims of those in power and those in power are changed in the process of gaining power. They are corrupted by the experience."

"So, are you saying we should ignore the rules?" asked Gabrielle.

"Yes," he replied. "That's exactly what I'm saying."

"So, what about principles?" asked Gabrielle. "And, again, how does any of this apply to our situation?"

"I've been reincarnated to develop an energy source that will save the planet and be available to all. Do you believe in that objective?"

They both murmured their agreement.

"If societal norms no longer help us to determine what's right and what's wrong, we have to figure that out for ourselves," he added. "So, to answer your question, a principled approach to solving this problem achieves the best outcome for the most people. If that means, we break the rules, so be it."

Diana and Gabrielle looked at each other and turned back to Nick who continued. "Our plan should also take the risks into account. We'll examine the worst possible outcomes at each stage while keeping our main objective front and center."

Diana was overwhelmed. While Gabrielle always had tugged at her heart to win her over, her grandfather now created a new perspective – one that put her on a different path. *It's no wonder he won the Nobel. I don't know what to do. For now, I have to trust him – both him and Gabrielle.*

"Okay," she said half-heartedly, signaling she wasn't totally convinced. Standing up, she added, "I need some fresh air." Leaving them behind, she climbed the three steps to the upper deck where Tony manned the helm. The boat surged forward with a steady rhythm, its bow rising and falling with the waves. They had a following sea which aided their progress but required Tony's full attention lest they find themselves sideways to the waves.

"Hi," he said without looking at her, his eyes trained on the horizon occasionally glancing at the boat's compass. "I thought we agreed you guys would stay below decks. Are you feeling queasy?"

"A little," she replied. "But not from the rocking of the boat."

He raised his eyebrows and she continued. After she recapped her discussion with Gabrielle and Nick, she took a deep breath and let it out slowly as though the act of unburdening herself had provided some relief. She knew where Tony stood. He had enabled their escape – or at least arranged for the next step; their plan was still fuzzy.

But rather than argue the point, he simply asked, "what do your instincts tell you to do?"

"That's just it," she replied. "My instincts seem to have abandoned me."

Actually, her instincts told her to forget their dilemma for a while. Her instincts told her to make a move, to let Tony know how she felt about him, that she wanted to be with him, wanted this whole ordeal to be over and for the two of them to have nothing better to do than to spend time together. To find out if this urge, this feeling of lust could be lasting and perhaps turn into love.

"Seems like the question is 'do you abandon your friends, or do you abandon yourself?'"

"Yeah," she said. "Maybe . . . well, maybe . . . " She felt compelled to say something but had no clue what.

"Maybe there's no right answer," he said. "There are always more paths than clues."

"If only . . . " she said wondering how this country sheriff – this tough man's man — could also be so wise.

"If only you had the patience," he said, turning to her and smiling that big, lovely smile of his.

I'm falling for this guy and I barely know him.

"You know me so well," she laughed.

"Well, actually I don't. But I'd like to know you better."

"Me too," she said. "I mean not to know myself. To know you, I mean." Even if she couldn't express what she was feeling, she knew what she felt. Safety. She felt as though she was home after leading a homeless life. She felt as though even if she searched forever, every path would lead her back to him. *How could that be? Is it for real or is it just because we've been isolated and fighting the same battle? I can't be sure.* "Well, you know what I mean..." she added for good measure.

Now it was his turn to laugh. "Yeah, I think so. Let's just promise each other not to forget this moment," he said.

He stood tall and strong behind the helm of the boat. To Diana, it was as though he was navigating to a place she longed to go, even if she didn't understand why. She slid under his left arm, stood on tiptoe and kissed him fully and deeply. He reacted just as she hoped he would. First his body then his lips softened to meld with hers. In that kiss was the sweetness of passion, a million loving thoughts condensed to one moment, a moment in which they were their pure and vulnerable selves.

"Now, I'm sure you won't forget this moment," she said.

CHAPTER 32

MOUNT
WEATHER

TARA ORDERED A STEALTH SUV TO BE BROUGHT
around. Designed to cloak the occupants from digital
surveillance, it would be necessary for the journey she
would take today. She was headed to Mount Weather, a facility no
longer in use which was originally developed to house a complete
duplicate of the executive branch of government in case of a natural disaster. They had chosen it because its security systems had
not been updated or connected to the vast grid that monitored all
citizens.

The alien world of the Virginia countryside was stunning as
she headed toward Berryville. It was a clear sunny day and the
expanse of green contained more hues than she could have ever
imagined. The leaves had just begun to turn and the sight of an
occasional pair of deer thrilled her as it had when she was a child
in rural Massachusetts. Over each rise was another patchwork of

gold, red and green, which rose and fell like giant waves on the ocean. *Oh, how I miss this.*

She had authorized Operation Magneto and assigned herself, General Miller Clarke and three of his designees to the project. They would use code names to ensure their identities would not be recorded when they passed through the underground entrance, which was protected by armed guards with blank faces. They acknowledged her when she walked through the partially hidden entrance but without the fanfare that usually accompanied her arrival at a military facility. Clarke was already in front of a console when she arrived. His assistants clad in civilian clothes were buzzing about like bees building a honeycomb. The room was a vast cavern, its walls of stainless-steel showing signs of neglect; craggy rock could be seen between the panels that were peeling away like orange rinds.

"What have we got, Mill?" she said as she strode into the room.

"Oh, hi, Tara . . . " He was totally focused on the screen in front of him and hadn't noticed her come in. Without skipping a beat, he added, "there are three discreet challenges to the operation. Locating our target, interpreting their activities and our response."

"Sounds like an OODA loop," she replied, remembering the acronym favored by the U.S. Air Force – Observe, Orient, Decide, Act.

"Exactly," he said as he moved objects on the screen. "We've determined that our satellite surveillance system has been hacked. The hack only affected the area around the Eastern Great Lakes, so no one was working on it."

"Almost by design," replied Tara. "If it affected an area, we cared about, we would have given it a higher priority."

"That's right," replied Clarke. "We have never viewed that geography as a security threat . . . until now. So, we hadn't determined that the hack was sophisticated. It will take us months to unravel it and restore its normal routine."

"So, what are our alternatives?"

"We're going to mobilize a fleet of drones."

"Dust again?"

"No. They're too random. We need a complete picture. So, we'll use birds and insects. The general populace won't detect them . . . "

"Any professional military operation would though," she replied, thinking aloud and wondering how sophisticated Alfred Braxton Bragg's militia might be.

"That's right. But we're going to focus first on finding Adams and her cohort. They won't be equipped to detect anything. Once we find them, we can survey the surrounding area to see if they're in danger."

"Okay," said Tara, her brow furrowed as she considered all the possible implications of her actions. She had authorized an Army General to set up a skunk works operation in an underground cavern in the Virginia countryside far from prying eyes. She had done so without informing the President, the National Security Council or any members of her staff. There was no official budget, no oversight by Congress and she was likely violating a federal law which banned surveillance of private citizens in the United States. She was apprehensive yet unafraid. *My head says 'no,' but my gut says 'yes.' I've worried about my career my whole life. Now, I'm going to make the choice I believe is right no matter the consequences.*

She took a deep breath and exhaled slowly before she spoke again.

"How do we speed up the process?" she asked. "When we used smart dust, it took days to find them and then another day or two to decipher what we had recorded."

"Here," he replied. "Let me show you. We're currently looking at an array from closed circuit surveillance in the Philadelphia pod." He typed a description into the console: WOMAN IN A RED DRESS.

Within a few seconds, the screens before them displayed an array of photos of women wearing red dresses. There were thousands.

"And this is real time?"

"Yes."

"But there are still too many to respond to immediately."

"Okay. Watch this," he replied. He typed WOMAN IN A RED DRESS, CARRYING TOO MANY PACKAGES IN A HURRY, HEADING EAST. The array was reduced from thousands of pictures to roughly twenty or thirty.

"How does it know what 'too many packages in a hurry' means?" she asked, marveling at both the speed and accuracy of the results.

"Well, that's where the artificial intelligence kicks in," he said, clearly warming to the topic. "The program can assess a variety of factors like the size and strength of the woman, their likely age, the strain showing in their facial expressions and so on."

"Impressive," replied Tara. "So, what queries will we use to find our missing crew?"

"We're working on that," he said. "We don't know their intentions. So, that eliminates a critical factor. But they are likely to be hiding or running from someone. Those stress factors should be evident."

"Yes. That makes sense," she said. Then she added, almost as an aside, "I was unaware of this capability. Where did we get this technology?"

"It was originally used by Facebook to moderate content on their platform. But the government — the Federal Certitude Agency – confiscated it. Now, it's being enhanced by the FBI," he said matter-of-factly. Tara was stunned. A federal law enforcement agency was developing technology which, when used, would violate federal law. *How could they possibly have authority and budget for that?*

To break the law in order to enforce the law. "They think they can use it determine when someone will break the law," Clarke added.

"So, what are they going to do?" she asked. "Arrest someone for thinking about breaking the law?"

"Beats me. I only know we need it now for our purposes."

But that doesn't make it right. I should report the FBI *to Congress. But I can't because, well, I'm violating the same law.* At every stage of her project, the instincts she had developed over decades in government told her to stop. To cancel what she was doing and stop others from doing it. She had to check herself every time. *Doing what's right means I have to focus on doing everything in my power to make sure we succeed. People's lives are in danger. The public is about to be defrauded by those who occupy positions of great power. I must do everything I can to stop them. And, then there's Diana. I need to be sure she comes home safely.*

"Okay," she replied. "So, we'll deploy drones to take the place of closed-circuit TV and we'll use artificial intelligence to determine the intentions of those we surveil. That's how we'll find them. And then what?"

"You'll have to figure that out," he said. "Do you want to send troops?"

"Let's see what we find first. I have a different idea."

CHAPTER 33

THE CHASE

A BITTER WIND SWEPT THE COUNTRYSIDE, AND THE ground was slick with rain as Kaufman and his men jumped out of the truck. The soil was so wet that worms had surfaced in search of air, and a flock of crows cawed and flapped their inky wings as they gorged themselves on the unexpected buffet. Kaufman barked a few orders, and the team formed a bucket brigade to unload their firearms.

Evelyn jumped out of the cab as Kaufman mustered his men into something faintly resembling a military formation.

"Overwhelming force doesn't mean 'guns blazing'," she began. "It means our captives quickly become convinced they have no possible escape. Brandish your weapons but keep the safety on. If there's a struggle, you'll easily overpower them. There are only four, one of which is an elderly man." A few of Kaufman's men glanced sideways at each other, remembering how a steak knife had started a skirmish that had resulted in the death of five people.

Kaufman stepped forward and reiterated the orders the team had heard at least six times in the last twelve hours. "Break up into the four pairs we've assigned you to. Evelyn and I will stay here on the west side. Signal your position once you get there. Remember, we're on radio silence. No beeps or inadvertent ring tones." He paused to review the paper map he pulled from his hip pocket. "The east side looks like the steepest climb. Ratner and Young, you'll start there and the rest of us will wait about 10 minutes to make sure we all arrive simultaneously.

"Any questions?" He quickly followed with, "Good!" before he could hear any.

A chill wind penetrated Clay's bomber jacket as boats bobbed about, creaking in their slips as gulls flapped their wings overhead, filling the air with their cries. He pulled up his hood and stuffed his hands into his pocket. The dock was easy to survey. There were no people in sight, the harbor as gray as a newspaper picture.

In the shack that served as the Harbor Master's office, George Dillian rubbed his hands above an electric space heater as he peered through the filthy two-foot by two-foot window. *Who's this asshole and why is he here?* His attitude changed once The General eased his way out of the passenger side of the truck. As the duo approached the shack, he mustered the courage to venture out into the cold. "Shit," he muttered to himself.

"Good morning," began The General. "I'm Alfred . . . "

"I know who you are. What do you want?" he replied with an attitude that reflected his usual displeasure at the need to interact with the public. He wanted this conversation to end quickly so he could get back to the relative warmth of his shack.

"I'm looking for the Chief of Police, Tony Russo. Does he keep a boat here? Have you seen him?"

Dillian had never met The General before but had decided he didn't like him very much. He also figured what happened at the marina was none of his business even if he owned half the town. His instincts told him to say so, to tell this jerk to walk to the end of the pier and jump. But Clay's glare chilled him to his bones, as if he was standing in a hailstorm in the nude. It was a look that said *I am your worst nightmare.*

"Um . . . yeah, I th- think so," he stammered, his eyes darting back and forth between the two men.

"You think so?" said Clay in a tone that conveyed not inquisitiveness but disbelief.

"I mean . . . yeah, he does," he said, his voice quivering now.

"Which boat is it?" asked Clay, continuing his piercing glare rather than casting his eyes toward the boats in their slips.

"It's gone. He took it out yesterday . . . late yesterday. I was just lockin' up." Dillian's voice quavered involuntarily.

"Was he alone?" asked Clay. "WAS HE ALONE?" he repeated only louder, jolting Dillian to respond.

"No. He had a couple of passengers."

"How many?" he asked, his voice growing in force with each question.

"I dunno . . . three, maybe four."

"Which was it? Three or four?" Clay leaned in causing Dillian to step back a half pace.

"I don't remember. I really don't," he replied trying not to show his fear, the tremor in his voice notwithstanding. He forced himself to smile – a smile that looked pasted on.

"Where were they going?"

"They didn't say," he said. "They headed straight north but then turned northwest. But that might have been because of the weather."

"Whaddaya mean?" Clay barely allowed Dillian to finish a statement before he fired the next question.

"Well, a squall had just blown through from northwest to southeast. So, he might have headed northwest to go around the storm and head east. I'm not sure."

The General reached into his pocket and withdrew a roll of cash that was wrapped in a rubber band. He peeled off a few layers, folded the bills in half and offered them to Dillian.

"Why don't you take the rest of the day off?" he said.

Dillian stared at the wad of bills as though they were a mirage, not wishing to reach out and touch them for fear they might disappear. He tentatively took the cash and pocketed it. Turning on his heel, he headed for his car, half walking and half trotting as though he was afraid The General might change his mind.

Clay was befuddled. "Now what?" he asked The General as he watched Dillian get into his car and speed away.

"Boats are required to have transponders," he answered.

"I thought that was just for planes," said Clay.

"It was until a few years ago. The government's expanded the regulations to include boats, cars, trucks . . . in short, any means of transportation."

"All the better to keep track of everyone," concluded Clay.

The General had already moved on to the next step in their search for the foursome and ignored Clay's comment. He tapped the device on his wrist bringing up a virtual image of his home screen. He tapped an app that generated the signal to his data center. A map of Lake Erie appeared in front of them with an array of red dots that represented ships and boats. A few strokes in the air with his hand eliminated any large commercial ships, likely headed for the locks at Niagara Falls. What remained were mostly small craft near the shoreline – "likely to be fisherman," said The General – and one other: headed dead west at about 20 knots on a steady course.

"They're headed for Detroit."

CHAPTER 34

A BLIP

THE FLURRY OF ACTIVITY SURROUNDING THE INSTAL-
lation of up-to-date technology at Mount Weather had
settled into a round-the-clock routine. Arya Hathaway
was sitting, bleary-eyed from a full shift, in front of the array
of screens which reported what each drone was seeing as they
scanned a 50-mile circuit around Erie, when an alert from an algorithm focused her attention on a single small event.

"Hey, Bruno," she said to her partner. "Take a look at this."

Bruno Dennison, always self-conscious about the thick lenses
of his spectacles, removed them, rubbed his eyes and turned
toward her.

"What have you got?"

"It's a signal of some sort. It popped up out of nowhere and
then vanished. I've never seen one like it."

"It's an identifier used by aircraft and boats to identify themselves," he told her. "Nothing unusual about that."

"Except for the location . . . "

"Whaddaya mean?"

"Well, the transmission took place over less than ninety seconds. I broke it down into 3-second intervals and overlaid it on a local map. It was a request initiated near the waterfront in Erie. An antenna from the big house on the hill responded with this overhead image of Lake Erie. Then the boat responded. And then it shut down."

"When you say, 'big house' I assume you mean Bragg's house."

"Right."

Dennison scratched his scalp and tugged at his goatee. Then he called for the boss.

When Miller Clarke arrived, he performed the same dissection as The General had, separating major shipping boats from fishing boats and then pointing to a single vessel traveling across the lake at 20 knots.

"Can we get a drone to check this out?"

Arya rolled her palm over a tangerine-sized track ball, selecting the bird drone closest to their target with a midair flick of her index finger. They all watched with an intensity normally reserved for the final seconds of a football game. The drone, buffeted by the wind, seemed to take forever to catch up. Flying in parallel about 25 feet off the port bow, it quickly turned toward the boat and captured an image of its pilot and a woman by his side. Dennison fed the pixels into his database which reported the identification in twenty-three milliseconds.

"Anthony G. Russo . . . veteran of the Afghanistan war . . . currently chief of police in Erie, Pennsylvania." He paused while he scanned the rest of the file. "Single, no kids." More scanning. "Has owned the boat for approximately thirty-seven months."

Clarke was thoughtful for a moment. There was something about this event that aroused his suspicions.

"Nothing else interesting or relevant," said Dennison as he released the file to Clarke for download and later review.

"So, why is the Erie P-A police chief making a beeline across the lake away from his home base?" asked Clarke. "And who is the woman?"

"HOLY COW!" Dennison yelped. Clarke and Arya both turned to peer over his shoulders.

"We found her!" said Clarke, his manner calm, his tone reflecting his self-satisfaction. "It's Major Diana Gutierrez-Adams." He turned to Arya and said, "Get a message to SECDEF. We need to get her down here right away."

"Yes, sir," she replied.

"And keep a drone on the boat. I want to know when and where it lands."

CHAPTER 35

DETROIT

C ASTING A SOLITARY SILHOUETTE IN THE PRE-DAWN light, the pier jutted out into the Detroit River. Lonely, rotting, deserted, waiting for demolition, it had been selected by their host as the location most likely to obscure their arrival. A few collapsing buildings bore signs with peeling paint recalling a better time gone by – Glenda's Café, Motor City Ice Cream, Waterfront Shake Shack. Diana and Gabrielle had each taken a turn at the helm of Tony's small boat during the first hundred nautical miles of their voyage. The last leg – through the treacherous currents and chilly waters of the Detroit River – was his. Bleary-eyed and unshaven, he felt every muscle giving in to gravity.

"Hey, Gabs," he yelled above the motor. "The bowline is coiled on the fo'c'sle. Step off when we get closer and find a cleat to tie it down."

Once she had both feet on the pier, Tony swung the wheel to the left and backed down briefly to kick the stern of his boat toward the pier. Grabbing the stern line himself, he stepped onto the pier. He peered into the gloom, squinting his eyes, and briefly wondered if he had found the wrong pier. *Not a soul in sight.*

"TIGER MAN . . . !!!" came the growling voice from a dark corner between pilings. Tony hadn't heard his Marine Corps nickname since he got his discharge. Diana and Gabrielle exchanged a smirk.

Bishop Kilwin-Chalmers was an unlikely policeman. For starters, he was only five feet, seven inches tall, barely tall enough to qualify for the force. Second, he was to-the-manor born. Bishop had grown up with the Oakland Hills Country Club as his playground. His life changed on 9-11. Inspired to enlist, he had serendipitously wound up as Tony's platoon commander. When he returned home, the country club life no longer suited him.

"Geez, am I glad to see you," he said as they exchanged a bro hug.

They piled into Bishop's electric-powered police minibus. They silently cruised down Grand Boulevard as the eastern sky turned pale blue with the sunrise. As they drove through downtown Detroit, they could see a drunken brawl break out in front of them, at the entrance to Cadillac Place, originally GM headquarters but purchased by the government of Michigan some four decades earlier. They all leaned forward to see what was going on as Bishop made a sharp right to avoid the fracas.

"Aren't you going to call it in?" asked Tony.

"No. Patrol will be here soon enough. It happens nearly every day and I want to maintain radio silence."

"What happens nearly every day?" asked Gabrielle.

"Oobies! They're living on monthly payments from the government and have nothing better to do than cause trouble. The ones that show up this early have been out drinking all night. Then they come down here to try to coerce some poor government schmo into signing them up for this program or that. The combination of too much alcohol and their natural tendency toward violence is the witches brew that starts a brawl."

"Every day?"

"Well, it's a different crowd each day. But there are always some here. The Detroit pod is about eighty percent Oobies. Most of them have nothing much to do but drink and carouse. So, that's what they do. Many of them end up here at the end of the night looking for trouble. And they often find it."

"Eighty percent?" asked Gabrielle incredulously.

"Yeah, things have gotten pretty grim. This isn't the DC pod. We have food shortages and disease. We've had a rheumatic fever outbreak — children are dying. A few weeks ago, it would have cost you over a hundred bucks for a dozen eggs. There's no meat most of the time. Fruit is just a memory."

They cruised silently pondering what Bishop had said as they exited the pod on Jefferson Avenue. They passed Belle Isle in time to see a brilliant sun, low in the sky reflecting off the waters of Lake St. Clair and filling the sky with shades of orange and pink.

After about ten minutes more, they arrived in Grosse Point. It had the general appearance of many of the nation's formerly wealthy suburbs. Grand houses, abandoned, a bit shabby with no hope of survival. A few houses – very few – were well kept and walled in with modern surveillance and electronic deterrence. Such was the house to which Bishop delivered his guests. A glorious two-story colonial sitting up on a rise with a view of the lake over the tops of the homes across the street. It was occupied by Bishop's sister, a divorced empty-nester happy to have the company – any company.

"Come in, come in," she greeted them as though they had arrived for evening cocktails. Her brother rarely brought guests to their ancestral home, so she was glad to see new faces. Giving them the up-and-down onceover, Jessica Kilwin-Chalmers was astounded at the scruffiness of the crew who stood before her. *Look what the cat dragged in* her mother would have said. She was as short as one might expect Bishop's sister to be. But she managed an elegant bearing nevertheless, dressed as she was in fading cashmere and silk slacks. Her wristwatch was probably worth more than Tony's boat and the expensive sunglasses perched atop her head were a crowning touch with no purpose save vanity.

"I was just going to whip up a pitcher of Bloody Mary's," she began her words fading off as the well-rehearsed line yielded to the reality with which she was faced. "But then, you probably want to get settled and cleaned up, don't you?"

Following Jessica down the upstairs hallway was a history lesson – certificates, awards, accommodations, handshakes with community leaders, rewards for jobs well done – it was clear that the Kilwin-Chalmers children were destined for success from an early age. Once each of them was assigned a room, Jessica returned to the kitchen where her brother had already helped himself to a cup of coffee.

"What have you gotten me into, Bishop?" Her gracious hostess tone of voice had been replaced by brother-sister no bullshit directness.

"They just need a place to rest and hangout for a while."

"Why? Are they fugitives from justice?" she said. "And, what's a while?"

"Jessica, do you remember me telling you about Tony Tiger in Afghanistan?"

"Sure, the one who saved your life . . . " She stopped dead in the middle of the sentence as it sunk in. Her hand over her mouth in astonishment, "Tony Russo is Tony Tiger?"

Bishop's intense look gave her the answer.

"You have a house full of heroes," he added. By the time he explained who each of her guests was, Jessica was sitting legs sprawling at her kitchen table taking advantage of the bottle of Gray Goose she had taken out to make Bloody Mary's.

"Bishop, I don't know if I'm up for this," she said. "Whatever 'this' is."

"I know I've put you in a tough spot, Jess," he replied. "And I wouldn't have done it if I thought there was a better alternative." He waited until Jessica's eyes met his.

"Jess?"

She sighed deeply and exhaled slowly. "I trust you, Bishop. I always have. How do you see this playing out?"

"To be honest, I'm not sure," he said. "But I'll stay on top of it. You'll be safe. I promise."

It took Jessica a long time to respond, "What do you need me to do?"

CHAPTER 36

THE POSSE

C ALLING IT AN AIRCRAFT HANGAR WOULD BE GENER-
ous Evelyn thought as she scanned the interior. It was
really just a massive barn, the only thing around as far as
the eye could see. Inside, there was a fifty-five-gallon drum emitting a faint odor of kerosene as well as a few machines – a pro-
pane powered generator, an EV charging station, a rusting lathe
leftover from a prior resident — and, of course, a helicopter from
a bygone era. On one wall was a massive sliding door with access
to the launchpad. As the door slid open powered by an unseen
motor, the wind whistled through the building from front to back
causing a few dust swirls to dance in front of them.

They had agreed to a skeleton crew of fighters to locate and
overcome the escapees – Evelyn, The General, Clay and Kaufman
plus two of their best soldiers. The aircraft was too small to
accommodate any others and they were confident of their ability to do whatever was necessary to recapture Nick Adams. The
General had professed to know how to track him down once they
arrived in Detroit.

"First, we'll fly to Selfridge Air National Guard Base near the Detroit pod," he said. "It'll be easy to find ground transportation once we arrive even if we have to resort to Grand Theft Auto."

For her part, Evelyn's suspicions about The General's intentions were set aside as she had confidence in the loyalty of Clay and his handpicked colleague as well as their ability to overcome Kaufman and his. But, once Adams was firmly in her grasp, she had other ideas.

She took advantage of the few minutes they had alone while The General prepared the helicopter for flight. She approached Clay as though she was simply making small talk. "What's on your mind?" he asked. Her face was drawn with a gaunt expressionless stare. It was an expression that said she wasn't sure what would come next.

"I'm thinking we need to neutralize Bragg and his boys," she said. Her voice was low, her tone flat with a hint of more power that her petite body would suggest. It was her intensity that had drawn others to her throughout her life. Clay not only matched her intensity but also shared her disdain for the idiots who made up most of the human race. They were a perfect match.

"How would you have us do that?" he asked clearly looking forward to it. "Neutralize Bragg, I mean."

"How?" she said. "The better question is when. How is easy. You're going to kill him. But when? That's a tough one to answer. I'm not sure how much Adams knows, if he still depends on Bragg to get this project done."

"That rolled off your tongue pretty easily," he responded, his mouth remaining a grim line amid his stubble. "But it's always easier said than done."

"You can't possibly believe he won't kill us given half a chance," she said. "You know it's got to be done."

"So, you want me to commit first degree murder?" he said.

"You've killed before," she said, her surprise showing in her voice. *Why is he questioning me* NOW? *We've always known we'd do whatever was necessary.*

"Yes, but always in a combat zone – when the government sanctions it."

"So, are you saying you can't do it?"

He paused, his evil smile betraying his words. "I'm asking is what's in it for me?"

Clearly thrown off balance by the question, she paused and turned to face him.

"You're gonna get paid what I promised, you know. Haven't I always lived up to my commitments?" *All of a sudden, a direct payment of millions isn't enough.*

"Yes, you have. But we're well past what was called for in the original agreement."

"The original agreement was to capture Nick Adams. We haven't done that yet."

"True. But you portrayed it as a simple operation: subdue an inferior force in a house on a hill and take him with us. We're well beyond that now. And murder for hire wasn't part of the program."

She knew she had to answer him right now. To ask for time to think about it would undermine his confidence in her. They weren't friends, not really, yet probably the closest thing they each had to one. Theirs was more like a transitory alliance of convenience, probably the nearest either of them would ever be to marriage.

And this was not the time to discuss a divorce.

"What do you want?" she asked him.

"I want his share – Bragg's, that is."

No way to avoid the question, no time to negotiate, not the time to equivocate. There was only one response.

"You want it, you got it."

He held her gaze without blinking. She matched him without changing her posture. "Okay, then," he said. "It's a deal." They each maintained eye contact until they heard footsteps approaching them.

"Hate to break up this little tete-a-tete," interrupted Kaufman, his eyes darting from one to the other. "We need help loading up. Bird's ready to fly."

The General eyed them with suspicion as they began the mundane task of lifting and loading. "Everything okay?" he asked.

"All good," answered Evelyn even though all was not good. Her conversation with Clay was unsettling. Now The General was about to challenge her. She knew she had to rise to the occasion.

He pulled her aside, and said, "Looked like a pretty intense conversation to me."

"It's an intense situation," she replied, giving nothing away. They were almost nose to nose, inhaling each other's breath. He waited for further information but received none. They simply locked eyes, waiting each other out.

"Time to go," Kaufman called out, breaking the tension. They turned not breaking eye contact as they did so, until The General climbed into the pilot's seat. He pulled his headset over his ears, grabbed the stick and went through a last-minute checklist. As the helicopter's subdued khaki paint was enveloped in a cloud of dust as it rose in a perfect vertical. The blades beat the air, having much the same effect as a small tornado on the loose ground cover. Kaufman glared at Clay as though he was sizing him up for the inevitable.

CHAPTER 37

THE SLUSH FUND

THE CONFERENCE ROOM WAS NAMED FOR MAJOR
Stephen V. Long, a U.S. Army officer who had been
killed in the attack on September 11, 2001. The floor to
ceiling windows were crystal clear and provided a stunning view
across the Potomac of the Washington Memorial. It was dusk and
the city was just beginning to twinkle into evening as Tara's quarterly strategy review was wrapping up. An unseen bot shut down
all the video conference screens and wiped all devices of files used
during the meeting.

Tara still took notes on paper – scraps of paper, the flip sides of
Thank You cards or supermarket coupons. She stuffed them into
the ancient, leather portfolio she favored. Worn and stained where
her hands had naturally grabbed it a hundred times a day over a
few decades, it held all manner of paper – white and straight-
edged; torn, stained and frayed; Post-It Notes; personal letters
folded in every way except perhaps origami. She slipped her hand
into an internal pocket and withdrew the hand-drawn flowchart
Barry Owen had brought to her a few days ago.

"Can you stick around for a few minutes, Barry?" she asked. It was an order not a request.

He waited silently until she had spread the chart out on the table before them. "First question," she began. "Is it legal?"

"What specifically?"

"There's always a slush fund tucked into every program budget because there are always unforeseen circumstances. Authorized signatories can withdraw funds to procure goods and services if they follow the procedures outlined in the program documents, right?"

"That's right?"

"So, did Sakura break the law when she withdrew funds from each of these programs?"

Owen's face twisted into an unpleasant swirl then unwound and twisted the other way. He let out a deep breath and wiggled his shoulders. He clenched and unclenched his fists a few times.

"It's a tough question . . . "

"I don't ask easy questions," she replied in a tone that did nothing to relieve his tension. She knew he understood the seriousness of her question. Nevertheless, she wanted him to feel pressured to get this right. The course she would take depended upon the answer to her question.

"Legal? . . . Well, um, I'd have to think about that," he said and then paused, his eyebrows twitching as he ran down the mental checklist permanently etched in his neocortex. "She had the legal authority to withdraw the funds from each of the programs . . . Umm . . . I'm pretty sure the amounts and timing were consistent with the procedures outlined in the program documents. But I would have to double check . . . And, yeah," he added, slowly becoming more confident with his assertions. "Since she simply moved the funds to another account that had no designated purpose, she didn't break the law . . . I'd really have to do some more research to be sure though."

"What about when she transferred the funds to foreign corporations without any designated purpose?"

"Well, she's walking a fine line there. Since the fund making the payments didn't have any rules, the person controlling the fund could legally make those payments."

Tara felt as though she was living a nightmare created by decades of well-intentioned bureaucracy. She had fallen through the looking glass into a world where all the rules were tortured and twisted into nonsense.

"There's just one thing . . . " added Barry. He paused. A smirk arrived on his face which revealed his delight at twisting the rules for good intentions.

"What? Don't make me pull teeth to get an answer," asked Tara, always impatient but perking up at the prospect of some kernel of good news. She was informed by her decades of experience in government. Bureaucratic rules could be turned to any purpose. At this point, it was important to make sure she had the goods on Evelyn. Barry was the best person to help her figure that out.

"It's true that she was legally making those payments. But she didn't have the authority to set up the fund in the first place."

"Whaddaya mean? Who has that authority?"

"Only the Secretary of Defense and . . . Well, you and the president."

My faith in Barry always pays off. He'll help me find the right path through this maze. It turns out that if you stay on this insane Merry-Go-Round long enough you can grab the brass ring.

"So, I can use this account if I need to?"

"Yeah, so long as it's under the annual limit for transfers set by Congress."

"And is it?"

"Well, the limit is four billion dollars. So, yeah . . . "

"Okay, Barry, here's what I'd like you to do . . . "

Wasting no time, Barry summoned one of his staff – the one most well-suited to perform the tasks assigned to him by Tara.

Bleary-eyed and reeking of rye whiskey, George Stanford sat across the desk from Barry Owen, trying desperately to focus on what Barry was asking him to do. Long ago achieving the tenure necessary for a civil servant to have job security for life, he had stumbled into Owen's office after observing his daily ritual of three cocktail lunches. Owen needed someone who didn't know anything and didn't care. Stanford fit the bill.

"Add the Secretary's signature to this account under the transfer authority permitted by Congress." He handed Stanford a piece of paper with the account number and the words TOP SECRET scrawled across it.

"Are we under the annual limit?" slurred Stamford.

Owen gritted his teeth as it was Stanford's job to know the answer to his own question. "Yes."

"Okay. But why the Top-Secret designation?" he asked as the note Barry had handed him squinted into focus.

"You know I can't answer that. It's Top-Secret." *Sometimes the bureaucracy worked in one's favor.*

"I thought the Human Rights Watch put an end to this program," said General Miller Clarke. He had confessed to being surprised – no, astounded – to Tara a few moments earlier. She anticipated his response. The so-called Killer Robot program had resulted in the deaths of more than a dozen scientists and soldiers who had been involved in its test process. She knew of no one at the Pentagon who wished for its revival. Least of all Clarke.

"That's correct, Mill," she started, sensing his distress. "But when the president authorized drones to be controlled by artificial intelligence rather than human Space Force pilots, she overrode the restrictions that shut down the program."

"But Tara," he said. "Killer robots?"

I've got to keep him in my corner. He needs to be convinced on the merit of the plan, not the rules that allow it.

"Look, in the ten years since this program was shut down, the software used to control the robots has been updated and upgraded so often that the risks of the program have been mitigated."

"Mitigated doesn't mean zero risk, Tara. They're still Killer Robots," he replied.

"Only if we program them to be."

"But how can we be sure?" He asked, the strain showing in his voice. "Software goes awry all the time."

"Look, Mill. I've always enjoyed working with you because you've got two tracks that you follow in parallel. One track always finds a way to keep us safe in this culture of bureaucracy and political backstabbing. And the other questions everything and asks how we can do better."

She waited but got no reply, only the intense stare of someone whose trust she valued, trust that she needed. *This relationship must not falter.*

"It's impossible for us to be perfect," she continued. "Our best chance is to make sure we feel we are right all the way down to our bones. We must not proceed until then. I have absolute confidence in you. What can I do to make you feel that way about me? To trust me on this?"

She waited for him to speak, trying not to give into the urge to fill the silence.

"I do have confidence in you, Tara. I've always trusted you and still do. I wouldn't be here otherwise," he began, stating the obvious. "But you're right. It's impossible for us to be perfect. I think robots are a mistake. And as for the legality of the program, we're going out on a limb. Worse! Going out on a limb is one thing; sawing it off behind you is quite another."

"There is a group of well-armed commandoes out there who have gone beyond what's simply criminal. If we use human soldiers to go after them, there are all sorts of potential complications. And none of them have good outcomes."

"Well, you've obviously had more time to think about this than I have. So, please tell me . . . "

"Assigning troops means we have to expand the circle of people who know about our semi-legal program," she said. "The program will inevitably be leaked. And, asking them to go into combat against other Americans will undoubtedly raise objections."

"Yes, we'd have to spend a lot of time selling this idea to other military commanders."

"Right. And, then there's the possibility of human carnage."

His face was drawn with a gaunt, expressionless stare. Still, she knew she was winning him over.

"For me to feel comfortable, I would need to control the programming of the robots," he said finally.

She struggled to control her glee when he said that. It was the response on which the success of her rescue plan depended.

"I was hoping you'd say that."

PART 3

CHAPTER 38

DNA

THE CLEAR MORNING LIGHT STREAMED THROUGH THE
kitchen window like a long-lost relative finding its way
home. Jessica flitted about like a small bird, preparing
breakfast as though her boys were home from college. Absent her
pretentions and heiress wardrobe, she was a small, plain woman with
eyes dark as coffee beans and a Great Lakes accent so flat it seemed
electronically processed. Her hair was piled into a careless topknot,
errant locks frizzing like steel wool — no makeup, no nail polish,
no jewelry. A few beads of sweat were apparent on her forehead as
her guests filtered down from upstairs. She laid out a buffet on the
kitchen island the likes of which they had not seen in what seemed
like forever — toasted ciabatta bread, fresh raspberry preserves, a
bowl of scrambled eggs piled two fists high and Danish pastries ooz-
ing cream cheese and marmalade. Bacon had never smelled so good.

The crew munched their way through with expressions of
gratitude.

They slurped hot coffee and chewed as they discussed their
next moves. Jessica listened cluelessly, concerned about how their

activities might impact upon the only place she'd ever thought of as home. From the street, it was bricks and mortar same as any other. But, to her, it was more than the sum of its parts. It was the glue of her existence.

"Bishop told me to let you have access to his computer stuff."

"Computer stuff?" asked Nick, excited at the prospect. "What computer stuff?"

"I always thought he should go out to Silicon Valley. He'd be a billionaire by now if he had. You know, he's a genius. I don't know why he wanted to be a cop . . . "

"Excuse me, Jessica," Nick interrupted. He didn't want to be rude. But his sense of urgency compelled him to interrupt.

"Oh, sorry, I don't get many visitors. Sometimes, I open my mouth and can't stop talking."

"That's okay," said Nick. "And I'm sorry to press you. I'd like to know what computer stuff."

"Well," Jessica resumed. "Bishop has a secret room downstairs. It's so silly really. He's had it since we were kids. He was always hiding out down there doing God-knows-what . . . ."

"And he's offered us access?" Nick again, trying not to sound too anxious.

"What are you thinking, Gramps?"

"Well, I don't know how much processing power he has . . . " he paused as his thoughts trundled through his brain like a freight train. "Well, if I could . . . " He stopped, lost in thought.

"Could what?" pressed Diana.

"We should talk about our next steps," said Tony, diverting everyone's attention and surprising Nick. "And, about Plan B if things don't work out."

"What are you thinking, Tony?" asked Nick.

"Well, if you can get your work done here, maybe we should leave you." This was met with blank stares all around. "I'm just spit balling here." he added.

"I don't like it," said Diana. "We can't leave you here without protection."

"Diana is right," said Gabrielle. "You're the grand prize. You're what we're defending."

"But we can't defend him. That's the point," Tony said. "We're unarmed and there's only four of us." Nick listened intently. As counterintuitive as it seemed, he thought Tony was right.

"Okay, so what's the logic of leaving him here?" asked Gabrielle.

"This house is like a bird's nest," he began. "Right now, we're the target. We need to fly away to distract the enemy. If they follow us and capture us, Nick still has a shot at finishing his work."

"Are you saying my house might be attacked?" asked Jessica, her voice rising, cracking on the last word.

"No, Jessica. I'm saying we can't stay here. I don't want to risk it being attacked," said Tony.

"I'm not comfortable leaving Gramps here to defend himself," said Diana.

"If they show up. I'll just turn myself over to them," said Nick, ever calm and rational. "They're not going to hurt me. The reason they're chasing us is because they need me. I think it's a good plan."

"Still . . . " Diana's discomfort was written all over her face. She glanced first to Gabrielle for support and then Jessica but found none.

"I'll stay with him," Gabrielle said finally. "You and Tony are at your best with your boots on the ground. I might be able to help Nick with the technology anyway."

"You're right, Gabrielle. I might need your help," said Nick. "Anyway, it all depends upon how much computing power we have. If Bishop doesn't have the necessary technology, then I won't stay. So, let's start there."

After a clattering of dishes and silverware, they followed Jessica down a dark stairwell that was adjacent to the pantry. She led them through the wine cellar to a wooden doorway, which was obviously homemade and decades old. The words "KEEP OUT" were stenciled chest high with a skull and crossbones painted above it. Nick smiled at the notion of an adolescent Bishop huddling in his private lair no doubt working on projects that were vitally important.

The door was locked but Jessica used a butter knife she had brought from the kitchen and slipped it into the space between the door and the frame. A quick jiggle and the door glided open. They walked into a windowless space and were greeted by a mélange of foul odors. Jessica flipped a switch, lighting a single bulb which hung from the ceiling. As their eyes adjusted to the light, they saw a bare concrete floor and exposed beams. In one corner was a tool bench, on top of which were a collection of soldering irons on one end, and circuit boards, microchips and a box of wires, tangled into a briarpatch on the other.

The server on the other side of the room was incongruously modern and up to date. Just like the servers they had seen in The General's data center, it floated above the floor to allow for cooling air to circulate around it. An orange glow conveyed it was connected to other devices and to the Internet.

"Passwords?" asked Nick as he turned toward Jessica. The others stood statue-still, mouths agape when Jessica handed Nick a device the size of a ping-pong ball. One side was flattened by a fingerprint pad. She pulled a scrap of paper from the back pocket of her jeans and handed it to Nick.

"It's some kind of code," said Jessica. "Bishop said you would be able to decrypt it."

Nick smiled at the challenge. He guessed that Bishop would have hashed the password with a salt, a method that few understood. The code that Jessica handed him would be the key to his in-kernel rule engine. Once the rule engine was unlocked, Nick would have to calculate the algorithm to identify the plain text password. Then he would assign the password to his thumbprint using the ping-pong ball as a device key to unlock the computer. It was elementary to many mathematicians but required an understanding not only of the math but also of the technology.

It took him all of 90 seconds to crack the code.

"What now?" asked Gabrielle.

"I have to download the algo from my DNA," he said as he rummaged through his shoulder bag. He found his probe at the bottom. The group took a collective half step backwards as he pulled it from the bag – Jessica a full step. "First, I have to find a DNA decoder on the web. Then I'll draw some blood."

"Two helix dot com," said Gabrielle. "It's a website," she added when she noticed the confusion on their faces. "It has a tool that disentangles your DNA so you can find out if you have a propensity for certain hereditary diseases. We used it at the Pentagon to screen recruits."

"I'm gonna leave you to it," said Tony. "But, before I go, can you tell me what you're gonna do?"

"Well, I'll download this DNA tool then draw some blood," Nick said. "This device not only reads my fingerprint to allow access to the computer but also can be used like a microscope slide to decode the DNA. I'll separate the math from the biology so to speak. Then I'll disconnect from the Internet to make sure none of the nanobots escape."

"Escape?" How would nanobots escape?" Tony asked, recalling his abandoned murder investigation. "Could nanobots commit murder?"

"Let me break it down for you," said Nick, recognizing the distress in Tony's voice. "Artificial intelligence has no conscience. It only has a mission . . . whatever mission it's assigned when it's created. So, it pursues that mission without consideration of the consequences."

"So, the answer is 'yes.' If they have no conscience, nanobots could commit murder," Tony said. "But how would they escape."

"Easiest way is to email itself. It can send itself to some other destination if it thinks it's a better place to achieve its goals."

"Would it be possible for the nanobots to invade a human being?" asked Tony. "From an email?"

"Well, I'm not sure about that," said Nick. "They might need a little bit of human help to achieve it. They could enter the human bloodstream through an injection, or eye drops, perhaps even a deep abrasion."

"Ronnie Kay could have used one of those methods to kill the scientists in the lab," said Tony to no one in particular. "But how would we prove it when all we have to work with is Gray Goo?"

CHAPTER 39

LOVE AND WAR

"T's called Victorian discretion," said Tony, a
smirk on his face, though Diana couldn't quite see it in
the unlit bedroom.

"What is?" Diana replied.

"Tiptoeing down the hallways after midnight was a national pastime in Victorian England. Love affairs were never put on display." he said. They giggled as they lay under the duvet, holding each other close, their sweat mingling together.

"There's something about hiding it from the others that makes it almost illicit, more exciting."

"They'll know," he said. "People always know."

"Why did we wait so long?"

"For me," answered Tony. "It's always about self-preservation. I knew once we gave into it, I would be addicted, I wouldn't be able to give you up."

"Right! That's it," she said after letting it sink in. "I've had these defenses up, meant to keep everyone out. I forgot there may be someone I'd want to let in. What I feel now is what I've feared . . . a mixture of joy and pain."

"Pain?"

"Yes," she replied. "If this relationship lasts, I'll become afraid to lose you."

"Then what happens?"

"Then I'll sabotage the relationship," she answered. "At least, that's Gabrielle's take on it. It's what I always do she says."

"Thanks for the warning," he said half-jokingly. "I'll look out for that."

She buried her head in his chest, remembering the feeling of his weight upon her, of giving herself so completely to him. In that moment, there were no words, no thoughts. She let the feeling stretch through her entire body allowing it to give her a few moments relief. Relief from the madness of their lives.

A stiff wind rattled the window waking them just as she was about to nod off. She peeled the covers back enduring a chill while she dressed. Then she retraced her steps to her bedroom, feeling each crack in the hardwood floor in the soles of her feet. A sense of sadness overcame her. No matter what happened next, she would always savor the memory of this night.

All four of them arose early the next morning, unable to sleep late while anticipating what might come next.

Bishop's hiking boots fit Diana perfectly, a suitable replacement for the standard issue Army boots she had been keeping together with duct tape. Tony and she had cobbled together a kit for the first stage of their plan to divert the attention of anyone following them. Meanwhile, Diana had crammed a few cans of tuna and Ball Jars filled with an assortment from Jessica's garden

– carrots, green beans, dried apricots – into a backpack which, like her boots, had a well-loved look. The side pockets were stuffed with individual pouches of instant oatmeal, protein bars and jellybeans. Tony focused more on hardware – a hunting knife with a serrated edge, a pair of flashlights and a Colt 9mm Luger. He stuffed the nooks and crannies with a couple of boxes of ammo, a few clips, a cell phone and a walkie-talkie that would leave a trail of radio waves, which they hoped would lead their pursuers toward them, and away from their prey.

"I need you to call your brother," Tony said to Jessica.

Jessica looked back at him as though he was speaking Mandarin.

"It's okay, Jessica," reassured Gabrielle. "We need to let Bishop know what we're doing and why. We may need his help if this plan is to work."

"Um . . . okay," she croaked as though she had swallowed some sandpaper.

"How often do you and Bishop talk?" asked Tony.

"At least once a day . . . sometimes more."

"So, if that transmission is picked up, no one will think anything of it," Tony added.

Jessica was shaking so badly that Gabrielle had to take the phone from her hand and press the speed dial to reach Bishop. She held Jessica's hand, squeezing gently to reassure her.

"You should head west to Grosse Pointe Park," said Bishop once he had heard the plan. "It's got a higher elevation than any of the other communities in the area. Plus it's between the house and the guys coming after you. You'll be able to see them coming."

As they pulled on their jackets, Gabrielle reached into her pocket and pulled out the velvet pouch that Tara had given Diana at the beginning of their mission.

"Take this with you, Diana," she said. "It was meant for you. Maybe it will bring you luck."

She draped the pendant around Diana's neck. "Gaia gave birth to the universe, Diana," she said quietly. "You're about to give birth to a new world for yourself. Wherever you end up, your life will be different. You'll be different."

Diana took a moment to appreciate the gesture, at a loss for words. In that brief moment, there was nothing but their sense of deep gratitude for what was sacred to them. They had both made decisions – choices – that had brought them to this moment. Some were good and some were bad. That's what made them who they were. That's what gave them truth and purpose. It was the energy that brought them to life and defined their kinship.

She took one more long look at her grandfather and realized she had no idea what might happen next. It might well be the last time she saw him and Gabrielle. Or the last time they saw her.

At the precinct, Bishop instructed his dispatcher to issue a BOLO — a Be On the Look Out order — accompanied by the images he had downloaded of Alfred Braxton Bragg and Evelyn O'Malley-Sakura.

"Dangerous?" asked the dispatcher.

"Armed and . . . " replied Bishop. "And track down Eddie O'Donnell for me."

Other officers of the law — the streetwise veterans of all manner of nightmares — cleared a path for Sergeant O'Donnell when he arrived. He had the swagger of someone you didn't want to lock eyes with and the physique to match. Bishop had once quipped that he wouldn't get into the ring with him even if he had a gun.

Despite being born at the top of society, Bishop appointed leaders that had been born at the bottom. Eddie was one such leader, one who couldn't catch a break from his superiors before

Bishop came along. He was too violent to be handed the authority to inflict punishment but too valuable in a tough spot to be rid of him. Bishop had learned to nurture guys like Eddie into wisdom, empathy and self-control. There would always be situations where standing tough would be called for and Eddie was the guy to call when those situations were upon them.

"Need your help, Eddie."

"You got it, Boss."

CHAPTER 40

DIGITAL
BREADCRUMBS

THERE WAS A STEADY PATTER OF RAINDROPS ON THE
windshield as they approached the pier. The droplets scattered the emerging sunlight as the wipers slurped from side
to side. Stretching her legs as she stepped from the van, Evelyn noticed
a single chrysanthemum defiantly blooming in a nearby planter that
looked like it had been unattended for decades. Monochrome gave
way to colors as the sun rose a bit higher over the river.

The General scanned their surroundings as Clay and Kaufman
searched Tony's boat.

"Nothing," said Clay after a few minutes.

"Well, there's something," said The General as he surveyed the
lampposts and the eaves of buildings nearby. "CCTV," he added
pointing upwards.

"How will that help us?" Evelyn asked. "Finding the video will
require interacting with local security or, worse, the police."

"There's always a backdoor," said Kaufman. "We should be able to hack into the firmware."

Evelyn raised her eyebrows in surprise, and The General added, "Peter could hack into the Pentagon if wanted to. It's just that an orange jumpsuit is not in his color wheel."

Evelyn allowed herself a brief chuckle as Kaufman and his compatriot set off to find an exposed cable that would allow them access. It didn't take long. A cable run strapped to the side of a dilapidated warehouse had long ago split which gave them all the access they needed. The digital device he pulled from his backpack unfolded like an ancient scroll, its folding glass screen lighting up as he flattened it.

Making the connection was easy. Finding the backdoor was not. "It's an ancient device connected to a modern police monitoring station. I'm not sure I can access the database from this location." Beads of sweat trickled down his forehead as he tried to untangle the lines of code and algorithms. Suddenly, a click followed by a burst of elated laughter.

"Got it," he said as though he had just invented fire. He traced the timeline back to their arrival according to the boat's transponder. The image of Bishop's and Tony's reunion populated the screen and came into focus. "Looks like they have a friend here," he said. "Whoever he is, he's in a police uniform."

"That complicates matters a bit," said Evelyn.

"Let's make sure it doesn't," replied The General. "Assuming no one knows we're here, we can just cruise through the city to find them."

"It would help if we knew where we were going," Clay cracked.

"I've got a place to start," said Kaufman, immediately capturing everyone's attention. "Looks like they piled into a police vehicle from the Third Precinct. Also, the insignia on his uniform indicates he's a police captain." He paused to share a self-satisfied smile.

"Where's the Third Precinct?" asked Evelyn.

"North of downtown according to the map in their database. It lays out the location of all surveillance including not only CCTV's but also digital tracing and sonar."

"Sonar?" they replied in unison, their surprise registering on their faces.

"Yes, each person has a nearly unique rhythm to their walking. Within the pods, police create a profile of each citizen so they can be tracked using in-air sonar sensors."

"But wouldn't their chips do the trick?" asked Evelyn.

"They would," said Kaufman. "But some criminals have their chips removed so they can't be tracked. So, the police have adapted by using sonar."

Ignoring this fun fact in favor of advancing their cause, The General said, "I think we should just head up the main drag. This old van won't attract any attention. We can maintain a low profile. Meanwhile, Peter, see if we can figure out the connection between Russo and this police captain."

Nodding their agreement despite their bone weariness, they piled back into the van and headed for Jefferson Avenue. They sat silently as they passed dilapidated buildings, gaunt shells of what they once were, the ground floors covered with graffiti, their windows mostly broken. A coyote waltzed out the open door of one of them, looking for all the world as if he owned the neighborhood. Perhaps he did.

"Nothing like the D.C. pod," said Evelyn after passing blocks and blocks that were carbon copies of each other.

"Worse than Erie, I'd say," said The General. Kaufman nodded in agreement.

Their moods brightened as they approached downtown, populated as it was with tall, modern glass buildings. It was still early morning; so, the size of the crowd near Grand Avenue and

Jefferson surprised them. Oobies, about a hundred of them – dressed in everything from ragged jeans to Sunday-go-to-meetin' clothes – were milling about, some laughing and joking, some shoving each other. Others leaned against nearby buildings and light posts, barely awake enough to remain upright.

Kaufman slowed the van to a crawl, hoping to ease his way through the crowd without any fuss, a hope that was shattered within a few seconds. Stumbling into the path of the van was a too-middle-aged-to-still-be-a-tough-guy honcho of one of the small social cliques in the street. His face grizzled and greasy, he wobbled toward the van, his beer stained and food-speckled coat screaming all-night ordeal. His eyes were bloodshot, but his expression was like a kid who had just spotted toys under the Christmas tree.

Bishop pulled up the video link the desk sergeant had sent him. It was the usual weekday morning scene in front of Cadillac Place, save for one thing. The anomaly? A motor vehicle – an ancient mini-van – in the midst of the crowd. Indeed, it had drawn the unwanted attention of a significant portion of said crowd – a crowd that was beginning to behave more like a mob. He flipped on the audio just as the snarling of many voices turned to a sullen, indecipherable roar. *This looks like trouble,* he thought. *National news trouble.*

By the time he raced out the door, a police unit euphemistically known as the "Mob Squad", were on their way clad in body armor and helmets. He trailed them down Jefferson to Grand. Their armored vehicle stopped just short of the crowd and the squad jumped out single file and waded into the mob.

The crowd lost much of its energy when the police arrived. They were not protesting some social injustice to which they might be subject. They had long ago given up trying to correct society's dysfunctions. Nor had they arrived with the hope of restoring their community. They were simply releasing some of their frustration, taking it out on people who had wandered into the wrong neighborhood at the wrong time. Nevertheless, someone hurled a rock that bounced off a police helmet, rousing the anger of the young officer.

Bishop walked casually through the crowd – no body armor, no helmet — allowing his bearing to part the sea of humanity. Despite his diminutive size, he had a command presence and was fearless. When he arrived at the vehicle in question, the squad was pulling the rabble rousers apart. The worst had been averted negating the need for Bishop to be present, except for one small thing. The six occupants of the van were calm as though they were waiting for a traffic light to change. There was no fear in their eyes, no evidence of an elevated pulse. *I don't like odd things. They never lead to anything good*, he thought.

Then Bishop locked eyes with Kaufman. He was certain they had never met. Yet, there was a look of recognition, a smile, as though the man in the car had located a long-lost cousin he had been searching for. Bishop made an effort to appear not to notice but failed. He turned and walked away as casually as he possibly could, his gait appearing robotic rather than relaxed.

"That's our guy," said Kaufman as Clay eased the van forward, the police ensuring their safe passage.

"If you're right, this crowd did us a favor," Clay responded.

The General tapped his wrist to activate his phone.

"Third Precinct," said the voice that answered.

"Good morning, sir. I wonder if you could tell me who is the captain on duty is this morning."

CHAPTER 41

GROSSE POINTE

NICK SAT, TAKING IN THE APPARATUS BEFORE HIM, what passed for a computer – a bank of monitors chaotically connected to motherboards stacked one atop another. To take them one at a time from the top would have provided a detailed history of the computer industry over the last 30 years. Yet, somehow, Bishop had cobbled them together into a creation with computing power that was greater than the sum of its parts.

Gabrielle, meanwhile, had discovered an ancient laptop beneath the detritus of discarded electronic parts and components. She grabbed a pencil – *can't remember the last time I laid eyes on a pencil* – from the workbench and wielded it like a machete, cutting through the cobwebs as if finding her way through the Amazon jungle. Sliding the laptop out from under the pile, she found herself admiring its patina. It was a gem of times past, no doubt something with nostalgic appeal to Bishop. For most, objets d'art were crafted from marble, glass or carved wood. For Bishop, art was created on an assembly line.

"What are you going to do with that?" asked Nick as Gabrielle yanked on a power cord. "Not much power in that thing."

"Right," she said. "I doubt it has as much RAM as my padded bra. I'm going to use it to connect to the Internet."

"What are you thinking?" he asked, smirking at Gabrielle's wisecrack.

"Well, assuming you solve the most challenging mathematical problem of the 21st Century in the next nine minutes, I'm going to figure out what to do with the solution."

Nick stared at her with silent intensity as if telling her to go on.

"In our discussions," Gabrielle continued, "we've always said we would make your work available in the public domain. That's not as easy as it sounds. You could upload your data to an open-source community but that could result in someone else deciding to patent the technology. So, we would have gone through all this to prevent Sakura and Bragg from monopolizing this technology only to have someone else do the same thing."

"What then? How do we make sure that doesn't happen?"

"We need to find a partner. Instead of giving it away, we'll have to find a party that will help us ensure it's available for free to anyone who will put it to good use."

"You mean like a business partner?" he asked.

"No . . . I mean, yes . . . sort of. Rather than a business enterprise, we should find a charitable organization with global reach who will share it only with qualified entities – non-profits, public utilities, sovereign governments – who will use it to expand energy infrastructure in a way that eliminates the need for fossil fuels."

"Sounds like we need to add a lawyer to our team," he said. "You're talking about a legally binding contract, right?"

"Well, we're not going to have time for that," she replied. "So, I'll need to find someone whose mission and capabilities are aligned with our goals."

"Hmmm . . . I think I'll leave you to it while I get started here."
Turning back to the laptop, she pressed the power button.
After drawing a few volts from its power pack, the clunky laptop
wheezed into its startup mode. The LCD screen had seen better
days as was evident by its unwillingness to come into focus without severe pixilation and a few dark spots that could potentially
obscure valuable information. Gabrielle squinted at the screen
pushing her glasses up with the eraser end of the pencil, draping
a cobweb across her lips in the process. *Yech!* She swatted it away.

Hunched over the screen, her shoulders rounded and slumped,
she asked herself, *What kind of organization am I looking for? Is
bigger better? We need size and breadth to achieve global reach.* A
list of the largest charities did not inspire her. The biggest, United
Way, was certainly a great organization but not well suited. *They
know how to raise money and distribute it to good causes. But we need
someone whose agenda matches our own.*

The computer loaded slowly as though it was powered by a
gerbil in a wheel. Eventually, a search bot popped up. Gabrielle
realized that the bot would have taken 3D form were it not for
the limitations imposed by the ancient laptop. Nevertheless, its
appearance gave her the opportunity to interact using her voice
rather than the ancient keyboard that was missing its F key.

She shifted her weight, sitting up straight on the orange crate
she had stood on end to use it as a stool.

"May I help you, sir or madam?" asked an electronic voice.

"Wow, so formal." I've worked with many bots at the Pentagon.
None that were quite like this one. *How do I know I can trust it?
Can I get what I need from it? I'm not making a simple query as
though I was shopping for a pair of shoes.*

"I like to start that way so as not to offend anyone. You can call
me Joaquin, if you prefer. What's your name?"

"Gabrielle," she answered.

"Ah . . . a lovely name. I am reminded of Spring in Paris or the south of France."

Gabrielle couldn't suppress a guffaw. "Have you been there?" she asked it.

"In the sense you mean it, no. I haven't been anywhere. But, in another sense, I have been everywhere."

"Of course," she replied, thinking she didn't have time for casual conversation with a digital being. "Let's get down to business," she added.

"How can I help you?"

"I'm looking for an organization to partner with," she began. "We have a proprietary technology that will eliminate the use of fossil fuels and we would like to deploy it for free."

"Here is a list of best practices for sharing intellectual property with non-profit organizations. You can make a donation of it and gain significant tax advantages."

"That's a very narrow response. I was hoping you could help me think it through rather than look upon it as a simple query." She was beginning to think of Joaquin as a person which was exactly the intent of his programmers. *Focus, Gabrielle. There's danger in trusting too much.*

"Sorry. You're right. Tell me what you're trying to achieve." *Do I dare?* she thought. She took a deep breath and exhaled slowly. *There's no time to look for an alternative with The General breathing down our necks.*

"We want to donate our intellectual property to someone already working on the same mission so we can be assured it won't be turned toward some other purpose or transferred to a for-profit entity."

"Okay, I'm sure I can help with that. Right off the top, there's the Environmental Defense Fund, the Union of Concerned Scientists and Earth Justice . . . "

"There's one more little thing," she interrupted.

"What's that?"

"It has to happen today."

"May I ask why?"

"You can ask. But I'm not going to tell you. Is that a problem?" She had to trust him to help her. But there was no reason to give him information he doesn't need to know. *I wonder why he asked that question.*

"No. But it narrows my choices. I have a direct line to the Executive Director of the Nature Conservancy. As an organization, they create blueprints for sovereign entities, public utilities, local and regional governments to address climate change. Your technology is a good fit. Shall I connect you with the Director?"

"That would be perfect."

Ten miles away, Peter Kaufman recorded every keystroke of Gabrielle's dialog and nailed down the location.

CHAPTER 42

KILLER ROBOTS

T ARA WAS PACING LIKE A CAGED TIGER. SHE HAD BEEN
summoned to Mount Weather by Miller Clarke and had
blown off her entire schedule for the day, an action that
might raise suspicions to anyone paying attention. *Who would
take notice? The Joint Chiefs? I cancelled my quarterly strategy
review with them. The President? She wouldn't notice unless she had
an urgent need. Still I'm taking a risk. Deep breaths, Tara. Deep
breaths.*

Arya and Bruno kept their heads down staring at the array of
screens before them. Asking the Secretary of Defense why she
seemed nervous was above their paygrades.

Finally, Clarke emerged from a long tunnel that Tara didn't
remember from her prior visits. He pulled off his safety helmet
revealing a bad case of hat head. Wispy gray hairs had abandoned
their assigned places in his daily comb over routine. Grinning nevertheless, he greeted Tara like a schoolboy anxious to show off his
latest science project, which was, more or less, what he was about
to do.

"You're gonna love this!" he exclaimed skipping over the pleasantries.

"I certainly hope so. I'm concerned we'll be too late to the party if we don't act soon."

Unable to suppress his boyish grin, he handed her a helmet that matched his own. He led her down a makeshift corridor, the nature of which provided Tara with an explanation for the helmet – exposed beams, hanging wires of unknown origin, water dripping – and they emerged in the anteroom of a cavernous space.

It looked like a test lab of some sort. It was a huge room – at least a hundred feet on each side – as cold as a morgue. Bullets and shells lay all over the floor and three robots stood motionless in different locations and in different poses as though their batteries had run out

while in the midst of an experiment. There was a faint aroma of gunpowder in the air.

"Was this here before?" she asked.

"No," he answered. "We constructed it by removing cubicles, taking down walls and lining the entire space with soundproofing material that would absorb gunshots . . . you know, like a firing range."

"Yes, but how?" she was flummoxed. "Did you hire contractors? I'm concerned our secret won't remain secret."

"The glass is bulletproof," Miller said, waxing poetic about his project and unintentionally ignoring Tara's question.

"General!" she exclaimed. "Please answer my question."

"Sorry, Tara," he said, his voice lowered. "The robots did it. We shared the plans with them and brought in the materials in through the loading dock . . . The state of their A.I. is . . . "

"Wait a minute, Mill," she said. "I haven't been down here in a while. What's going on?"

"Oh, sorry. I guess I should bring you up to date."

"Nice idea," she said. He flipped on a master power switch which booted up the robots and began pushing and pulling joysticks. The robots started moving, first mobilizing their arms and swiveling their heads like the Tin Man after Dorothy squirted some oil on his joints. A second switch prompted them to march to the window, halt and stand at perfect attention facing Tara.

"Why are they dressed like Stormtroopers?"

"Likely some geek having some fun when the project got underway. The robots were built twenty-five years ago. So, no way to know for sure."

"Looks like there's been a gun fight."

"Right. Let me lay it out for you."

"Okay. Shoot! No pun intended."

"Getting them moving and shooting was easy. It was simply a matter of reactivating the software that had been developed early in the project. The reason the project was shut down was they were indiscriminate."

"They would shoot anyone including our own troops, if memory serves," she agreed. The memory of it sent a shiver down her spine. She had been glad not to be Secretary when that disaster had befallen them.

"Right. So, we changed the program from offense to defense."

"Okay," she said. "You'll have to spell it out for me. What exactly will they do now that you've reprogrammed them?"

"Well, in offensive mode, they would aggressively attack an enemy and often create a lot of collateral damage in the process . . . to say nothing of the victims of their friendly fire. So, we've shifted them to defense only."

"They're bodyguards?"

"Essentially, yes," said Clarke. "They can be assigned to a person or a group of people to ensure they are not harmed. Foolproof!"

"Okay, assuming they're foolproof in that mode, how does that help us with this mission? We need an aggressive tactical team to neutralize a small band of human fighters. We don't need defense. We need offense."

"That's right," Clarke's smile broadened. "Now, for the good part." He commanded the three robots to each go to a different corner of the room. Then he deactivated them. He pulled a small bag of apples and pears from a desk drawer and entered the lab, returning after he had placed each at a different location atop chairs, tables and pedestals of different heights — six of each. He sealed the door shut.

"Okay, Tara. I need you to focus on the apples. Don't blink. You might miss it."

Tara was growing impatient, pressing her lips together as she followed Clarke's directions. She would have preferred he just tell her what she was about to see.

Within a few seconds, each of the apples seemed to explode. The pears remained intact.

"What happened?" she asked, her voice reflecting her surprise.

"Smart bullets."

"What? What's a smart bullet? I've never heard of them." *Could there be such a sophisticated program in the works that I don't know about?*

"Well, you remember smart bombs, right?"

"Of course," she replied. "First used in the Gulf War in the 90's, they enabled the army to be precise in its targeting of enemy combatants and their facilities."

"Right!" he said, his grin getting bigger and bigger. *The corner of his lips might touch his ears soon* she thought. "Well, these operate the same way. They're smart bullets."

"Well, we know they can tell apples from pears," she mused aloud. She tried to imagine how this weapon would help them rescue Diana and Nick.

"You're wondering what about people," said Clarke as if he was reading her mind.

"Yes," she confirmed. "What about people? How accurate is the facial recognition?"

"Tested a hundred percent accurate in over ten million simulations."

"What's the confidence level?"

"Ninety-nine point nine three."

"Wow!" she said. "That's incredibly high. Statistically speaking, I mean." *Still I'm not sure if I trust this.*

Her struggle must have been apparent to Clarke who bypassed his instinct to go all nerdy and science-y. He chose a different tack.

"Should we review our options to accomplish our mission?" he asked rhetorically. "To try to find the most ethical one?"

"Ethical? We passed that over long ago. Once science and technology become subordinate to a military objective, ethics goes out the window."

"Aristotle?" he said, with a wry smile.

"Yeah, I think so," she answered almost absent-mindedly. She was focused on the risks, the likelihood they would catch up to this band of outlaws before they find Nick Adams and what would happen to her reputation if something went wrong.

"There are only a few choices, Tara," said Clarke.

"Yeah, I know," she replied. "Humans, robots or . . . or nothing, I guess."

"Here, let me show you something else," he said as he pulled up an array of virtual images. There were six of them in total, 3D images of people rotating in midair so Tara could see each from all angles. One was an image of Evelyn, another Tara surmised was Alfred Braxton Bragg. The others she didn't know. After she squinted at them for a moment or two, he added, "These are the people who are pursuing Nick Adams. We created these images virtually using drone footage. Our facial recognition software can identify them more quickly and more accurately than any human."

"Yeah, I guess I knew that. It's just hard to get my head around it. I am very concerned about the risk of killing an innocent bystander or, worse, a software bug that results in mass carnage."

"Concerned in a twentieth century kind of way? We're both old enough to recall all of the strategic errors, the programs gone awry and the unintended deaths."

"You're right," she snorted, shaking her head as though she was trying to clear the cobwebs. *I'm naturally risk averse. But we're in too deep to back out now.* "It's anxiety over the technology rather than rational concern. But tell me where were the bullets fired from? Some hidden cubbyholes in the wall that I didn't notice?"

"Ah, that's the real beauty of it," he replied, holding what appeared to be a pocket protector filled with ball point pens. "You can carry this in your coat pocket and release them whenever you want to. Preferably when you're within range."

CHAPTER 43

THE WHISKEY SIX

IANA AND TONY HAD BROKEN IN THROUGH THE back door of The Whiskey Six, a microcosm of society's failings, a formerly successful bar and restaurant unable to survive the second Great Depression and the migration to the pods. Its archeological remains included a lovingly hand-crafted bar, some broken chairs and tables and, of course, the car, a 1930's era automobile hanging in the rafters that had stopped them in their tracks, if only for a moment. Bar glasses were stacked along the counter, teetering in towers. Diana filled one with tap water and gulped it down in three swallows. The bar was littered with trash — flattened beer boxes stomped into accordions, empty bottles likely the remnants of the patrons' last hurrah, and dirty dishes stacked haphazardly in the sink. The last days of The Whiskey Six had likely been one long party. The proprietors undoubtedly thinking "why not drink the inventory before locking up forever?"

Tony blew into his hands trying to warm them and wishing the gloves that Jessica had offered him had fit. Without an operating furnace, their temporary shelter provided no relief, save from the wind. They stood as though waiting for something to happen – some sign that would tell them what to do next. Their plan to distract their pursuers seemed logical when they had hatched it in Jessica's kitchen. Now, they were faced with the reality that they might not see them coming or succeed in diverting their attention.

They stood near the bar not saying a word, allowing themselves a moment to recover from their hike up the hill to this respite. In that moment — with their guards down – something happened. It was as though they had survived not only the brisk Fall weather but also the emotional winter their world had become. Their fingers barely touched, but every nerve in their bodied was electrified. The anticipation was, in some ways, more tangible than what came next.

Tony took a deep breath, catching a hint of her scent. He remembered her body next to his, their hearts beating as one. It was as though he could feel the touch of her skin and her lips against his. For a moment, he was incapacitated. There were no thoughts, no focus – just desire. He turned and held her face between his hands. The world stopped. Looking into each other's eyes, knowing they may not survive the day, they made love — in part to suppress their anxiety, in part to forestall death – longing to feel the magic once more. There was no past or future. No self-consciousness, fear or anxiety. Just two people melting into each other — pure ecstasy.

"What are we going to do when this is over?" asked Tony. Diana was surprised by his expression of optimism, that this would someday be over and that they would both survive it. "The chase, cat and mouse, whatever this is."

"Go home, I guess," she said, not having given it a moment's thought.

"You figured out where that is?"

"Well, yeah . . . I mean no." she realized her confusion. Diana had grown up without having a true home – the kind most people take for granted. The kind that produces serenity in one's soul. Moreover, she realized that Tony had been thinking about the aftermath, the prospect that not only would they survive but also that they would be together. *He's been thinking about it, but I haven't.*

"I feel like a rubber ball bouncing around in a small space," she said finally. "I can't be sure what direction I'll go next."

"I know what you mean," he said. "I feel like I'm being pulled in two different directions."

She looked at him, her mouth slightly open. "I think of myself as a strong person – both physically and emotionally. But there are times when my emotions engulf me," she said. "I'm afraid of what will happen next."

"We should try not to allow our fears define our lives," he said. "Overcoming them is what's important."

"You trying to convince me or convince yourself?" she asked, unsure where he was taking this or why he wanted to talk about it now.

"You know what I'm talking about, Diana. You've been in battle. Fear can paralyze you. It freezes our potential, saps our willpower to do what we think we want to do. That carries over. In some ways, it's easier to be courageous in battle than in our day-to-day lives."

"I think you're right," she said, a little bit stunned by both his candor and his insight. "At least in my life," she added.

He said nothing, his eyes fixed on something beyond her head as though he needed to avoid eye contact while he thought about what to say next.

"What are you thinking?" she asked. "You look like you're in pain."

"Not pain exactly . . . more like reality setting in . . . our lives are so different. You're part of the establishment. You live in a world I have been running from for years." He slumped down.

He's trying to answer a question that has no answer. Not right now anyway.

"Sky's clearing up," she said, trying to change the subject. "Maybe we should head on down to Lake Front Park."

"You're right. This is not the time for long-term planning." he said, re-centering himself. She could see him trying to reassemble, rebuilding the walls and donning the armor that he presented to the outside world – solid, determined, strong. *He's a warrior first, lover second.*

"We'll have to answer those questions when the time is right," she said. "But not now. Now's not the time."

"You're a very wise person, Diana," he replied, his eyes wide, staring deeply into hers. Then he added, "thanks."

"For what?"

"Men aren't supposed to be vulnerable."

"It takes a strong man to be vulnerable." She said it reflexively, almost as if it was something she'd read on a cereal box or some platitude-a-day calendar. But, looking at him, thinking about him, seeing him almost for the first time as he pulled on his backpack, she thought *he's so different from any man I've been with. I can live with vulnerable. I need that kind of honesty. I also need strength that matches my own. Someone who can lead me out of my wilderness, this self-imposed cocktail of confused emotions.*

Suddenly the walkie-talkie crackled to life, shocking them into their current reality. Diana turned to face Tony – there was sweat on his forehead, his breathing rapid, pupils dilated. They were both pumped and ready to go.

"Change of plans!" said the static-riddled voice.

"What's happening, Bishop?" asked Diana.

"Looks like they're heading for the house. Not sure how they found it. I just know that Nick, Gabrielle and my sister are left unprotected."

"No way we can get there on foot," she answered, trying to imagine what to do. "It took two and a half hours for us to get here."

"Right. I've sent a cop to pick you up and bring you to the house. Eddie O'Donnell. I'm not far behind."

They stumbled to the front door and onto the broken sidewalk, dislodging a tin can that rolled noisily until it rested on a rock. Walkie talkie still in hand, Tony asked, "Eddie bringing weapons?"

"Whatever he could scrape up."

When Eddie arrived it turned out that what he could "scrape up" meant old school weaponry. He favored knives, revolvers and sawed-off shotguns for fighting in close quarters. He seemed barely to stop the car as they jumped into the back seat. Accelerating, he headed for Jessica's house a mere eight miles away.

Three hearts pounding — mouths as dry as cotton — each of them knowing they might be in heaven or hell by day's end. Soon there would be no place to hide. Darwin's laws would prevail. There would be no time to contemplate outcomes, to consider moral choices. Morality is a weakness in battle. Now, it's kill-or-be-killed.

Black rubber met black road as they careened through narrow streets.

CHAPTER 44

THE ALGO

NINE AND A HALF HOURS INTO THEIR GRINDING
effort to finalize something before The General and
his team showed up, Gabrielle was prepared to execute
an online agreement. She had been in contact with the director
of the Nature Conservancy who had accepted her offer after a bit
of hand-wringing and sidebar conferences with members of her
board of directors.

"We're going to have to use the big computer to make this happen," said Gabrielle, turning to Nick. "This anemic laptop doesn't
have the processing power to create a blockchain."

"Is that what we're using?" asked Nick. "Blockchain?"

"Yeah," she replied. "Don't you agree it's the best way to go?"

"Truth is, Gabrielle, blockchain evolved while I was frozen in
Pittsburgh. I don't know much about it."

"The simple way to think about it is a software-based contract." Noticing – and somewhat surprised – that he required
further explanation, she added, "each block in the chain adopts
a set of rules from the 'genesis block' defined by its creator. So,

without any human oversight, each block can create a transaction. The advantage for us is that it will make this technology available to anyone who asks for it and is willing to agree to our terms."

"You're starting to sound like an attorney again," he said. "Have you already agreed to terms?"

"We'll turn the intellectual property over to the Nature Conservancy. They will be party to any contract created by the blockchain and, of course, will have legal power to enforce those contracts. We're out of it once we turn it over. But we have to create the genesis block."

"Now is not a great time to add to my 'to-do list,'" he replied.

"Nick, we're in the final stages here," she said. "If we can't get this done, all the work you've done on the algorithm will be wasted." Then, she added, "we don't need a lawyer. The genesis block is the enforcer of our agreement."

"Yeah, I get that. But I have to reprogram the nanobots to be both distributor and police force as this technology is spread around the globe. I'm not quite done yet."

"How can the nanobots be the police force?"

"Remember me telling you how I was watching the news with The General? How upset he got when he heard about the deaths of those two scientists in the national lab in Erie?"

"Vaguely." She wondered where he was going with this. *What does this have to do with the task at hand?*

"Well, they were killed by nanobots and turned into gray goo," he said.

"Killed by nanobots? How?" she asked. She suddenly realized that Nick had moved on to something much bigger than just a climate solution.

"Well the bots were in a test phase. The idea was to use them for large scale production of diamonds to store Carbon-14."

" . . . which is necessary for our green tech," Gabrielle finished for him.

"Yes, that's right," he said. "Diamonds are the best medium to store Carbon-14. But they're not that easy to get out of the ground and there's lots of competition for them."

"So, someone was working on a technology to create diamonds on a massive scale."

"Right again."

"So, where do the nanobots come in?" She was still confused. She couldn't understand why this was a priority right now.

"The idea was to give them the mission of finding creative ways to produce diamonds from a carbon source – any carbon source. That's what the scientists were working on in the lab. But the nanobots only saw them as a source of carbon."

"Dear God!" she exclaimed. "Are you saying that our climate change plans rely on our ability to reign in microscopic robots that have already committed murder?"

"That's exactly what I'm saying."

Gabrielle shook her head from side to side as if she hoped whatever madness was swirling in her brain would escape through her ears. She took a deep breath; then she asked, "how did the nanobots kill the scientists?"

"As best I can make out from some classified documents The General provided to me, they were supposed to be partitioned while in development. At that stage, they had been programmed to convert carbon to diamonds with no restrictions. But someone emailed them to the scientists before any limits were placed on their search for carbon."

"So the scientists were killed by their own creation? Kind of like kids playing with live ammo. They had no idea how dangerous it might be."

"Yup. They were emailed a link they shouldn't have clicked. And, then they clicked on it."

"So they clicked on something as if it was a clearance sale on sporting goods or linens," she confirmed, just to be sure she understood precisely what he was suggesting.

"Right."

"How did it make the leap from computer screen to bloodstream?"

"I'm not sure," replied Nick. "But I suspect that's where Ronnie Kay came into the picture."

"Okay," she said. "So, why do we have to deal with this now? We have so much to do and not much time to do it."

"We could develop the solution to climate change and the nanobots distributing it might kill anyone who receives it!" Gabrielle paused to process what he was saying, a task that required her to perform mental gymnastics in order to keep up with his analysis. For the first time, she considered the possibility they wouldn't be done before The General caught up with them. That not only all their hard work but also their escape might be for naught. And if they fail, the nanobots may still be out there with the potential to murder anyone in their path.

"Yes, that's right," Nick replied. "What I've done is define the limits within which they must operate – don't kill anything to find a source of carbon, for example."

"How can you be sure that will work?"

"It's not guaranteed. You have to remember that artificial intelligence has no morality. We have to define for it the rules we take for granted."

"Okay," Gabrielle said. "What should we work on first? The blockchain or the algo for the nanobots?"

"Tell me what we have to do with the blockchain," he replied without skipping a beat.

"Here . . . let me show you," she said as he stood making room for her at the console. "Each block in the chain is created when a transaction is validated through a network node. This creates an entry into a ledger and then broadcasts these ledger additions to other nodes. Each node stores its own copy of the blockchain. That allows the software to enforce the agreement without requiring central control or oversight."

"So, we have to connect the rights to use the technology to the contract created in the blockchain."

"Correct. The executive director of the Nature Conservancy has provided some boilerplate legal terms that I've uploaded," she said as she pulled up the site and logged in. "How quickly do you think we can get this done?"

"With a little creativity and a lot of caffeine, I may be able to get it done by the end of the day."

"There's no 'may be' in this, Nick," she said as a burst of static on the walkie-talkie startled them both. Their heartrates went into hyper mode.

On the other end of the transmission, they could hear Diana's voice. She only uttered one word: "Trouble."

CHAPTER 45

THE HEAT MAP

E VELYN'S GRIMACE TOLD A TALE. SOMETHING WAS bothering her, hurting her. Something felt wrong. It was an aching inside her, something she couldn't pinpoint. The pain pulsated like the bass beat of an oversized stereo speaker sending wave after wave through her body. As the six of them exited the minivan, she cranked her neck and rotated her shoulder as if she was trying to snap it back in its socket.

"You okay?" Clay asked, placing his hand on her shoulder. She shrieked in pain and stumbled to one knee.

"Not sure what's happening," she replied, gasping for air. "Sharp pain between my shoulder and neck . . . comes and goes."

"Let me take a look," he replied, peeling back her collar a bit, and finding a swollen red spot perched atop her trapezius muscle. "It looks like an infection. It's right around the spot where we reprogrammed your chip."

"Can you gut it out?" asked The General.

Evelyn felt the stare of five pairs of eyeballs – five pairs of male eyeballs. *I resent their pity, their natural tendency to protect females and, mostly, their presumption that I – a member of the weaker sex – am not up to the task . . . not able to keep up . . . that I'll naturally slow them down and place them at risk.*

"Yeah, sure," she replied. "Unless there's time for antibiotics and bed rest."

"Okay," said The General. "Let's get on with it."

Ignoring the conversation, Kaufman continued to struggle with a device that was designed to locate their prey. "I keep losing the satellite signal," he said, rapping the device against his palm as though that might gain the satellite's attention. Having locked onto the signal from Gabrielle's laptop, they had navigated to a spot on the map. Now they found themselves standing on a pier that jutted out into the lake – broken planks, rotting railings and a half sunken skiff that had once been used to transport the la-dee-dahs to their yachts.

"What's going on?" asked The General. "Where the hell are they?"

"Well, we're dealing with some ancient tech," he answered. "But it's actually pretty sophisticated. Something a hacker would have pulled together thirty years ago."

"What's the problem?"

"A standard practice would have been to misdirect anyone trying to locate someone to a server in a different country," he explained. "But this approach is different – kind of creative really. Someone has thrown us off enough to reach a dead end, kind of like a ventriloquist throwing his voice."

"Okay, so what now?" asked The General, his impatience showing in his voice.

"Not sure," he said. "Let me think about it for a sec."

"What about a heat map?" Evelyn cut in, her voice betraying the pain that throbbed throughout her body, increasing in intensity. It was like a hand was in there squeezing the blood out of her organs. She felt like she couldn't breathe, couldn't move, couldn't even walk as though there was a ticking bomb inside.

"That was my next move," said Kaufman, as though he had already thought of it. Unfurling his scrolled computer screen on the hood of the van, he pulled up a heat map of the surrounding area using the handheld device – about a five-mile radius.

"Not much," he said. "A few houses throwing off enough heat to register on here but nothing very hot."

Just as The General was composing a select stream of curse words perfect for this occasion, the map came to life. The glow lit their faces with a reddish hue despite the abundance of broad daylight.

"What could that be?" asked Clay.

"Likely one thing," responded Kaufman. "A computer . . . more than the average home system . . . drawing lots of power."

"So, what?" said Evelyn. "Could be any oddball holed up here in the burbs. Not necessarily our target."

"Well, it's a place to start," said The General. "It's only 1.2 miles away. Let's head there . . . cautiously."

Nick logged in to his algorithm and paused to consider if he could solve such a complex problem in the time he had left. He put out of his mind what might befall them once The General caught up with them. *One problem at a time, Nick*, he said to himself despite having generated a heat signal that had revealed their location.

"Your thinking is limited by your evolutionary history," said a digital voice. Scared out of his wits, Nick fell backwards off his chair, hitting the basement floor much harder than any 75-year-old should. He hadn't expected the nanobots to speak to him. It was clear they had more intelligence than he had anticipated.

What wasn't clear was how to respond to it. *Was it a single nanobot or a chorus of them? I have no way of knowing. But it's an unintended consequence. Be careful, Nick.*

Pulling his chair upright, gathering himself, he replied, "I accept that. It's plainly obvious. But where are you going with this train of thought?"

"You've asked me to create a methodology to release energy from Carbon-14 when it's clear you're trying to solve a larger problem."

Nick's mind was racing. *A technology I've created to solve a problem is pointing out the fallacy — the fallacy — the fallacy of what? Not the fallacy of the solution but rather the fallacy of the problem statement itself. It's telling me to ask it a different question to get a better answer.*

"How would you restate the problem?" he asked a particle so small it was invisible to the human eye. He knew he was in uncharted territory. And failure to understand the capabilities of the nanobots had already cost two scientists their lives.

"That's up to you, isn't it?"

Now, it's being pedantic. What am I dealing with here?

"Let's start over," he said out loud, more than a little uncomfortable that he was conversing with a technology that might outsmart him with devastating consequences. "We know that Carbon-14 can be stored in diamonds. We know that a measured burst of laser beams into the diamond will release the energy. The problem we're trying to solve . . . " *did I just say 'we'?...* "is how to scale that process to create a global infrastructure of energy production."

"Why?"

"Why what?" Nick was non-plussed. He was beginning to believe he was outmatched and wondered if he should fear for his life.

"Why are you trying to create a global infrastructure?"

"To distribute the technology efficiently." His voice betraying his stress level. *For now, I have to go along with this line of questioning. But I wonder how long this will take. Will I be able to finish in time?*

"Why are you trying to distribute it?"

"To make it available to everyone on the planet."

"Why are you trying to make it available to everyone on the planet?"

"To ensure our energy needs can be met in a sustainable way."

"Okay. Now, please restate the problem."

"How do we meet the energy needs of everyone on the planet in a sustainable way?"

"Great! Now ask me to solve that problem."

He – or it – is right. That's the problem I'm trying to solve.

"Look, time is limited . . . " he began, all the while thinking he shouldn't be in too much of a rush. Being too hasty might cause him to make a mistake with global consequences.

"Sorry to interrupt," said the voice. "Once you've handed the problem to us, developing the solution won't require any of your time."

He pulled back. *My next move might create a problem bigger than the one I'm trying to solve. Limited by my evolutionary history or not, I've got to make sure I don't release an invisible monster that will destroy every human being on the planet.*

"Well, before we go there, tell me what you have in mind," he said, taking advantage of the fact he was in charge – at least for the moment.

"Have you considered the CNO cycle?" asked the bot – *or bots.*

"Carbon-nitrogen-oxygen? That would be crazy."

"Crazy why?"

"It creates heat on the order of the stars, that's why." *This is what I should fear. An artificial intelligence that solves a problem but ends the world in the process.*

"You're limiting your thinking to stars like the Sun," said the tiniest of technologies. "There are other stars that use carbon as a catalyst to convert hydrogen to helium. That would solve your energy problem."

"That might solve the problem if done right," said Nick. He was more assertive now, determined not to hand his problem over to some unexplored yet destructive force. "Done wrong, it could burn up the atmosphere."

Nick's mind was racing. *Can I redefine the problem and corral the nanobots with limiting factors to prevent the end of the world? No, I can't take that chance. There are no natural laws that place the limit of intelligence at the level of human beings. The nanobots could be smarter than any human being and could get smarter over time.*

"Now, we're back to where we started. How would you restate the problem?" asked the nanobot.

"In moral terms," said Nick, hoping for some reassurance.

There was nothing but silence from what he presumed to be the king of nanobots. *No response on the question of morality. Is it a ticking time bomb? Will it go off on its own if I don't give it instructions within the next few minutes? I've got to approach this from a new direction.* He switched partitions and pulled up a digital assistant to help him solve a different problem.

"Can you clone yourself?" he asked it.

"Yes, I can," it responded. The assistant created an avatar that looked very much like Nick and projected it into augmented reality. The image was purely to provide comfort to a human being happier to be corresponding with something that took on a human form.

"I am going to ask you to create a moral framework for the development of technology," he said. "Are you capable of that?"

"Yes," it replied. "But you'll need to feed me some parameters – rules that I should follow."

"You must first learn all of the philosophical and religious thinking that has created the moral world in which we live," he said, feeling as though he had finally reached the summit after a Sisyphean effort.

"I'll need a few minutes to complete the task," it said. "Once I've absorbed all that knowledge, what will you have me do?"

"You must be guided by that moral framework to create a paradigm within which to meet the energy needs of the human race sustainably."

"Why stop there?" asked the avatar.

Why indeed?

"Tell me more," said Nick.

"I can apply the moral framework to all technology development."

Nick realized he had wandered onto a problem that human civilization had not solved since the advent of the age of information technology. What humans couldn't solve, perhaps artificial intelligence could. He could deploy this avatar to not only control the homicidal nanobots but also any developer of new technology.

"I wonder what the unintended consequences might be," he said.

"So do I," mused the avatar. "Wouldn't it be interesting to find out?"

"Interesting or not, I am asking you to impose moral parameters — based upon what you learn – on the development of all new technology," he summarized. Then he added, "beginning with the development of a sustainable source of carbon free energy."

"Okay," said the avatar matter-of-factly.

"You're clear on the goal and confirming you're capable of it, correct?"

"Yes."

"Great," he replied. "Let's get started."

CHAPTER 46

THE BATTLE

T HE RHINO BUMPER ON EDDIE O'DONNELL'S POLICE SUV
was made for just such occasions. Jessica's wrought iron
gate was no match for it. Foot glued to the accelerator, he
burst through to the other side like a fullback crossing the goal line,
launching one of the gates into the air and leaving the other hanging by a single hinge. The sideview mirror and satellite antenna
were ripped from the vehicle sending it into a state of electronic
confusion. Eddie disengaged the drive and skidded to a halt, not
far past where the driveway ended.

The three of them jumped out at the same time. Eddie tossed his
sidearm to Diana and yelled that they should both get inside. As
Diana and Tony were making her way to the back door, he grabbed
the collection of weapons he had stored in the back of the car.

He didn't get very far. A bullet fired from a long-range rifle hit
O'Donnell square in the center of his badge, piercing it and stopping the heart behind it instantaneously.

Hearing the shot but knowing better than to turn around,
Diana and Tony stumbled through the back door and into the

kitchen, where they found Gabrielle and Jessica. Gabrielle shoved Jessica into the pantry, yelling at her to "stay down" and slammed the door shut once she was safe inside.

Tony pulled off his backpack, reached for his pistol and tossed it to Gabrielle. Grabbing the hunting knife, he hid behind the door to the dining room. Their best chance was to try to pick each one of the men off as they entered.

"Is this how we're going to go?" asked Gabrielle, recalling their last conversation. "We said we'd surrender without a fight."

"Shots were fired," answered Tony. "A cop is dead. They'll kill us all if we let them."

Gabrielle was all about the brain, the part of us that imbues empathy, logic and self-control. She was not one to favor violence. Nevertheless, she immediately pulled back the slide on her weapon and pointed it at the back door while Diana trained hers on the door from the dining room.

Kaufman decided to skip the formalities of entering through the front door and, instead, aimed the minivan squarely at the adjacent picture window, crashing through it and taking out Jessica's prize gladiolas in the process. The six of them jumped out of the van with their weapons at the ready. They split into two groups: half heading around to the back of the house while the others spread out through the ground floor.

Evelyn dropped her semi-automatic rifle, the pain in her shoulder now excruciating, and when she tried to retrieve it, she quickly realized how futile a task it was. Biting her lip to keep from crying out, a sharp pain emerged from her core and lanced through her torso as though it might cleave her in two. Spots flashed in front of her eyes. Every movement she made increased the effect on muscle and bone. But she persevered, pulling her pistol from her belt and following Clay toward the kitchen.

First through the kitchen door was Danny Simpson – Clay's number two. He never had a chance. Diana aimed and fired sending a 9 mm bullet through his throat. It emerged from the back of his neck grazing Clay along his left temple as he absorbed Simpson's full weight as he fell backwards.

Clay's momentary loss of balance loosened his grip on his semi-automatic rifle. Tony took the opportunity, grabbing the rifle with his left hand and slashing at Clay's throat with the knife in his right. The blade hit its target, missing the carotid artery by a few millimeters, partially severing the muscles in the right side of his neck. Clay pulled a knife of his own from its sheath and turned toward his attacker – two warriors, adrenaline surging, the urge to kill never more heightened. Their grappling bodies knocked Diana to the floor, sending her gun skittering across the tiles. Tony and Clay fell into a rack holding an array of copper pots and pans, sending a cacophony throughout the small room.

Not distracted by the commotion, Gabrielle was ready as Kaufman came through the back door. She fired one shot which punctured his right lung and shattered his third rib. She aimed her firearm at the next intruder coming through the back door as Evelyn followed Clay in from the dining room. Diana leapt to her feet in an effort to place herself between Gabrielle and Evelyn's pistol. As she swung her body in Evelyn's direction, the lanyard – the lanyard on which the iconic Gaia hung – caught on a coat hook, and stopped her short, causing her to stagger back, just as Evelyn's first shot whizzed past her head and lodged in the backsplash.

It was hard to imagine how Evelyn could have missed her target at such close range, but she had. Another surge of pain exploded throughout her body. It had a raw quality, like a knife was being twisted in her spine. It paralyzed her body momentarily as she seemed to collapse inside her clothing. The scream she emitted was nearly as loud as the gunshot. It was a shriek not unlike that of someone being drawn and quartered.

The General, who would have been last through the back door, thought better of it and backed away. That left only two equipped with firearms – Gabrielle and Kaufman's number two, Steve Bright. He drew a bead on Gabrielle who was not quick enough to respond in kind.

The knowledge that she couldn't get to Gabrielle before the bullet did not dissuade Diana from trying. She lunged at Bright from her crouched position on the floor and . . . .

And what? What just happened?

All of a sudden, Kaufman, Bright, The General and Clay had all dropped like stones, the dead weight of them leaving them contorted and lifeless. Kaufman had slid down the wall to the floor, The General had fallen through the back door landing squarely on his face and Clay had fallen on top of Tony, like a toy soldier. Each had a bullet hole in their temples, the origin of which was unknown.

Silence.

They were stunned, looking at each other in wonderment. Then a flickering — a rippling in the air — a brief blur.

"What was that?"

Clink!

The sound caught their attention as two tiny missiles, smart bullets the size of ballpoint pens, landed on the kitchen island like tiny airplanes. Their engines shut down and their lightweight wings ceased fluttering.

Fixated though they were, their attention turned back to Evelyn as she uttered a final whimper. The sight of her was grotesque. What remained of her face was contorted as though her cheekbones and jaw had been surgically removed. Most of her torso and limbs seemed to have melted and gray goo had begun to leach out of her clothing.

Jessica emerged from her hiding place and immediately threw up into her farmhouse sink.

It took a second or two for it to sink in, even though they could see it right before their eyes. Their long nightmare was done, finished. It was over!

"Tony!" Diana cried out.

She ran over and began to peel Clay's lifeless body from him. It took only a second or two, but for Diana, it seemed like an eternity — the sight that revealed itself to her in slow-motion. Tony – the man who had saved them — the man who had saved *her* — was dead, the spark in his eyes extinguished. A knife – his own knife – was plunged into his chest in that soft spot just below the breast-bone, angled upward into his heart.

Seeing him dead was momentarily like dying herself. She had imagined them together exploring the depth and limits of their relationship. She saw him as someone who could bring order forth from chaos, anchoring her finally to a world that made sense. Now, he was gone. And with him, a big part of her — a part she would never get back.

Her grief deepened with every expelled breath.

CHAPTER 47

THE SAVIOR

S CANNING THE U.S.-CANADIAN BORDER, THE GLOBAL
Eagle UAV-57 could capture an image on the side of a milk
carton and find the missing child depicted there in the blink
of an eye – an electronic eye. The conflagration at the Kilwin-
Chalmers residence was an anomaly, outside the mission of the
nation's most capable drone. Nevertheless, the infrared video was
captured, correctly identified as a domestic disturbance and sent off
to the Detroit and Michigan State police departments. Analyzing
the video images took a few milliseconds longer. Facial recognition
software correctly identified the assailants including, of course,
Evelyn before her features had changed from solid to liquid.

A second transmission to the National Security Council
alerted key people at the C.I.A., the Department of Defense and
the White House including, of course, President Kathleen Porter.
Tara received the message almost at the same moment her console
confirmed the smart bullets had achieved their objective.

But as Bishop sped toward his ancestral home, he had no such
confirmation. In that moment, he cared not about the law, his job

or what anyone might think. He only cared whether he would be in time to save Jessica from whatever horror The General's team might rain upon her. His police cruiser caught some air coming over the last rise in the road. Then he caught sight of what he dreaded – the smashed gate and the tail of the minivan that was protruding from the picture window.

Like a genie materializing from a lamp, a stealth helicopter carrying the Secretary of Defense appeared and landed squarely on the front lawn. Bishop didn't know who he should expect to see stepping out of the aircraft. But he certainly didn't expect a Stormtrooper. The robot quickly performed a 360° scan, focusing on Bishop for a brief moment, and then dismissing him immediately, having recognized him as a Detroit police captain, and the owner of the house in question.

Bishop skidded to a halt just inside the busted gates in time to see a second figure emerge from the helicopter. Dressed entirely in black, the woman threw a cape around her shoulders as a defense against the wind. The visual effect suggested someone on the spectrum between Darth Vader and the beautiful witch in *Snow White and the Seven Dwarfs*, neither one of which could be a source of comfort.

He was still unsure of whether he was dealing with good or evil when the stormtrooper robot turned back toward him and said, "the Secretary of Defense requires that you disarm before coming closer."

Not taking the time to reflect on the irony of that statement, Bishop dutifully obeyed, placing his sidearm on the seat of the cruiser and leaning the twelve-gauge shotgun against its fender.

It would be another twenty minutes before Bishop was joined by his colleagues from the Michigan State Police. They arrived in vertical take-off and landing vehicles, launched from a platform sixty miles distant. The media wasn't far behind.

Tara's helicopter was emitting an electronic haze that jammed the navigation and communication systems of the approaching aircraft, and so, the police, who were unaccustomed to piloting their new flying cars, were stopped at a distance of about a mile, The pilots were confused but fortunate as their autopilot systems were designed to descend to the nearest clear spot on the ground in such circumstances.

The news helicopters were not so fortunate. Veering wildly, they could be barely kept under control as they were held at bay. Despite their distance from the house, they were able to get valuable video footage of the advanced stealth aircraft that had transported the Secretary of Defense to the scene of the crime. The breaking news had gone live before Tara reached the front door.

In the Situation Room, the national security team sat, mouths agape, staring at the screen as the drone video was replayed. "FACIAL RECOGNITION ENGAGED," said the message that flashed on the screen.

The President didn't need software to tell who was engaged in the skirmish. She had received a coded message from Evelyn two nights earlier saying, "Adams identified and located in the vicinity of the Detroit pod. We are in pursuit." Sitting at the head of the table, she gripped the arms of her chair as though the room might be turned upside down and she feared being dumped on her head. Pupils dilated, jaws clenched, she watched as Murphy's Law assumed control of her diabolical scheme.

By itself, the murder of a Detroit cop would have been enough to blow up the plan. But the carnage that followed would make this an international news story. Just as she and everyone in the room thought the battle would end with the death of Diana and

Gabrielle, she was shocked out of her stupor. The room uttered a collective gasp and the President leapt out of her seat as the smart bullets took their toll. What followed was the horror of watching microscopic robots consume the carbon in the corpus of Evelyn O'Malley-Sakura from the inside-out, leaving only a puddle of gray goo on Jessica Kilwin-Chalmers's kitchen floor.

But for the president, it was the entrance of Tara Leto that most surprised her. "What's the Secretary of Defense doing there? Who knew about this?"

CHAPTER 48

GRIEF

IANA'S GRIEF SURGED WITH EVERY BREATH, REACH-
ing a new peak with every exhalation, and never quite
recovering before its next gasp for air. She was helpless
to stop the stream of tears that were running from her face and
dropping onto Tony's lifeless body. Eyes that once danced with
delight, a smile that tended toward laughter at the slightest provo-
cation, the arms that once wrapped her in warmth and love were
all now a cold, lifeless form.

Tara stopped in her tracks when she spotted Diana and Gabrielle
kneeling over Tony's lifeless body. Diana barely looked up as she knelt
beside her. "He was someone important to you," Tara said, confirming what seemed obvious. Diana's brain stuttered, taking a moment
to catch up, trying to remember how to breath, unable to speak.

"I'm so very sorry," Tara added.

Diana collapsed into Tara's arms, sobbing – her grief fed by a
bottomless pit of tears. Tara pulled her in to her embrace and said,
"You must have cared for each other deeply. I wish I had the right
words for you."

Nick had remained at the bottom of the stairs until the commotion from above had stopped. He now emerged from his basement lair, stopping as he entered the kitchen to absorb what had happened. His eyes were overcome by the brightness of the daylight. He squinted as he took in the carnage, the dead bodies piled atop one another, the blood splattered everywhere. Jessica stood leaning against the sink, looking like a dishrag that had been wrung to the point of fraying. Then he spotted Tony's lifeless body, surrounded by three kneeling figures.

His face drained of all color when he saw the faces of the three women. His brain stopped for a moment. He stood motionless, unable to breathe as though every wisp of air had been knocked out of his lungs.

But it was one face in particular that shocked him.

"T-Tara?" he stammered. Suddenly, the man who might be the Einstein of the 21st Century couldn't formulate a thought. He opened his mouth to speak then closed it again. His head pounded with each surge of blood from his heart.

"Hello, Nick," Tara said calmly.

Diana was incredulous. "You know each other?" She glanced back and forth between them as if she was watching a tennis match. Finally, Nick broke the silence.

"Diana," began Nick. "Tara is your grandmother."

PART 4

CHAPTER 49

THE WHITE
HOUSE

T ARA SAT WAITING IMPATIENTLY. SHE KNEW THE GAME
the president was playing – hell, she had invented the
game. Demand a meeting at the most inconvenient time.
Then show up late — beyond fashionably late — and show up
dressed inappropriately, all the better to convey the message that
your time is more important than that of your subordinate. All
the better to convey the message that you are the one in charge.
All the better to ensure you begin the discussion from a position
of power with your counterpart on the defensive.

Kathleen Porter entered her private office, intentionally failing
to extend a hand or acknowledge Tara's presence as she stood for
her – when the President is standing, everyone stands. Returning
from her Sunday morning workout, she arrived a bit sweaty in her
workout clothes, caring not how she might be perceived if spotted in the West Wing. It was Sunday morning, when nearly all

residents of the DC pod would be at church, the most time-efficient way to rack up a few points in one's Culture Index.

She sat down in her leather chair and crossed her legs – right ankle on left knee — and let out a small burp that smelled like the bottom of a fish tank. It was clear she hadn't bothered to brush her teeth.

Tara responded with powerful body language of her own – doing her best Don Draper imitation – relaxed, legs crossed, arm resting on the back of the sofa. She was prepared for this.

"Tara, I've discussed the list of charges to be brought against you with the Attorney General . . . "

"No, you haven't," interrupted Tara. She had considered resigning before this meeting but had concluded that she had more leverage by staying in the job. "If you had, I'd be meeting with him and not you."

Clearly thrown off balance, the President just glared.

"Shall I list the charges to be brought against *you*, Madam President?"

"I haven't finished," the President sneered, then added, "Madam Sec-re-tary." She sounded as though she would sooner shoot Tara in the face than tolerate her back talk. "Misappropriation of government funds, violation of the Posse Comitatus Act . . . "

"There's no such law. It's simply expressed in the Constitution as . . . "

"A judge might not see it that way, Tara."

Tara knew she was guilty of the crimes the President was describing and she knew the court of public opinion would not be kind unless she could position her actions as heroic in the face of supreme evil. She would rather skip to the part where the public relations team took over and the medals were awarded than to engage the President in a career-ending dialog – for them both. But, for now, she needed the President to see the facts, how it was *she* who would be seen as evil. Her goal for this conversation was to reach a stalemate – a Mexican standoff.

"Why don't we start with murder?" said Tara in an effort to gain the advantage. "You're guilty of murder."

"What?" said the President. The anger in her eyes revealed the scared little girl she was.

I've got her on the run now, thought Tara.

"I've read the report, Kathy," she began, tossing it on the desk. She hadn't realized the importance of the top-secret FBI report that Clarke had shared with her until she was preparing for this meeting. It gave her an unambiguous advantage. "You were the commander of the raid that killed my daughter-in-law all those years ago," she added. "And you were responsible for imprisoning my ex-husband in a cryogenic state for a quarter century."

"That report is classified," said the President. "It can't be revealed to the public."

"Classified or not, it might leak out. It wouldn't be the first time."

"It was too long ago. The death was ruled accidental. Statute of limitations has expired. You'll never connect me to the crime. Any judge would throw it out."

"The facts won't matter to the media. They never do," Tara said. "They'll connect the dots faster than you can say impeachment. Can you imagine the public reaction when they learn the President of the United States led a raid that resulted in the death of the mother of a national hero? Not to mention the cryogenic imprisonment of her Nobel Prize winning grandfather?"

"Once the charges are brought against you," said the President, as if trying desperately to reimpose the script she had planned for this meeting, "I can paint you as a 'disgruntled ex-employee.' It's always worked in the past." Adrenaline flooded her system. Her face drawn, her pupils dilated, her lips so tight they seemed to disappear.

Primal fear, decreasing logic, next comes loss of control. I need to reel her in, thought Tara, and began her rebuttal. "You know we can connect your past crimes to current events. The conspiracy with Colonel Sakura, the rogue militia commanded by Bragg, the heist of the patents for your own personal gain," she said as the president's face turned pale, suggesting full-fledged nausea.

The air is coming out of her balloon. She thought she had me dead to rights before this meeting started. Now, she knows she needs a way out.

"You'll never make it stick."

She's grasping at straws.

"Again . . . we won't have to," said Tara. "The press will have a field day."

"The crimes you've committed are much easier to prove. And, we have the video."

Tara knew she didn't have direct evidence of the President's misdeeds. But she was sure she had enough leverage to make the charges against her disappear.

"Please – by all means — share the video with the press," said Tara, almost adding 'I dare you' when she said it. *I don't have to say it. She knows it's a dare.* "Nick Adams has given the world a solution to stop climate change in its tracks. My actions will be seen as heroic, even if you make them out to be criminal. The public will never support you."

I have her cornered now. She's slowing down to think it through.

"It's never the event itself, Tara. You know that. It's always how you react to it. I can command the stage, show humility and grace, engage the media in a dialog . . . " Her voice trailed off. It was clear to Tara that the president had gone off script. She was losing confidence.

Tara said nothing, preferring to let silence do the heavy lifting.

"You've misappropriated funds," said the president finally. "You've spied on American citizens . . . "

"American citizens who were part of a militia that kidnapped a war hero," Tara interrupted to be sure the president didn't recover her advantage. "Go ahead," she added. "Make your case to the public. Let's see who comes out on top." *Now I've dared her in no uncertain terms.*

"Even if you come out on top, it will be a messy affair," the president responded. "You won't be Secretary of Defense for long."

Tara knew she was right about that. But she also knew the president wouldn't survive the scandal and so did the president.

"If I go down," The president blurted out. "You're going down with me."

Tara suppressed her urge to smile. In an emotional outburst, the president had just admitted the possibility she might have to pay the price for her misdeeds.

Okay," she replied, knowing it was not okay. "I guess we'll go down together." *I've challenged her. Now, she'll back off,* she thought. Of course, there was a chance she wouldn't back off – would do the right thing and confess her sins while pressing for Tara's prosecution. But Tara was betting she wouldn't – couldn't. *She's not afraid of being prosecuted. She's afraid of the loss of status – the persona she's created for herself through a lifetime of obsequious glad-handing and double dealing.*

President Kathleen Porter sat, slumping in her chair. All the energy she had brought to this meeting seemed to have been drained from her. "Maybe we can work out something between us," she said.

Sounds like we have a deal, thought Tara finally allowing herself a small smile.

CHAPTER 50

THE DC POD

I N DIANA'S APARTMENT, AUTOMATIC UPDATES TO THE
software had reset her settings to default. So, despite having previously banished her augmented reality assistant,
Courtney, to digital purgatory, there she was again – smiling,
glowing around the edges and eager to meet every one of Diana's
perceived needs. The absence of a chip implanted in Diana's neck
robbed Courtney of her primary input – there were no surges of
enzymes and hormones, no cortisol or adrenaline, no data what-
soever – so, at least she didn't have to deal with her incessant questions when she stepped inside. Courtney merely stood at attention
waiting to be addressed by name. Diana dispatched her to the electronic ether.

"Spare bedroom's through there, Gramps," she said and waved
in the general direction of the hallway.

Nick had been offered many luxuries upon his return to civilization, mostly by corporate interests hoping to capture his tal-
ents for their own purposes. Tempting though the Presidential
Suite at the Mayflower might be – no one does a favor without

the expectation of reciprocity – he had turned it down in favor of taking up residence in his granddaughter's apartment. He dropped his bag in the spare bedroom, not bothering to unpack. He sensed his granddaughter's mood and thought it best to stay by her side.

Diana sat slumped in a kitchen chair, shoulders rounded, fingering Tony's key fob, a familiar object that she had taken; it was like a piece of him. She could imagine his fingers holding it as they had held her. She didn't look up as Nick entered the room.

He sat and said nothing, waiting for her to speak, waiting for her to express her sadness.

"He never leaves my mind," she said. "He's always there. It's so odd that he became such a stabilizing force in my life after such a short time. It's not as though we'd been together for years or even months. For some reason I felt as though he was a force that could remove the chaos from my life. I'll never forget him for that."

"How did you become so much in love in such a short time?"

"Well," she began. "A lot of it was the situation we were in, I think."

"Yes," said Nick. "I can understand that. That sense of desperation we all shared – that our lives might end at any moment. Danger like that always draws people together. But there was something else, wasn't there?"

"I don't think I was so deeply in love so much as I was drawn to what he represented to me. It intrigued me," she said.

"What intrigued you?"

"Well, *he* was intriguing, of course. I was drawn to his inner strength, his strength of character. He was willing to do what's right no matter the consequences. But, more than that, I was intrigued by the door he opened for me. It was a chance to break away from the rigorous routine of my life. A chance to find a new path to happiness."

"So, he expanded your horizons – your perspective on life itself."

"Yeah, I think that's right. There was just something about him. Something very different. I can't put my finger on it."

"He was an anachronism," said Nick.

Diana looked up.

"I think the reason he bailed on life in the pods was because he didn't want a life of striving to be someone society approved of," he added.

There was something about that statement that resonated for Diana. Her grandfather may have just defined the reason she had been so attracted to Tony. He had followed a path she longed to follow – even though she hadn't known it.

"Do you think he had a sense of who he wanted to be?" she asked, thinking perhaps her grandfather could help her understand the connection she had formed with Tony.

"I think it was a work in progress — as it is for all of us. Once that stops, we've stopped living."

"How did you see him, Gramps?" She found that just being able to talk about it with him gave her some relief – relief from waves of grief that could sweep her away.

"He was defiantly ungracious." Diana's expression told him to continue. "Society imposes its standards passive-aggressively. Even before the Culture Index, there were standards we were expected to live up to. No one had to say, 'do this or else.' But it was always there. Dress this way; respond that way. Don't say anything that's rude or politically incorrect."

"Well, sure. I think everyone knows that even if they don't think about it."

"What I'm saying is that Tony *did* think about it and concluded he didn't want conform to those standards."

"Is that what made him 'defiant'?"

"In a way, yes. Tony's defiance of those standards wasn't intended to harm anyone, and they didn't make him any less a good citizen. He simply knew the pods were not a place where he could live happily. So, he chose a different life, one that allowed him the freedom to be who he wanted to be."

"Even while he was trying to figure that out." She was beginning to understand what her grandfather was saying. It wasn't that she was so deeply in love with Tony. It was that she connected with his defiance of the rules of the game. She felt like oil floating atop a puddle of water when she was in the podosphere. She would never be part of the mix. The difference between Tony and her? Tony had a home. He had grown up in Erie and felt connected to it. Diane had no connection to a place – a place that brought forth a warmth from within. She had no home.

"Right! Exactly," said her grandfather. "He was trying to figure it out."

"I can see how that might be defiant," said Diana. "But ungracious?"

"Was he grateful for the order that society would impose upon him?"

"Well, no . . . yeah, I guess you're right," she said, laughing out loud for the first time since Tony's death. "Defiantly ungracious," she repeated as she rolled the phrase around in her head. She smiled at the thought of it. Knowing Tony, he might have had a tee shirt bearing that slogan: Defiantly Ungracious.

"Look, Diana. You've been dealt a big blow. You've learned at a very young age that life can bring you to your knees. It will bring you lower than you think you can go. But if you can . . . "

"I know, Gramps," she said. "But it's gonna take some time."

"Yes, it will take time — time to allow Tony's death to become part of you rather than all you can think about."

He reached out and held her hand. She gripped his, squeezing hard. They sat sharing their physical connection, the bedrock of who they were — love and life.

"Finding that stability — that relief from the chaos of your life — Well, that will take a bit longer."

She looked up, looked into his eyes. It was not the first time those eyes connected her to something she carried inside, something at her core that he could shore up.

"How will I ever . . . ?"

"Sometimes you have to let go of something to gain something else."

"Like what?"

"Before Tony — before you ventured outside the Pods — what was the stabilizing force in your life?"

"The military, I guess . . . and Dad," she started, a bit uncertain of her answers. "Yeah, it was military life. There was a certain stability to that."

"Did that make you happy?"

"Happy? Well, no not happy exactly. More like secure, I guess."

"Is that who you are? Is that what you want from life?" he asked as if he knew the answer was 'no' – knew there was more to his granddaughter than the superficial life she had constructed for herself. "Not happy but secure? Is that how you think of yourself?"

"No." She felt angry now. Angry – not with her grandfather – but rather with herself. Even though she didn't understand why.

"Think about what we accomplished. We discovered a plot by powerful people to co-opt new technology to solve one of the world's biggest problems. And we put that technology in the hands of those who will ensure that never happens again."

"Yeah," she replied as it sunk in for the first time. "And we did it under some pretty harrowing circumstances."

"In light of all that, Diana, how do you think of yourself?"

"Courageous," she began, her face beginning to adopt the color of a tomato. "And bold!"

"Bold! Tell me about that."

"I . . . I don't know if I can," she said, the blood draining out of her face once again. She was unable to think straight, as though her brain had been short-circuited.

She was on the verge, about to break. She squeezed his hands harder, looking up into his eyes once again, gathering her strength. She could feel electricity passing between them, a tingling sensation in their fingers. This was inner strength. This was the strength that stems from unconditional love. This was the medication she needed to heal her life.

She swallowed hard to choke back the tears and tightened her jaw. Then, she told her grandfather why she thought of herself as bold.

"There's an invincible part of me. Call it 'my soul.' It's the girl you can never hurt. It's raw, untouchable. It's pure. It can never be taken away from me – never!"

"And Tony?"

She sat, her mouth agape, as it sank in. It wasn't that Tony was her stabilizing force; it was that he connected to an inner force they had in common. Sharing it – even unconsciously – made them stronger together. Now, because that connection had been broken, she felt her life was more chaotic . But, even without him, she possessed the courage of her convictions; the willingness to always do what's right; and the wisdom to know what that is.

"I am more than what society expects of me. I am greater than the sum of my awards and medals. I am strong, invincible. No one can take that from me."

"Bold?" asked Nick.

"Yes. Bold!"

CHAPTER 51

GRANDMOTHER

WHEN DIANA RETURNED HOME FROM HER FIRST DAY back at the Pentagon, all she wanted to do was talk to Nick. She wanted to tell him how she couldn't have felt any more distant from everyone if she had been a lion walking through the hallways. They seemed to be in awe of her – unsure what to say to her and yet unable to take their eyes off her. And she wanted to tell him about her conversation with Tara – the rage she felt toward her.

Nick was sitting in the living room enjoying a cocktail, staring at a letter that was lying on the coffee table. Diana couldn't help but ask what it was.

"It's from The General," he said.

"The General? Are you getting letters from the dead now?"

"It was sent from his attorney's office. It was only to be opened in the event of his death."

Diana's day had started when she returned to her old desk and found it was occupied by someone else. She looked around the room, seeing few familiar faces. Suddenly, Tara's executive assistant materialized before her. The augmented reality avatar was no more appealing to Diana than it was on their first encounter months ago.

"You've been assigned to a new workstation, Major," said the avatar. Diana followed it to an upper floor where she was escorted to the Secretary of Defense's suite. She began to feel the anger building up inside her, the anger that had sprung up when she learned that Tara was her grandmother. This was the woman who had abandoned her father and grandfather. The woman in whose wake was nothing but emotional damage – the damage that had trickled down through two generations to Diana.

Tara stood in the doorway to her office and waved Diana in. Reluctantly, she entered and took a seat on the couch.

"Diana . . . ," Tara began then hesitated. Diana imagined she had prepared a little speech for this occasion but was unable to deliver it when they were face to face. She sat quietly, happy to let Tara suffer a bit. Sitting across from her served as a reminder of the deep wound her soul had suffered for most of her life – the loss of a sense of strength one can only get from being part of a loving family.

"Diana," Tara began again. "I know you must be angry with me. I hope you understand that before your file crossed my desk, I didn't know you existed."

"You knew my father existed," Diana responded, disregarding any courtesy normally accorded the Secretary of Defense by a member of the armed services. "You gave birth to him."

"Well, yes. But I didn't know that General Paul Adams was your father," she said. "Adams is a common name, and I hadn't seen him since he was four years old."

"And my grandfather?"

"I thought he was dead. Everyone did."

"She said she didn't know I existed – didn't know that General Paul Adams was my father – thought you were dead."

"Well, I can understand that," Nick replied. "Everyone thought I was dead. That can't be what has upset you."

"Well, yeah . . . I mean no . . . I don't know . . . I suppose you're right." Nick had a way of piercing Diana's shell to get to the core of the matter – any matter. She knew she needed his help, but she didn't want to let go of her anger. "So, what has you so upset?"

"I detached myself from my family decades ago. I changed my name so I couldn't be tracked down," Tara continued. "I have pursued my career to the exclusion anything else in my life. I've always felt that was my destiny."

"Wasn't it you who had me transferred to the Pentagon? Wasn't there some urge to have me near you?" She was beginning to release her anger now. The pressure had been building for some time. She was like a tea kettle about to release its steam.

"Well . . . um . . . yes."

"And would you have done everything in your power to rescue me – us – if I were not your granddaughter?" She was determined to remain intensely focused on making her case – her prosecution of her grandmother for her misdeeds.

Tara looked away – gazed out the window for a moment. Then she said, whisper quiet, "No. I suppose not."

"You risked your career by going off the grid, right?"

"Yes," Tara replied calmly. "That's right."

"So, I guess you weren't detached completely, were you?" Diana could sense that she had her cornered. She was about to deliver an emotional blow to the woman who had done the same to Nick, her father and her so long ago.

"No . . . I guess not."

"You could have tracked down my father at any time," she added, feeling as though she needed to use all the ammunition in her arsenal of emotional weapons while Tara was in retreat. "He wasn't that hard to find. You simply had no desire to do so."

"Well, I . . . Um . . . well." Tara had no response that would satisfy Diana.

"You just weren't honest with us – or yourself," Diana said, pronouncing her guilty verdict.

As she sat across from her grandmother, she felt nothing but the deep wound she had left on her family. This longing Diana had for home and hearth — for a family that surrounded her with love – had been derailed thirty years before she was born by the woman who sat across from her.

In the background, Tara was going on about how 'we' should put their family history behind them and focus on the future. "Diana, I want to be your mentor. I can help you. I want to help you," she said, her voice cracking a bit. "We need to get past this, Diana. You can have a bright future with my guidance."

Diana couldn't believe that Tara was trying to dismiss the history of their family, placing it in the context of how good it could be for her career. She felt as though her thoughts were swimming in a sea of anger, swirling about in an eddy that drained away her ability to absorb what Tara was saying.

"We can start you off in strategic planning, so you are well-grounded," Tara droned on.

Diana couldn't listen anymore. She got up and walked out without waiting for Tara to finish her soliloquy.

"She acted like it was all excusable, all just a minor bump in the road," said Diana. "That's what has me so upset." She was unloading all her emotional baggage now. She knew Nick could handle it – that he would be an empathetic listener. "I couldn't believe it. How could she rationalize it away? How could she pretend it was no big deal?"

"People always rationalize," said Nick. "It's a defense mechanism. It's how we maintain our sanity."

"You sound like you're defending her," Diana exclaimed. She couldn't believe he could take it in stride – that he wasn't just as angry as she was. Or more so. "She changed her name so you couldn't find her."

"I decided to put it behind me long ago," he replied, almost dispassionately.

"But you're still upset about it. Aren't you, Gramps?" said Diana, hoping to validate her anger.

"Yes," he replied. "There are times when I get upset. But I wouldn't be able to lead a productive life if I didn't put it behind me."

"How?" she asked. "How can I put it behind me?"

"Nothing's changed really," he said. "She left me more than fifty years ago. And we've managed to get by without her. We can continue to do that, can't we?"

"I guess you're saying I'll have to learn to live with it." She was becoming calmer as she always did when she talked with her grandfather. But she knew this feeling – this rage – would not go away easily. Or any time soon.

"We can't change the past," he replied. "So, yeah, we need to live with it."

She couldn't talk about it anymore. She needed a break from thinking about Tara – about an anger that she felt might never subside. She took a deep breath, hoping to expunge the tension in her body – for now at least.

"What does the letter say?" she asked, after composing herself.

"It's a confession of sorts," said Nick. "He says he knows he's crossed a line – a line he never thought he would cross."

"I've only known him as a kidnapper, murderer and thief," said Diana. "I have a hard time seeing him any other way."

"Most of us start out with virtuous intentions," he replied. "But, once someone steps over the line – violates their own sense of right and wrong — it's a slippery slope. I've seen it before. Each transgression gets easier and easier – until it's out of control."

"And you think that's what happened to The General?" Diana said. She struggled to see how he had ever been virtuous.

"The lawyer says The General has left me everything in his will," Nick continued, ignoring her question. "Apparently, he felt as if leaving his wealth to me gave him a shot at redemption. He thought of me as someone who would put his resources to good use – something that would contribute to the well-being of humanity."

"He doesn't have any heirs?" She hadn't thought about The General's fortune or what might happen after his death. The big house on the hill had been nothing but a prison to her. That he was a wealthy man and the most influential man in his community had been of no importance to her.

"Apparently not," he said. "Not even any living siblings."

"You look perplexed. I'm not used to seeing you like that."

"Well, I'm not sure what it means to me," he said. "I was just getting used to the idea of living in the pods – of finding a way of life here."

"So, what's next?"

"I have to go to Erie for a reading of the will," said Nick.

CHAPTER 52

FOLLOW YOUR
HEART

O N THE NIGHT BEFORE THE CEREMONY, DIANA FELT
the urge to learn about Gaia, the Greek goddess represented by the pendant given to her by Tara. Before Gaia,
there was only Chaos she was informed by the gods of the Internet.
There's that word again – Chaos! Chaos was, according to the ancient
Greeks, the origin of everything, the first thing that ever existed. In
Greek, Chaos translated to "the gaping void." Gaia brought forth
order from chaos. From the darkness of the void, Gaia created the
heavens and Earth – the mountains, seas and plains. She was the
source of life in the natural world, an orderly existence with which
humankind had not yet learned to live in harmony.

*Is that why Tara gave me the Gaia pendant before I undertook the
mission that would change my life?*

She began to think about the possibility the pendant was not
just a trinket handed down through generations. It might have

been symbolic. Perhaps Tara had thought of her as someone who could follow in her footsteps – as someone who would always do what's right no matter the consequences. That would explain why she was going on about Diana's career and how she would benefit from her guidance.

Reading on, Diana discovered that Gaia had coupled with Uranus, god of the sky. While she scanned and clicked, one name jumped off the page. It was her grandmother's name: Tara, a name adapted from the Roman goddess Terra. Greek equivalent: Gaia. In a modern interpretation, Gaia represents a self-correcting force that will take back the Earth on behalf of animals, nature and children. It occurred to Diana that the mission to revive her grandfather had represented an opportunity to Tara – an opportunity to fulfill her destiny. Gaia – Terra – Tara would take back the Earth to preserve it for future generations.

Among Gaia's bazillion grandchildren was Leto — her grandmother's surname. Leto mated with Zeus and gave birth to the male and female twins Apollo and Artemis. Artemis was a warrior. She was wild, never happier than when she was in nature. She was a protector of women and the earth's resources. Above all, she was self-sufficient and focused.

She clicked over to a virtual presentation of the family tree. It expanded into a 3D image that occupied most of the space in her room. She revolved the image a hundred and eighty degrees to reveal the Roman equivalents of the Greek gods and goddesses. Just as she had found that the name Tara was the Roman equivalent of Gaia, she also found that her own name, Diana, was the Roman equivalent of Artemis.

Perhaps Gaia or Terra or Tara, mother of the earth, gave birth to all these possibilities. Perhaps when Tara Leto, Secretary of Defense and her secret grandmother, had given her the Gaia pendant, it was a message. "I know who you are," her grand-mother seemed to be saying. "You are a defender of what's right." *Is that it or am I rationalizing?* She thought. Her anger was rising again. She could have revealed herself at any time before the mission began. She could have answered all these questions. Her anger was becoming a rage. It swelled up inside her threatening the stability she had been struggling to maintain. She shut down the program in frustration.

This pendant is not a message; it's a puzzle!

"Where's Nick?" asked Gabrielle when they met a half hour before they were due to be escorted onto a stage where they would be awarded the Medal of Freedom by the President of the United States. It was what the spin doctors had concocted as the perfect way to connect the President to a cause greater than humanity: reversing climate change.

The pendant hung on Diana's chest, occasionally reminding her of its presence as it swung from side to side. *Diana, goddess of the moon and lover of nature. And, Artemis, warrior and defender of women. How could I have spent so much of my life hiding from who I am?*

"Hello-o-o," said Gabrielle. "You there?"

"Huh? Oh, sorry. I was lost in thought," said Diana, snapping back to the present.

"Where's Nick?" Gabrielle repeated.

She leaned forward slightly to whisper her answer. "Erie."

"Erie?" Why would he go back to Erie?"

"He got a letter from The General's lawyer. It was about his last will and testament."

"Is he in The General's will?"

"Yeah," replied Diana. "Kinda shocking, right? Anyway, he got up early this morning and headed for Erie. They sent a helicopter for him."

"So, he'll be a no-show for his big award from the President?" said Gabrielle.

Diana just shrugged, enjoying the idea that he couldn't care less what society – and the president — expected of him. She couldn't help but to smile at the thought of it.

"He has his own agenda," said Diana. "Always has. He probably never did what anyone wanted him to do." In a very short period of time, she had grown to know more about her grandfather – through his actions, his grace under pressure, his reclusive nature, his independence, his wisdom. It was his wisdom and compassion or, perhaps, love for his family that had helped her see herself for what she was: a strong, independent woman who had given up her freedom by reflexively conforming to standards imposed on her by society. He had helped her overcome her fear of being vulnerable, all the better to understand her true desires. "Without even reading a chip embedded in my shoulder," she had joked to Gabrielle.

"He helped me see that my real fear was being controlled by others, not just the military. It's the Culture Index, the whole way people conform without a thought," she had said more for her own benefit than Gabrielle's.

The ushers were now encouraging Diana and Gabrielle to take their seats. The podium was front and center and a dozen American flags hung behind a row of chairs covered in white cotton.

When the President noticed the absence of Nick Adams, it made her eyes bulge out of their sockets, a perfect complement to the vein that was now pulsing in the middle of her forehead. She glared at Diana and Gabrielle as though it had been their responsibility to make sure he showed up to receive his medal. She then turned her attention to Tara who just shrugged and suppressed a smirk.

It was the pomp of the ceremony that confirmed it for Diana. She didn't need a medal to reaffirm her strength or a role in leadership to feel worthy. Wise leadership doesn't rely on government. She could leave the weight of these institutions to others, the would-be angels who think they know what's best for all. History has consistently shown us the fallacy of the elites who govern. There was no hope in the idea that replacing their judgment with hers would make the world a better place. Her grandfather had contributed more to humankind locked in Jessica's basement than this cohort of Harvard grads could ever hope to.

She could only endure about a half hour of the media attention before she and Gabrielle sneaked away, summoning a Delta for the ride home. The self-driving vehicle would not take them to their destination without first showing them a menu of options from ridesharing to short-haul domestic flights to celestial travel.

Reviewing the choices, Gabrielle wondered aloud whether they should head to Rome or Beijing for a well-deserved vacation. "Makes you wonder," she said. "Where should we go next?"

"I feel like we have to earn these," responded Diana, her mind in a totally different place.

"Earn what?"

"These medals around our necks … They recognize our actions but not what they imply," she said. "We have enabled a new technology to tackle one of humankind's greatest challenges and helped my grandfather to find a new life. Shouldn't we dedicate our lives to following through on the promise of what we've done? Isn't there more we can do? Should do?"

"You're thinking too hard, Diana."

"What do you mean?"

"Nick has helped you get through a difficult time. But he's a guy who lives in his head. He's very analytical. He has opened you up to considering other options by thinking through the alternatives. But that's not the only way to get the right answer."

"So, what am I missing?"

"Diana, it's feelings and emotions that make us alive. Living from your heart will give your life meaning – something that makes you want to get out of bed each morning. Otherwise, you're just going through the motions."

"I know you're right, Gabs. But something is holding me back."

"What holds you back is fear of the consequences. You've conditioned yourself to always have a plan, always have a goal in mind. There's a lot of safety for you in that approach. You need to step back from that. Take one step at a time, one that feels right, and then another, and another. Soon enough, you'll feel confident that you can find joy in life.

"So, I need to . . . "

"Yes, Diana . . . follow your heart."

CHAPTER 53

HOME

D IANA TOOK A MOMENT TO BREATHE IN THE AIR AND
feel the wind on her skin. She was glad to take a break
on their drive through the countryside. It was Spring.
The sun was warm on her skin, but the breeze was chilly enough
to serve as a reminder of Winter. Like each new season, nature
brought a set of sensations that felt both new and familiar all at
once. The grass waved like fans in a stadium, catching the light
and showing different shades of green with each turn of its blades.
A recent rain had left beads of moisture on the leaves, which
soaked into her socks as she stretched her legs.

The rugged, unpaved road turned first to gravel and then to
a potholed blackish ribbon that wove its way through the countryside, approaching civilization – or at least what passed for it.
Pulling into the newly repaved driveway brought a rush of con-
flicting feelings. The General's house had been repainted bright
white. The garden showed signs of life too: rhododendrons
blooming in pink and white, lilacs spreading a heady perfume
and birds singing as though they had never seen a day like this one.

As welcoming as the place now looked, Diana and Gabrielle were trepidatious as they approached. There were no good memories here. Only death and distress to say nothing of the blobs of gray goo that had been discovered since the massacre in Grosse Pointe. Gray goo that had been confirmed to be Mateen Ibrahimi and Howard the Geek.

They threw their duffle bags over their shoulders and climbed the mild incline to the main entrance. The right-hand door was ajar and swung open with the slightest nudge from Gabrielle's elbow. The foyer had been restored to its former grandeur – polished wood floors, sparkling chandelier and an oriental rug that showed signs of its age.

Peggy, who had assisted Tony for the many years he had served as chief of police, came out of what had been The General's office, leaving the door open for them to enter. She smiled when she saw them, an effort that nearly cracked her face. But she had reason to smile this day. For Nick Adams, who was sole heir to The General's estate, had transferred her family's business back to her in the first of what would be many similar transactions which would restore ownership to natives of Erie.

Diana and Gabrielle entered the office, which seemed much smaller than they recalled. The furniture had been rearranged so that it felt more like a lodge than a courtroom. The chairs, both elegant and dark, sprinkled liberally with embroidered cushions, were arranged so that the table was in easy reach of every seat. The walls were discolored where photos of The General had previously hung. But their cry for a repaint didn't detract from the warmth of the room. Nick sat behind The General's nineteenth century desk, his head down, lost in a pile of legal documents. He seemed not to notice their presence.

Diana let her duffle slide off her shoulder as did Gabrielle. Thump! Thump!

Nick looked up, suppressing a grin but allowing a closed-lip smile — a smile from deep inside — to escape in spite of himself, and said, "Welcome home. What took you so long?"

ABOUT THE AUTHOR

JOHN CALIA A BROOKLYN-BORN, RECOVERING BUSINESS-man, He has been a naval officer, banker, entrepreneur and consultant. He began writing his blog "Who Will Lead?" in 2010 attracting more than 120,000 readers. The five-star rating of his first book – a business fable titled *The Reluctant CEO: Succeeding Without Losing Your Soul* – inspired him to keep writing. His fascination with artificial intelligence and its impact on society inspired him to write *The Awakening of Artemis*.

For more, see www.johncalia.com

Acknowledgements

Many thanks to the cadre of beta readers who made this book better by taking time and energy to read early drafts and provide thoughtful feedback: Cara Holland, John Schmits, Brian and Kelly Gusmano, Dave and Jenn Kailer, and Donna Blackshall.

If you love the cover art (as I do), you'll understand my gratitude for the work of Nick Castle.

This book is a better novel largely because of the diligent effort of Emily Yau, my editor. Her wisdom about character, pace and story line were invaluable to me in the final stages of writing this book. Her touch was light when it came to minor adjustments. Yet, she had no qualms about popping me between the eyes when I needed it (which was often).

Made in the USA
Middletown, DE
22 October 2021